FAT ANGIE

Homecoming

FAT ANGIE

Homecoming

e.E. Charlton-Trujillo

CANDLEWICK PRESS

This is a work of fiction. Names, characters, places, and incidents are either products of the author's imagination or, if real, are used fictitiously.

First edition 2021

Library of Congress Catalog Card Number pending
ISBN 978-1-5362-0839-9

21 22 23 24 25 26 LBM 10 9 8 7 6 5 4 3 2 1

Printed in Melrose Park, IL, USA

This book was typeset in Giovanni.

Candlewick Press
99 Dover Street
Somerville, Massachusetts 02144

www.candlewick.com

Carrie, because of you, Angie and I are both finally home.

There was a girl. Her name was Angie. Her life was finally perfect.

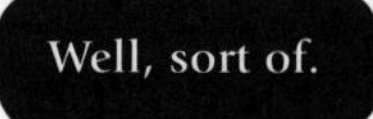
Well, sort of.

Chapter 1

This was not the beginning, again. Rather, it was an end. A fantastic end to an unbelievable, truly fabulous four weeks, three days, seven hours, and approximately four minutes since Angie's return from her road trip across Ohio. A trip marked by ups, by downs. By shifts in perspective. Since taking the stage with indie girl band Cat Scratch in the Queen City of Cincinnati and pouring her sister's ashes into the Ohio River, the once angry-depressed-devouring-candy-to-solve-her-problems Angie was more in control of what went into her body and her heart.

She was a girl on fire!

A fire that could be witnessed in the way she dressed, and especially how she expressed herself in and out of therapy. It was this version of Angie, riding passenger side in Jake's classic Datsun 280Z while blasting Katy Perry's "Teenage Dream," who was ready for something more. Because the moratorium on Angie's heartbreak regarding her first love, KC Romance (who had relocated to the greater Dallas metropolitan area, then ghosted her), had finally and thankfully expired. Which meant Angie was ready to make today, Thursday, mere weeks before homecoming, the day she officially asked Jamboree Memphis Jordan out.

Swoon!

Because Angie had never asked anyone out and was prone to nervous rambling, she had typed and glue-sticked what to say onto several three-by-five index cards. She wanted to leave nothing to chance because the last few weeks had been a life largely spectacular. Angie and Jamboree talking and laughing between classes, during lunch and late into the night. Their arms casually-not-so-casually brushing together during Random Movie Nights on the roof of the RV. The two of them lounging on crushed velvet sofas at The Backstory with Zeke and sometimes Darius. With Gary Klein now living several states away with his father, life was better for Angie. At least, when she wasn't home.

Home continued to be hard.

Angie's couldn't-get-it-together mother, a self-described unflappable corporate attorney, had found herself in a state of being, well, flapped. Her not-so-gradual descent into a semi-shut-in existence had followed her termination from work. Connie had spiraled into a life of rarely laundered pajama bottoms, disheveled hair, more drinking, and T-shirts that had belonged to her daughter Natalie. It was the lowest Angie had ever seen her mother. A low that Angie felt was partly her—

"You didn't hear anything I just said." Jake popped the top to a Pepsi.

"No, I heard," she said, attempting to cover her absolute not hearing anything he had said.

"Uh-huh," Jake said. "What are you studying for?"

"Um . . . They're just to keep me from rambling," Angie said. "Rambling is not sexy when you ask someone out."

"You still haven't asked Jamboree out?" Jake said. "Wang said something about hand-holding and milkshakes. He was unusually vague."

"Yeah, there were hands and kissing-not-kissing, staring, sort-of touching with frenetic energy. That's a thing, right?"

"I think it might be for you." Jake steered into the student parking lot. "Can I?" He motioned for the cards.

Reluctantly, she handed them over as he parked beside a lifted pickup blasting country music.

"Are you really going to quote a commercial?" he asked.

"Wang thought it would be funny."

"You're taking dating advice from Wang?"

"I panicked," Angie said. "You were with your dad."

"Not by choice." Jake continued to read.

The searing reality of Jake's parents' now-more-public separation continued to weigh heavy on his once light shoulders. Spending the weekend with his dad in his one-bedroom, one-bath apartment in the city was not what Jake had wanted. But Jake was a good boy, from a once-good home, who tried to make peace the best he could because that's what Jake did. Even if it hurt him. Deeply.

"Sorry," Angie said. "About how it is with your dad right now."

"It just is, right?" Jake said, still reading the cards. "Until it's something else."

Jake flipped to another card.

"I know what I want to say to her." Angie leaned against her headrest. "I just . . . I don't want to mess it up. The friendship part has been so . . . good, you know? And the other part is there. Like *really* there. I've just never asked anyone out. This is uncharted territory. It's a—maiden voyage. 'Love is a battlefield,' you know?"

"That's from a song isn't it?" Jake asked.

Angie grinned.

"Look, I get the cards, but I think you're overthinking this. Jamboree likes you. She always has, and if you hadn't put on the brakes after you kissed her, you'd already be a thing. A good thing."

Angie picked at a loose thread on her backpack. "Were you ever this nervous? Asking someone out?"

Jake nodded. "Sure."

"Liar."

"I *get* nervous," he said. "About a lot of things. Like—"

Before Jake could finish, Angie's eyes tracked Jamboree's car cruising past them, *BEAT THE OWLS* scrawled in white shoe polish across the back window of the not-so-trendy Honda Accord.

The wind whispered along the edge of Jamboree's skirt as she stepped out of the car. Her boho dress burst with color from beneath her oversize tweed coat, lapel dotted with miniature band pins. The sin of her was her smile, the way she said *serendipitous*, and of course, her mind filled with curiosity for all things retro and new. Angie's heart was undone, unfettered—floating well beyond her Pat Benatar *Get Nervous* super-soft baseball-style T-shirt.

When Jamboree's grin transcended the space between her and Angie right then, a rush crushed the soft parts of Angie.

Her cheeks flushed.

Her heart beat irregularly.

Her lips parted ever so slightly.

"You got this," Jake said, fishing a copy of *Every Day* from beneath his seat.

Angie reached for the cards, but Jake pulled them away.

"You don't need these," he said, jamming them into his glove box. "Just be you."

"You get that historically that hasn't worked out for me?" Angie said.

"Rewrite the narrative. Isn't that what your therapist says?"

"Kind of." Angie reached for the door handle. "More therapeutically."

A rotating wall of chatter and music circled Angie as she got out of the car.

"Hey, I get home around eight," Jake said, punching his arms through his letterman. "Stop by and tell me how it went."

Angie heaved her backpack on as Jake cut through the throngs of cars and teens. She took a deep breath, pressing PLAY on the Sony Walkman strategically clipped to the hip of her charcoal denim jeans. The melodic piano of the excessively retro REO Speedwagon song "Can't Fight This Feeling" vibrated through the orange foam headphones hanging around her neck.

The mood was set.

Angie began the longest yet physically shortest walk of her life. An estimated twenty-two steps, plump with rainbow, gay-girl-gay tension. She shifted her backpack straps along her shoulders. She smiled shyly. A dimple formed in her right cheek.

No longer the pariah, the freak of weighty gossip proportions, Angie was ready for this moment of walking toward Jamboree. She was Fat Angie and proud of it! A young woman who didn't shrink in shame at her size but celebrated it.

Most of the time, anyway.

It was this version of Angie, strutting in bedazzled combat boots, who continued, nervous-but-excited, toward Jamboree.

Jamboree grinned at Angie.

Angie grinned at Jamboree.

They were, by all accounts, in the midst of a sappy, cutesy, geeky grinfest for two.

This was it. This was *the* moment. This was . . .

"Hey," Angie said to Jamboree.

"Hey . . ." Jamboree said back.

Angie's mind went blank. Absolutely, unspeakably, yet realistically blank. Where was Katy Perry? Where was Angie's badassery? She had rehearsed her speech forty-two times in front of her bedroom mirror. A speech that she'd not only typed but spell-checked. Though it was still unclear why she had done the latter. In this free fall of what to say, Angie scrambled for her cool, her calm—making the fastest of prayers to the goddess of Amazons to return some crumb of her index-card speech to her consciousness.

"I stopped by The Backstory and got you this," said Jamboree. "Since it's their last day for the next few months."

"A Rock You Like a Hurricane Italian Cream Soda with a downbeat of espresso?" Angie said.

"Is there really any other kind of Italian cream soda?" Jamboree asked.

"No." Angie grinned. "There isn't."

Their fingers touched as Angie took the cup. Dozens of imagined butterflies burst from their invisible cocoons inside Angie. She gulped, fixating on Jamboree's soft, very kissable lips. The lips she had spontaneously kissed in an I-might-get-institutionalized-by-my-mom-and-never-see-you-again moment nearly four weeks earlier. The lips she had almost kissed over the weekend during Random Movie Night, had Zeke and Darius not been there. Had she had the courage to make the first move for a second time.

Had Angie simply said—

"I like your shirt," Jamboree said.

"Yeah? Wang got it for me. I think he had a coupon. Or something."

Why had Angie mentioned the coupon? It had no relevance to the conversation. This was why she needed the index cards.

"Hey, Ang." A girl from her bio class raised her fist. "Revolution!"

Angie did not follow the trajectory of the salutation and awkwardly responded, "Most def-i-nitely."

"What was that?" Jamboree asked.

"I don't know," Angie said. "I borrowed her notes once."

"You said you wanted to talk," Jamboree said. "When you texted from Jake's phone."

"Yeah," Angie said. "I did—I do . . . want to talk. Um . . ."

Angie cleared her throat.

"Is everything okay?" Jamboree asked. "Something happen with your mom again?"

"Yeah," Angie said. "I mean, no. It's not about my mom. Though it's an increasingly strange nightmare at home that would be best described as a—"

Angie had digressed.

"But that's . . ." Angie corrected. "It's not what I want to talk about . . . with you. What I want to talk about—it's a . . . a good thing."

"I like good things." Jamboree's smile wrapped around Angie's heart in layers.

"Yeah, me too. Liking of the good things." Angie took a deep breath. "I wanted to ask you . . ." The speech was returning. "First I wanted to say I really like . . ."

Angie was ready.

Angie was ready for everything.

Angie was ready for everything except what happened next.

The roar of a souped-up Honda Ruckus scooter engine ripped through the student parking lot. The headlights beamed in Angie's direction. As much as headlights could beam in the daylight on a cloudy day. Angie lost all sense of time, space, and even the fact that Jamboree was standing beside her because KC Romance, Angie's first girlfriend, had just unexpectedly cruised back into her life on two of the sexiest wheels possible.

KC killed the engine and lowered the kickstand. Her

punk-style cowboy boots crushed the pavement as she squeezed the hand grips. With a thrust of her hips, KC tamed the Ruckus into a freestanding park. The action, both powerful and slightly masculine, ignited an unexpected turn-on in Angie, who had all but written KC off. Written her off because KC had broken Angie's sugar-cookie heart.

Seeing KC again on the mysterious, matte-black Ruckus, all the excitement of the sweating Rock You Like a Hurricane Italian Cream Soda and asking Jamboree out slipped from Angie's consciousness. Because right then, the mystery of KC Romance had returned to Dryfalls, Ohio, and Angie was surprisingly curious.

KC slid her helmet off, her silky hair spinning in Angie-imagined slow motion. Puffs of blue and red streaked KC's hair, cascading to that unspeakable-yet-often-spoken-of purple heart tattoo along the nape of her smooth neck. She unzipped her vintage leather jacket; a flash of a new belly-button ring taunted Angie. Even from fifteen feet away, Angie could imagine the smell of KC's signature cherry ChapStick.

Angie's lips parted. The thinnest parcel of breath escaped, much the way it had when she'd seen KC for the first time in gym class a year earlier. What was this feeling? This feeling of longing when Angie had undeniably been:

A. Hurt by KC.

B. Done with KC.

C. Involved in something, though not yet defined, with Jamboree.
D. All of the above.

Angie looked at Jamboree, who had clearly seen Angie's no-poker-face reaction. This was when Angie decided she was in a conundrum.

Conundrum (n): A problem or question of intricate difficulty. Often presented in various fictional narratives to allow character growth.

Angie did not like conundrums, even when presented to her in the newest iteration of her more confident self.

"You two should probably"—Jamboree began to back up—"talk."

"What?" Angie said. "No, wait."

"I know what she means to you," Jamboree said.

"Meant." Angie reached for Jamboree's hand but hesitated.

"That wasn't a 'meant' look. It's okay. Really. It's . . . it's KC."

But it wasn't okay, as evidenced by Jamboree's forced smile. Angie cradled the Rock You Like a Hurricane Italian Cream Soda against her chest, not sure what to do. This was not part of the index cards.

"Um . . ." Angie managed.

Jamboree paused. "I forgot. Zeke said to find them before class."

"Hey," Angie called out. "See you at lunch, right? Just like, um, usual."

"Of course," Jamboree said.

"Is that 'of course' spelled N-O?"

Jamboree smiled halfheartedly. "It's spelled Y-E-S, actually."

Jamboree half waved, disappearing into the school. Angie turned as KC strutted confidently toward her.

"Hey," KC said.

Angie's thumbs jammed beneath her backpack's shoulder straps. "Hey."

"New look," said KC. "Retro with a slit of indie in the jeans."

Angie looked down at the ripped knees of her jeans, not sure how to follow up.

"Definitely, cool tee," KC said.

"Thanks."

AWKWARD!

"Benatar is beast," KC continued. "Sincerely, edge times pi. First time I heard her was in one of Esther's prized throwback flicks, *The Legend of Billie Jean*. You know it, right? 'Fair is fair.'" KC's fists pumped into the air.

"No, I, uh—I don't," Angie said.

"Oh, it's a must-marathon on VHS. Definite double feature with *Over the Edge*. No, wait, wait. Even better. *Foxes*.

Yes, *Foxes* with Jodie Foster. Oh my goddess, why can't she be our age right now?"

Angie thought this was rhetorical, but the lag time seemed to suggest maybe it wasn't.

"Because she's an adult?" Angie said.

"The perils of aging," KC said. "You and I will be forever young, though. I've decided I'm never getting old."

Why was KC acting as if they'd just seen each other at The Backstory last night? Things had happened. Lots of things had happened.

"I thought . . ." Angie began. "You were going to stay in Dallas. Life repaired by a Disneyland excursion or something."

"That buy-my-affection trip was a bust. Plus, I was over Dally. I mean, it's fine for a city in Texas. There's a sizeable underground VHS collector scene, queer-friendly in spots, but I was one hundred and ninety-nine percent over my dad on my ass twenty-four/seven. Dress like this. Act like that. Go to a megachurch so you can be megastraight. Highlight moment of his overt misogyny was when he said, 'KC, smile. You're prettier when you smile.' I was like, really? How did you ever impregnate my mom?"

Angie chuckled.

"Anyway," KC said. "I was literally suffocating in that suburban minimansion complete with heated pool and phony facade of a marriage to Mitzi, his man-wife. The woman literally has balls on the back of her truck."

"What?" Angie laughed.

"No joke," KC said. "Red rubber testicles hanging from the tow hitch. She's this ex-mechanic-turned-book-club-housewife who sells loads of cutesy shit on Etsy that she finds at estate sales. Her kids hate her as much as I do, but no alliances were ever to be made because they hate my dad and anything connected to him. Which is understandable. He's a tool. Massive."

Quiet.

More quiet that wasn't really quiet because people were talking all around them.

"So . . . I missed you," KC said, an unexpected vulnerability lingering. "A lot, actually. Probably more than I've ever missed anyone, you know?"

This was the part in the reunion with the witty, funny, intelligent, sexy first-but-now-very-ex-girlfriend where Angie was supposed to say, "I missed you too," because she had at first. She had missed KC to the point of longing that felt like a sickness. Angie hadn't simply filled that hole with Jamboree. Had she?

Before Angie could launch into contemplating the depths of her mixed feelings, which were many, the bell ceremoniously rang. Angie had literally been saved by the bell. The irony was not lost on her, and she would make note of it in her therapeutic journal for later reflection.

"I, um . . . need to go," Angie said.

"I'll walk with," KC said.

"If it's okay, I'd rather you didn't."

KC nodded. "Gotcha. Too much, too fast . . . too me. So, I'll see you later."

"Seems likely."

KC held steady for a beat longer before she left.

"Can't Fight This Feeling" faded out as Angie pressed STOP on her Walkman. Leaning against Jamboree's car, Angie wondered not just about KC's surprise return, but why she had let Jamboree simply walk away.

Chapter 2

It started with a few looks between classes later that morning. Nothing particularly noteworthy, or so Angie thought. But by the time she stood in line at the cafeteria, something was unquestionably amiss. Dozens of eyes launched from their phone screens, locking onto her. Staring wasn't an aberration in Angie's high-school experience, but *how* people were staring was. Their expressions teemed with a kind of awe and . . . excitement?

Skater Girl Rosie threw a nod to Angie as she walked past. Angie craned her neck toward her just as Zeke jogged up, camcorder in blinking-red record mode.

"Ooo, I like the hair color," Angie said. "It's very . . ."

"Pelt-the-Patriarchy Purple with hints of Anti-fascist Azul."

"I'm guessing that's not the name officially listed on the box," Angie said, picking up a food tray.

"No, but it should be," Zeke said, tugging at their ostomy bag through their shirt.

"You okay there?" Angie asked Zeke.

"Pinche adhesive. My skin is all pissed. Anyway. Girl, I sent you, like, six texts yesterday."

"My mom still has my phone," Angie said as the line finally picked up.

Zeke adjusted the weights stabilizing their DIY Steadicam. "Wasn't your dad gonna negotiate an early release?"

"It didn't exactly work out that way." Angie perused a pan of sickly rehydrated broccoli that looked like it had been dipped in the murky waters of the Hocking River. "They're still fighting about everything and nothing. He calls. She hangs up. She calls. He hangs up."

"And adults say *we're* immature."

"Right," Angie said. "Oh, and last night. You would have loved it. Absolutely camera-worthy. Wang and me and John/Rick were sitting at the dinner table right after my mom hung up on my dad. John/Rick asked her to pass the chicken tikka masala, and she threw it against the wall behind him."

"No shit!" Zeke said.

"No, um, shit. Then she threw the rice. Even the naan."

"That's hard core," Zeke said, camera back in record mode.

"I know," Angie said. "I really like naan. Anyway, she broke up with him. Right then and there. Wang started clapping. She started yelling. And John/Rick started spouting some self-help/couple counseling whatever-whatever. I'm just sitting there thinking after every idiotic thing John/Rick has said or done in the last year, it just took 'Pass the chicken tikka masala'? Strange."

Angie signaled the cafeteria server for fish sticks.

"It's never about the chicken tikka masala," Zeke said. "Adult relationships are a fervent spawn of lies and bored ideations."

"Huh," Angie said. "Yeah. Maybe. Anyway, sorry I didn't get your messages or meet up for songwriting yesterday. We were on an unofficial lockdown post–dinner drama. Wait. Did you get back with Raquel?"

"Yeah, no," Zeke said. "That would take divine intervention from the goddess."

"Or you apologizing for being weird. About the whole bag thing."

Zeke sighed. They did not like to be called out. It just wasn't something they knew how to handle, as evidenced by them saying—

"So, no one has said anything to you today?" Zeke continued to film.

"You can't deflect forever," Angie said.

"I'm not . . . deflecting about the O-bag and Raquel's freak-out."

"She didn't actually freak out," Angie said. "You kind of—"

"Angie," Zeke said. "You didn't talk to Jamboree? Darius?"

Choosing not to comment about her Jamboree blunder before school, Angie simply shook her head.

"Woman, I've got something good to tell you," Zeke said. "Really unbelievably good. My mother would call it a milagro. My father would make fun of her for calling it that. Which, my pinche dad. I can't even."

Angie grinned while paying the cashier. "What is it?"

"Okay, but at first it may seem like it's not good, but it's good, so you can't get mad."

In her brief knowing of Zeke, when they said *you can't get [fill in the blank]*, it often meant fill-in-the-blank was the inevitable outcome.

"You get that's holding me hostage?" Angie said. "Saying I can't get mad. My therapist would say it's denying me my mad."

"Yeah, okay, but you still can't get mad."

Angie waited.

And waited.

And when the waiting seemed like it might extend well past lunch, Zeke said, "I posted a video of you on YouTube."

This was a moment of unbridled terror, as evidenced by Angie's expression.

"Wait—what video?" Angie asked.

"Girl, you *can't* get mad."

"What video, Zeke?"

In the pause that followed, Angie knew that Zeke was withholding information for dramatic, on-camera effect. Angie was reaching for the lens when Zeke blurted out, "The one with you singing with Cat Scratch in Cincinnati."

"What?" Angie's loudness put the table closest to her at pause. Angie's head whipped left—right. The looks in the hallways . . . between classes . . . before school. There in the cafeteria . . . They had seen her—singing?

"It's not a bad thing," Zeke said. "People like it *a lot*."

The world of Angie Tilt-A-Whirl spun. All while holding a plate of greasy fish sticks and congealed cheesy tots sprinkled with freeze-dried parsley.

"It's viral," Zeke said. "Angie, it's—"

Wang crashed into Angie from behind, chewing a mouthful of cheeseburger. He shoved his phone in her face. "Dude, why didn't you tell me?"

Angie's eyes widened.

Her mouth dropped open.

By all accounts, she was in a state of disbelief.

She had to write the number of views as an algebraic equation in her mind.

Angie + Video of Song = 833,242 views!

She looked up from Wang's phone, Zeke's camera still filming her.

"Right?" Zeke said.

"That can't be real," Angie said.

"It's for real, yo." Wang threw his arm over his sister's shoulders. "Your shit's viral, and not even for doing anything dumb for once."

She shoved him. He continued to laugh as he stumbled back.

Zeke circled Angie with their camera, pelting Angie with a litany of questions. "How do you feel? What do you feel? When are you dropping your next video? What do you want to say to your fans, chica?"

"Fans?" Angie chuckled.

"The numbers don't lie, Ang," Zeke said. "What did I tell you? I said you have a story and people wanna know. You got fans, girl."

The number of views continued to orbit the gravity-dense atmosphere of her confused mind. Angie had been a joke in online videos—in GIFs. A joke until recently at her high school.

Wang gathered a handful of cheesy tots from Angie's tray as she tilted his phone toward her, scrolling through the comments. The obvious *Fat Bitch with a mic* and *Shamu out of the tank* were there, but many of them were like *Badass!* and *U ROCK! Love this song! Go, Fat Angie!*

"You called me Fat Angie?" she said to Zeke.

"You said was it was your superhero name. I wrote it with nothing but reclaimed-word respect. I can change it if you want."

"No . . . it's . . . I just . . . never thought eight hundred thousand people would know it. Not hate me for it."

"It's the opposite of hate," Zeke said. "It's like a big, beautiful body celebration. Tyler Oakley retweeted the video, and it blew up," Zeke said. "Facebook, Tumblr, Twitter, Instagram. It's everywhere."

Angie's pseudo-fame euphoria crashed with the word *everywhere*. The video could not be everywhere because that meant—

"My mom doesn't know I did this," Angie said to Zeke. "She doesn't know I went to Cincinnati."

"She knows you dumped your sister's ashes in the Ohio River," Zeke said, matter-of-fact.

"It's a very *big* river, Zeke!" Angie said. "She's going to kill me. Not like in a family television series where kids get in trouble and say 'My mom's going to kill me.' I mean, like, she may physically harm me. The naan, remember? She hasn't said a word to me since Gary Klein got suspended. Not a word. This might elicit . . . all of them. The bad ones anyway."

"She wouldn't hurt-you-hurt-you, right?" Zeke said. "Ang? Would she? Has she?"

Wang shot off a text, leaving Angie to continue to hide the volatile reality of their home life.

"I'm just—she's on the edge of whatever the edge looks like," Angie said. "She's been sitting in her room almost all day and . . ."

"Being a pain in my ass," Wang said, finishing his text. "And Angie's right. Our mom sees this, she's gonna shit like fifty-five angry bricks."

Wang's questionable descriptor was remarkably accurate.

"Why didn't you ask me, Zeke?" Angie said.

"It just—sort of happened." Zeke rested the camera rig against their shoulder. "Like, I showed it to my friend Finster who dropped it to her friend in California, who sings for the Raging Rachels, and she loved it. And she was like, 'you have to post this,' and I tried to text you, and then it just kind of went from there."

It was a good thing, a bad thing, and a potentially very ugly thing if Connie saw the video. Angie was not sure how to proceed.

"Dude." Wang nudged her.

"Not a dude, and I'm thinking," she said.

"Look, I don't want to," Zeke said. "But if you want, I'll pull the vid."

"No. I don't know. I mean, maybe?"

"It's not a maybe," Wang said. "It's a for-sure pull. It's one thing if it was me. I could give three steamy, long shits what happens."

"That's disgusting," Angie said.

"But you." He shook his head. "You gotta just not set her off."

Angie looked at Wang's phone. The video froze on

her and her primal-scream face. Seeing herself standing onstage, confident, fearless, not the Dryfalls Angie the world had come to know, it was a wow moment of the strangest variety. Maybe her mom wouldn't find out. Maybe if she did, she wouldn't go nuclear on Angie. On that stage, Angie wasn't meek or weak, and those were the two things Connie disliked the most about Angie. Well, behind her weight and mental health problems. And her love of her father's favorite music and—Angie had to stop listing because she was starting to panic.

"Just promise me you won't post *anything* else without asking," Angie said.

"I promise," Zeke said. "Gender-nonconforming honor."

Angie half chuckled.

"You guys wanna hug it out or something?" Wang asked. "Because—"

Wang's attention tipped toward the glass double doors as KC strutted inside. Zeke's and Angie's gazes soon followed Wang's as KC effortlessly maneuvered through the crowd of kids gathered near the salad bar.

"The plot thickens," Zeke said, camera back in record mode.

"Hey," KC said to Angie, before, "What up, Wang? Thanks for not passing on my text to Angie that I was coming back."

Angie's look to Wang was laced in not-so-subtle daggers.

He shrugged. "Must've forgot."

Clearly, he had not.

"That new ink is rabid, yo," Wang said, eyes on KC's wrist.

KC pulled up her shirtsleeve, revealing a witch's hat propped against a steampunk broom with the words

Witches Don't Play

"I wanted something a little smoky, little buttery, you know." She lowered her sleeve. "One body. One life. Make it count, right?"

"Aren't you, like, sixteen?" Zeke asked.

"I was three hundred when I handed him the cash," KC said. "The place was legit. Health department gold star. Just a little after-hours stop. Friend of my mom's."

The exchange of looks between KC and Zeke was more adversarial than Angie might have expected. A moment that she would surely note in her therapeutic journal for later reflection.

"Check this." Wang regrettably rolled up his T-shirt sleeve to show off what seemed the result of a painfully drunken night for both him and the tattoo apprentice.

KC cocked her head to the side ever so slightly. "It's . . ."

But before she could finish, Wang said, "Bruce Lee. *Game of Death.*"

It was truly, without question, a death of some kind, but *Game of Death* would have been a stretch of epic proportions.

"Yeah, I'm not seeing that," KC said. "More Middle Earth

Frodo with some . . . is that spaghetti in the background?"

He dropped his sleeve. "It's not literal Bruce Lee. Not entirely. Besides, I need some touch-up."

"You need a cover-up," KC said. "Listen, bad tattoos happen to even moderately good people. Come by Esther's shop. She's hella good with cover-ups. It's like her tattooist superpower. Sincerely. This weekend a woman came in. She got inked in Vegas because all things bizarro tattoowise happen there after twelve hours in a windowless casino downing three-dollar drinks while playing the slots. So, this woman is crying on my mom's shoulder. Full of ink remorse because she had two sunny-side-up eggs tattooed in a fit of irony."

"What was the irony?" Angie asked.

KC shrugged. "Irony is irrelevant. Relevant is that a few hours on my mom's table, her cover-up was ultra-even. Exquisite. Look."

KC slid her phone from her back pocket. A couple of taps and a few swipes and there were the before and after tattoo photos. Angie leaned in, the bareness of her arm touching KC's and igniting a twinge of unwanted attraction—of a familiar ache.

"You'd never know someone cracked eggs on her skin, right?" KC grinned at Angie before turning to Wang. "Besides, Esther will give you the friends-and-family discount, which is probably free because she loves Angie like a second child."

"Wang!" Cody Riley shouted from across the cafeteria.

Wang waved that he'd be right there before Angie pulled him to the side. "Why didn't you tell me she was coming back?"

"Yo, slow your roll," Wang said. "I didn't tell you your ex was coming back so you wouldn't punk out on asking Jamboree out. You did it, right?"

"Wang!" Cody called out, again.

"Look, I gotta go," Wang said to Angie. "I can't give you a ride after school, so hit Jake up."

"Wang . . . you promised not to hang out with Criminal Cody. He's the actual definition of trouble."

"Even famous you're weird," Wang said, backing up. "Relax. I'm an expert at avoiding trouble."

That was a canard. Wang was an expert in attracting trouble. From the opposite sex, from the same sex, from police officers, teachers, his mother, his father, and his court-appointed therapist, who had been sleeping with their mother until recently. Trouble was synonymous with Wang, only Angie understood less and less exactly why.

Wang threw Criminal Cody a snap-shake. Angie's stomach tightened because he was next-tier trouble. Unlike Wang, there was nothing poser criminal about him.

"Should I've lied?" KC asked Angie. "About the ink?"

"You could've modulated the emasculating," Zeke said, a defensiveness in their voice.

"Esther raised me to never lie about a bad tattoo. The

only person who's happy after bad ink is the jerk who pocketed the cash."

Zeke turned off their camera. "Weren't you supposed to be, like, in Texas?"

KC gave Zeke an up-and-down before saying, "I was in Dallas, and now I'm here. It's like a rabbit in a magic hat."

Uncomfortable.

Super uncomfortable quasi-confrontation between Zeke and KC.

"I feel like I just crashed into the middle of a joke with no punch line," KC said.

"Yeah, it's not a joke," Zeke said. "Ang doesn't hear from you . . ."

"Zeke—"

"Then you just show up, rabbit and magic, cracking on people's ink." Zeke stepped toward KC.

"Zeke," Angie said.

"What?" Zeke asked.

"Not yours," Angie said. "Okay?"

Zeke nodded, then leaned into KC, whispering, "Don't mess with her head."

Zeke stepped back, heading out the glass doors plastered with homecoming posters.

"So . . . who is that, and why does she hate me to the nth?" KC asked Angie.

"*They* or *them*. Pronoun-wise. It's new-ish—to me, not to them. And hate . . . maybe more protective instead."

"Because they're your girlfriend?"

"We write music together," Angie said. "Watch a lot of foreign films."

"Didn't know writing music was your thing," KC said.

"The world of your not knowing about what matters to me . . . is pretty vast right now. Like what it felt like when you left. When you stopped texting. When you just . . . moved on."

"I didn't *just* anything. And I definitely didn't move to anything except Dallas. I told you. I missed you. Like, by the seconds."

Angie nodded. "And the avocado-green-haired girl? With all the piercings that you posted pictures with? Which seconds of the missing was she in?"

KC paused, and it was in this pause that Angie felt a prickly, hot anger sprint along the corridors of nerve endings and flush her face.

Angie did not like anger.

Angie did not like knowing that while anger could be healthy, she rarely felt it that way.

Angie did not know how to navigate the complexities of this specific anger.

"Look, I had to make friends—try to fit," KC said. "I still missed you. I just didn't know . . . how to miss. But I'm here now. I wanna know about writing music and foreign films. Like, are you more the Clash or Beyoncé? French New Wave or Bergman?"

KC reached for Angie's hand. A confusing flutter expanded in Angie's stomach. She was mad. She didn't want KC holding her hand, but somehow it felt familiar and oddly alluring. Angie stepped back.

"But you didn't want to know then—when I needed you to know," Angie said. "And now you do? Don't you get that it's not— Don't you get how much you hurt me?"

"Let's just—have a do-over. You plus me and a sugary substance at The Backstory. A roll of quarters and *Galaga* in the arcade."

"What's wrong with you? Things have happened, KC. You weren't here."

"I made a mistake and I'm trying—"

"Yeah." Angie backed away from KC. "You did make a mistake."

"Angie . . . C'mon. It doesn't have to be fatal."

"You ghosted me," Angie said. "I can't. This. You."

Angie paused at the glass doors facing the courtyard. Jamboree sat, legs crossed, on top of their unofficially reserved table. Darius's head was characteristically buried in a textbook. Zeke filmed Jamboree now twirling her drumsticks, telling what was likely a funny story. Jamboree had the best stories. Maybe ever.

Pops of orange and red leaves rained around the trio. The whole scene could have easily been a snapshot from a trendy clothing ad in a number of magazines. All of them there smiling, laughing—that was Angie's new life minus

KC. A life where she had finally belonged. But for the first time since returning from the road trip, she questioned whether she truly belonged in that commercial-smiling-laughter version of her life. That version had a shelf life, with Darius determined to enlist in the air force after graduation, Zeke applying for film school in California, and Jamboree deciding whether to do another semester abroad. Where would Angie fit then? When the table was empty?

Angie looked over her shoulder at KC with her back to her. It hadn't all been bad with KC. It hadn't been all good either. There were many downs. Maybe more than ups, but KC was—she was KC. All that emulated the rugged rebellion of a feminist badass. Even if KC's slang was largely a creation influenced by her *Buffy the Vampire Slayer* television series fandom, it was KC speak, and it still made Angie feel . . . something she would have never expected. Confused.

Given the girth of Angie's perplexed and cluttered heart, she did what any empowered young woman with budding Internet fame would do. She retreated into the girls' restroom and waited for lunch to be over.

Chapter 3

Lockers opened and slammed shut while Angie stuffed her backpack, testing the limits of its threadbare edges. Her mind continued to spiral, as it had most of the afternoon, with both the excitement and the fear of being viral for something she wasn't ashamed of.

"Hey," KC said, her back collapsing against the locker next to Angie's.

Angie shook her head.

"I get it," said KC. "You're mad. You're right to be mad. Okay?"

"I don't need you to tell me that," Angie said. "That I get to be mad. It's just that. Me being me and not trying to fit whatever works for you."

"Wow." KC rolled onto her shoulder. "Is that what you were doing?"

Angie sighed. Articulating her feelings was not a strength in her relationship with KC because KC had been fragile-ish. For all her talk of ultra-even and feminist fury, she was just as wounded as Angie. Sometimes maybe even more so.

Angie noticed a series of scratches—fresh cuts—peeking from KC's shirt collar. KC quickly shifted her stance to hide them.

"When did you do that?" Angie said.

"Life is a maze with a lot of turns," KC said.

"Did you do that after lunch?"

"No," KC said defiantly. Maybe defensively. Angie was not entirely certain. "There is nothing to worry about. I'm working on it. New therapist. New plan."

Which was what KC had said many a time in many different ways when she had fallen off what she called the cutter's wagon. Not a phrasing Angie had ever been entirely comfortable with, but she acknowledged it was KC's way of minimizing it.

"Listen," KC said. "I saw your video. It's so extra-ultra. I never thought I'd hear 'transcranial magnetic stimulation' in a song, and it totally works because, you know, inherently that shit freaks me out. Happened to a friend of mine in Cali. But this song! Ang, I can't wait for girls to start burning the teen magazines coaching them on frivolous lip gloss techniques and fall fashion fixes in effigy. That would be essential."

"I guess," Angie said, flatly.

"You guess," KC said. "Okay. I know you don't want to talk to me. Fair. Kind of. But there's this competition. I found out about it when I was still in Dallas." KC slid her cell from her jacket pocket. "Look. Rock Riot. It's been going on for a few years. See? They're looking for all-female bands. Everything happens online. Which, bonus, you have a massive fan base. All you have to do is video a couple of original songs, make a promo vid, et cetera. You gotta enter."

Angie closed her locker. "I don't have a band. And even if I did," she said, glancing at KC's phone, "the deadline is in, like, three weeks."

Angie zipped up her backpack, shouldering it.

"You could do this," KC said.

"I don't want to talk to you."

Angie turned, but KC followed, cutting in front of her.

"What can I do? What?" KC asked. "I'm sorry that I—didn't handle leaving better or whatever. I'm sorry for it."

"You can't say sorry if you don't even know what it's for."

"Remember us?" KC said. "You. Me. *BTVS* marathon. Vanilla Coke in the bed of my mom's truck. Fourth of July. Eyes on each other. Like a queer country song if *ever* one was written. You could write it! I, of course, would be the heartbroken, boot-wearing damsel not in distress. I'd have a dog. A hound dog. We could name him Elvis."

"What are you talking about?" Angie said.

"Our country song."

Angie sighed. "We don't—KC, we're not a we."

KC reached for Angie's hand. "I love you. You're my best friend."

And that was when it happened. That moment in movies where the smart-sexy-troubled-ex-girlfriend professes her love only to have the current heart's interest come around the corner and see it all unfold. Jamboree's stride slowed down before backing up.

"I have to go," Angie said.

Angie jogged around the corner, the bottom of her backpack slapping against her lower back. It was a truly painful feeling.

"Jamboree!" she called out. "Jam."

Jamboree paused just outside the building.

"Hey," Angie said.

"Hey," Jamboree said, arms crossed over her stomach.

"I, um," Angie said, drawing a blank.

"Wang texted me to give you a ride," Jamboree said. "I was . . . coming to tell you I have auditions for Jazz Band and if you could wait until after. I didn't mean to interrupt."

"You didn't, um . . . interrupt. Anything." Angie's heart and head flooded with half-written sentences scribbling toward completion.

Quiet.

More quiet.

"Zeke told me about KC and lunch," said Jamboree. "Are you okay?"

Angie considered the question for an unmeasured amount of time as she was prone to do when put on the spot.

"I'm sorry," Jamboree said. "I probably shouldn't have asked."

"No, of course you should ask," Angie said. "You can ask anything. We're friends."

Jamboree's head lowered ever so slightly. A clear indication that she was under the assumption that there was more between them than friendship. And there *was* more between them. A lot more, though not yet defined. And while REO Speedwagon's chorus to "Can't Fight This Feeling" began playing in Angie's mind, something kept Angie from saying what she really wanted—felt. Carpe diem Angie was not.

"I'm not saying anything right." Angie looked down at her boots. "It's been a really weird day. Viral video, an A on an English test I was absolutely sure I failed, and Wang continuing to be . . . And my mom. That's, like . . . I don't know."

"Is she talking to you yet?" Jamboree asked.

"She sighed in my direction yesterday, which is better than seething, I guess," Angie said. "It's still mostly Netflix bingeing in her bedroom and micromanaging this ridiculous film about my sister. Which I can't even put together that it's happening."

"Zeke said they're filming here in a couple of weeks?" Jamboree said.

"Yeah. Plus we have to do this stupid family interview when they're here. I hate the interviews so much. There's nothing real about them except how uncomfortable they are. But I just . . . with my mom. I keep thinking maybe she'll hate me less if I go along with it."

"She doesn't hate you," Jamboree said.

"I did pour the remains of her firstborn in the Ohio River. Which really sounds twisted when I say it out loud."

Angie looked away, recalling Connie's coldness to her since she'd returned from her unsanctioned road trip, urn empty. The days and weeks that followed procured a hole in Connie unlike anything Angie had seen, leaving Angie to feel responsible for Connie's descent from high-functioning alcoholic to her "leave" from the law firm and pouring a glass of wine before ten most mornings. Regardless of the many ways Connie had wounded Angie, Angie had never meant to hurt her mother.

"Hey." Jamboree's fingers brushed against Angie's wrist.

"Sorry," said Angie.

"You don't have to apologize," Jamboree said. "You don't have be anything but whatever you are. Just you."

"How do you do that?" Angie asked.

"What?"

"Be so . . . kind?" Angie said.

Jamboree laughed. "I guess it's my superpower."

The wind sprayed Jamboree's hair across her face. A face faintly dotted in freckles and two small blemishes along the edge of her chin. Blemishes she could have covered with concealer but hadn't. Her smile was slightly crooked. Her eyes were wild and calm, and it was in that duality that the noise about Angie's family and the movie and all the other things dropped out to . . .

"What?" Jamboree said.

"Um," Angie said. "You know, we're not just friends. I wanted to say that before—earlier. Not that we're not friends. Because we're definitely, absolutely—you know."

The anxiety from the rambling—the nonsensical tripping over her feelings was utterly confidence crushing. She simply had to say—

"Yeah?" Jamboree offered.

"Maybe . . . I could come by later," Angie said. "I've got this dinner thing tonight with my dad and his newish-not-newish wife. I mean, it's really just a stop on the way to a conference in Cleveland, but he's made it out to Wang that it's about us, so I kind of have to go. And that was, like, the longest sentence ever."

"It was a perfectly fine sentence," Jamboree said.

"So . . . I could come by after?" Angie said. "If that's okay."

Jamboree grinned. "Sure."

One Grin + One Sure = Tingles

"Swell," Angie said. "Exponentially."

"So, maybe around eight or so?" Jamboree said.

"I'll text you from Wang's phone when we're done," Angie said.

"Good luck," Jamboree said. "With your dad and his . . . what do you call her?"

Angie smiled. "His newish-not-newish wife, Sharon."

"Good luck with her, too," Jamboree said, heading toward the band hall.

Angie would ask Jamboree out while they did homework, perhaps with Prince or Bowie spinning on vinyl in the RV. She would move past her confusion with KC and forward in her new life with Jamboree, however uncertain it might be. All she had to do was get through dinner.

Angie's palms pressed against the top of her mother's dining room chair while she stared hopelessly at a series of headshots stretched across the table. Twenty full-color photos had been assembled in two precisely aligned rows of ten. Angie was dumbfounded by the character names matched to the actors. It was—

"Your dad called," Connie said, her voice startling Angie. "He said they'll be late. Surprise."

Connie stood across from Angie, a glass of chardonnay in hand, as she reviewed the headshots. Nervously, Angie's index finger rubbed a jagged nick along the back of the expensive, hand-carved-to-Connie-perfection chair. Unsure of her exit strategy, unsure what her next best move was because even with a table between them, being alone with Connie felt too close.

"He wants you to meet him there," Connie said, not looking up from the table.

"Um, okay."

The imperfection in her mother's dining room chair slit Angie's finger. A line of blood exhaled along her thumb. Angie looked up from her hand at her mother, trying to understand some part of Connie, wearing a moth-chewed HORNETS' NEST TRACK T-shirt with designer jeans.

"What?" her mother said, sipping from her glass.

"So, these are the cast options?" Angie said.

Connie shuffled some of the headshots, studying their new pairing quietly. "The director and a small film crew are coming to film some kind of cinema verité B-roll during homecoming. That's how Joan explained it to me."

"I thought you weren't talking to anybody," Angie said.

"Why would you think that?"

Angie thought that mostly because Connie had rarely left the house the last few weeks, letting messages stack up on the landline answering machine, one of the few relics Connie clung to in what was becoming a largely digitally updated home.

"Anyway. They've asked me my opinion on a few of these people. It's more of a courtesy, but they want to get it right."

"Those actresses don't look anything like me," Angie said.

"They don't have to."

"But isn't that the point?" Angie asked. "The point of getting it right?"

Connie shuffled another series of headshots, seeming pleased with her new pairing. Angie, however, was not.

"These guys." Angie pointed to two headshots in the far top corner of the table. "Wang's Vietnamese. Not Korean or Filipino."

"They're people of color."

"They're the wrong color," Angie said. "You can't just swap out whatever version of ethnic you think is better."

"They screen-tested very well," Connie said.

"But it's a lie."

"It's a reframing of the narrative. I don't expect you to understand. You understand so little."

Angie clenched her jaw.

"This is really how you're going to do this," Angie said. "You're just going to rewrite us—cast people to play us to fit whatever idea you wish we could be."

"This is not about me. It's about honoring— It's an interpretation of your sister's life."

"Whose interpretation?" Angie said. "This is nothing like her life. That actress—right there. She doesn't even look like her."

"It's a headshot, Angie. Why do you have to make everything—"

"Wang's Vietnamese. I'm not a size eight. Dad doesn't have a scar above his eye like a cheap Harry Potter. Coach Laden is bustier and more . . . not that. And Imelda Sanchez, who played on the team, she's Afro-Latina, not white with curly hair."

"Stop." Connie's hand went up. "Just stop it."

"Mom, it's—"

"Can you just stop?"

Angie shook her head. "I don't want to fight with you. I just . . . This is so—wrong. Can't you see it?"

Angie and Connie shared a look that easily could have been timed at eight seconds. The length of time necessary for a rider to stay saddled on a bull in a rodeo. It seemed equally long and hard for Angie and her mother to look at each other. It was in this moment that Angie saw something shift in Connie's expression. The chiseled coldness loosened in the smallest of increments. Her eyes seemed to soften. Her heart was—

"Change your shirt before dinner," Connie said. "That one has a stain."

Closed. Her heart had closed as quickly as it nearly opened. A thorny ball of anxiety swirled in Angie's diaphragm.

"What happens when you try to just talk to your mother?" her therapist had recently asked Angie.

"You can't talk to someone who thinks you're invisible."

"Maybe . . . her grief makes it hard to reach out."

Angie had considered the notion, and then said, *"So, what about before? Before, when Nat was still home. She didn't see me then. She looked through me, around me . . . to see Nat, Wang, the landscaper. Anyone who wasn't me."*

Angie stood at the table alone. The sound of her mother's footsteps clapped along the stairs, her bedroom door soon closing. Tom Petty and the faint smell of a joint would likely follow.

Angie picked up one of two headshots marked:

ANGIE, AGE 16

The actress was television fat, which was way different from real fat. There was only the hint of a possible second chin, and in no world of acting did she appear sixteen.

Angie put the headshot back on the table, precisely in alignment with all the others, and walked toward the stairs thinking one thing: something had to change, but it wasn't going to be her shirt.

Chapter 4

Angie had waited for approximately twenty-three minutes, per the crooked clock behind the register of Jamie's "Truly Authentic" Chinese Dynasty. She had waited because Wang and her couldn't-be-accountable father and his newish-not-newish wife were, of course, late. She shifted on an unpadded bench while two white waitresses gawked from a pair of stools. It was a set of looks that normally would've made Angie cradle her stomach with her arms as if to somehow conceal the girth of her. But tonight she was not going to give them the satisfaction of reducing her body to something to be ashamed of. She was fat and beautiful, and they would just have to get used to it.

There had been a time, not that long ago, when Angie

would've salivated at an all-you-can-eat buffet. Tonight was not that night. As tempting as it was to eat her problems away, most notably those with her mother, she knew it would fix nothing.

The bell over the door jangled. Sharon walked in toting a large, sparkly gift bag though there was no reason for said bag. As far as Angie knew.

Angie readied herself for the uncomfortable hellos, *how are you, I-don't-know-what-else-to-say* as her dad stumbled in, attempting to wrangle a bouquet of balloons. Mylar balloons to be exact, with the phrase YOU'RE SO SPECIAL printed on each of them.

Angie cringed. The word *special* was specifically cringeworthy for her.

"Hey, honey." He proudly presented the balloons to her. "There are M&M's in the base."

Angie stood there literally speechless. Not that she didn't have something to say, it was just that—

"What?" he said.

"You drive a Prius and you bought me Mylar balloons?" she said.

"I don't understand," he said.

"They're nonbiodegradable. Baby sperm whales get them stuck in the lining of their stomachs and die. They cause power outages if they get tangled in electrical lines."

"But you love balloons," he said.

"No," Angie said, handing them back to him. "Nat did."

It was at this infraction that the invisible space between them widened. One of the balloons went rogue, bouncing into her father's clearly fake-and-bake face as he batted it away.

"Oh . . . um," he scrambled for something to say, but only came up with an expression of embarrassment. "Nonbiodegradable, huh?"

Angie sighed. She simply wanted this portion of the evening to be over. She wanted to lounge in the back of Jamboree's RV, listening to Blondie, Bowie, Prince, INXS—anything but—

"Latex too?" her father asked.

Angie sighed. "Six months to four years. The length of time it takes to degrade."

"Wow. I didn't . . ." He turned to Sharon. "Did you know that?"

"Yeah, I did," she said. "That's why we didn't have them at the kids' parties."

"Huh," he said.

"Booth or table?" the waitress asked, eyes leaving a sizable trail of judgment Angie's way.

"Booth, please." Angie's dad turned to her. "Unless you want a—"

"It's fine," she said.

It was, of course, not.

The waitress escorted them to one of three U-shaped, tall-back booths. Angie worked to wedge herself into the snug-fitting booth. While she attempted to push the table away from her, the waitress blurted out, "It's bolted down, sweetie."

"We can move to another table," Angie's dad said, tugging at his ear.

That was when Angie noticed that he had pierced his left ear with a diamond stud. From a suit and tie to flip-flops, dark-washed jeans, and a diamond earring, her father was truly a screaming example of midlife crisis.

"No, I'm fine," Angie said, surrendering to the pressure against her stomach.

She was not fine. She was annoyed. With the tightness of the table. With the electro-pop music accompanied by operatic vocals. With the fact that Wang, who wanted nothing more than to spend time with their dad, was late. With the Mylar balloons now floating in the center of the table.

In short, she was annoyed with the entire scene.

"Buffet or menus?" the waitress asked.

"Buffet. Right, Angie?" said her dad.

"If she wants that," said Sharon.

"Of course she does," he said dismissively.

"Sure," she agreed, just to have them stop talking about her like she wasn't there.

Finishing their drink orders, the three of them scooted out of the booth and perused the remarkably long line of buffet options. Pan after greasy and often sugarcoated pan of foods, including chow mein, fried rice, steamed rice, egg rolls, crispy noodles, beef broccoli, sesame chicken, orange chicken, shrimp with snow peas, crab rangoon, egg foo yong, seafood delight, and to Angie's confusion, even pizza, meatball pasta, mashed potatoes, fried chicken, orange Jell-O, and tiny squares of vanilla cake with hints of ice along the frosted edges.

Angie wanted none of it.

Not a single bite.

She simply wasn't hungry, and she should have been famished.

"Angie?" Sharon said. "Everything okay?"

Angie sighed and plopped an obligatory small serving of fried rice and lemon chicken on her plate.

"You want more than that," her dad said, his plate heaped with a mountain of General Tso's chicken.

He pierced the vat of lo mein with a pair of food-encrusted tongs. The noodles dangled helplessly as he craned them over Angie's plate, plopping them on top of her rice and chicken.

Just breathe, she thought. *Even if he can't see you.*

"What's wrong?" he said. "You love lo mein. I mean, you do, don't you?"

One, she was a food separatist. She didn't like her food touching much less slopped together like in a trough. Two, had he really just decided what she wanted to eat?

"I didn't want it," she said.

"Oh," he said, clearly befuddled by her response.

"Jesse," said Sharon. "She can figure it out."

He proceeded down the line. Sharon mouthed to Angie, "He's trying" before following him.

Angie considered the egg drop soup as Marcus Murphy dumped a fresh container of egg rolls onto the buffet line.

"Hey, Ang," said Marcus.

"Hey, Marcus," she said, a bit surprised they were talking.

Surprised because . . .

Marcus Murphy hadn't said much to her since freshman year. While they had classes together in junior high, they'd parted ways after she flunked ninth. They weren't particularly unfriendly to each other. They just had little in common aside from an affection for '80s and '90s music, B-horror movies, and the steak fingers served on Wednesdays in the cafeteria. Which, to be honest, should have bonded them for life, but it had not.

"Dinner with your folks?" He nodded toward the booth.

"My dad and his newish-not-newish wife."

"My parents got divorced too," he said. "My mom remarried twice. I don't think I ever told you that."

"No," Angie said. "I guess that would be kind of weird."

"Yeah, mostly," he said. "She's in SAA now. Sex Addicts Anonymous."

"Which . . . isn't all that anonymous because you just told me?" Angie said.

He shrugged, wiping spilled food from the counter. "She tells everyone. We were at The Slice picking up a pizza, and she told Sydney Oliver. Whole school knows now."

"I'm sorry."

"I saw your video."

"Yeah," she said. "Weird, huh?"

"It was really cool," he said. "Like, really."

"Thanks."

He nodded. "Want some moo goo gai pan? We got some in the back."

"No, I'm okay."

"Okay," he said.

She started to walk away, but stopped. "Hey, Marcus."

"Yeah?"

"Sorry about your mom," she said.

"It could be worse."

Angie waited for the worse, only he couldn't think of anything.

"At least she's not a serial killer," Angie offered.

Marcus grinned. "At least."

He swiped food debris into a bucket before disappearing behind a set of double doors.

Angie's father was pouring soy sauce onto his meal when she squeezed back into the booth.

"Did you see that they have those puffy fried donuts?" her dad asked her.

She twirled her fork around the mound of lo mein, not looking at him. "Yeah."

He sucked soda through a straw, peering over the sauce caddy at Angie's plate. "You didn't get any. They're your favorite."

"Not really. Not . . . anymore."

Sharon, eating in small precise bites, smiled at Angie, who had begun to count. Eleven times. Sharon had chewed one bite eleven times. Surely, that level of mastication was exhausting to one's jaw.

"We could get something else after we leave if you want," Angie's dad said.

"Dad, just stop it." Angie's fork dramatically clanged against the plate though she had not meant it to. "Stop fixating on what's on my plate or what my favorite whatever is."

Confused, her father said, "What is that about?"

"This dinner. Tonight? You don't return calls or show up when you say you will, and all of a sudden you're here? Do you get this is the first time I've seen you since Nat's funeral? You said you'd come to the dedication ceremony, but you didn't. Not that I can entirely fault you because it was an epically disgusting fiasco, but I kind of do."

"You know we were still settling in . . . and," her dad said, "Sharon had knee surgery."

"Leave me out of this," Sharon said quietly.

A surprise volley of looks bounced between Sharon and Angie's father.

"Angie, I know your mom is hard," her dad continued. "*Very* hard. But . . . running away—"

"I didn't run away."

"That's not what she says," her dad said.

"And she's a reliable narrator, why? Do you get that—what she—"

What Connie really was. Not just the version that he knew. The version she and Wang lived with. The mother who had hit her, had privately fat-shamed and actively threatened to send her to a modified conversion therapy facility. The woman who had done all of that, and sold her sister's story to the highest buyer only to arrange twenty headshots of actors who were in no way even remotely similar to the real people of Nat's life. Still, there was Angie, not saying what was true out of some . . . she didn't even really know.

Angie stared through the bouquet of floating Mylar balloons at her dad. A man who was reliving his teen years one vintage concert T-shirt at a time. What was he really going to do to help her?

He laced his fingers, elbows propped along the sides of his plate.

"Why did you pour your sister's ashes in the river, honey?" he asked.

"Is that really a question?" Angie said.

"I think so," he said. "Don't you think it should be?"

"Why didn't you tell Wang and me that the ashes even existed? Do you know how many times he went to the cemetery? Like, he thought she was there—the parts of her that came back, anyway."

It was that image that put a full stop to Sharon eating.

"I think we're confusing the issue," Angie's father said.

Angie leaned back against the booth, arms crossed.

"Angie, you know you're my special girl and—"

"For the love of the goddess, don't say that. Don't call me special. Please."

"Um . . . okay," he said, caught off guard.

They sat in a palpable tension for an unmeasured time before the waitress came by. "Everything good?"

"We're fine," Sharon said.

"Can we have some water when you have a moment?" said Angie's father.

"Of course," the waitress said, seeming to sense the unease before leaving.

Leaving them in silence.

More loud and deafening silence with Angie screaming from inside. Screaming—

"What's going on?" her father offered weakly. "You're sullen. You're argumentative. Is the therapy not helping? She came highly recommended for kids who have experienced trauma and . . ."

His attention fell to Angie's wrists. To the scars. To the "Free Fallin'" moment in the gymnasium bathroom when she had given up. Normally, Angie would've hidden her wrists beneath the table. "Normally" didn't work for Angie anymore.

"Attempted suicide?" Angie said. "Is that what you're trying to say?"

He shook his head and went back to his meal. Went back into his shell like the human turtle he had become prior to leaving Angie's mom. Went back to pretending nothing had happened to Angie or Nat or Wang or even himself. This was his way of hiding—his way of coping.

"Food," Angie had said to her therapist. *"My dad was always hiding it. In his bedroom closet. His desk at work. The garage. I mean, we all knew. Everybody but Mom. I mean, maybe she knew."*

Angie wrung her hands, feeling a wave of nausea rise. Then pass.

"When I was, um, maybe four or five, I had this really bad dream. And, um, I woke him up, but he didn't want to talk about it. He just walked me into the closet and gave me a prewrapped brownie. He said, 'It's all better now.' But it wasn't, and I didn't get that it wasn't. I mean, it was a brownie. Who doesn't want a brownie in the middle of the night?"

The therapist nodded.

"When things got harder, between him and my mom after Nat went overseas, he took me and Wang to Big Dave's Diner. Bought us these huge banana splits with extra everything. Whipped topping. Nuts. Cherries. But he didn't order anything

for himself, which was weird because he loved those banana splits. Wang just sat there. He wouldn't eat his. He knew. He knew what was coming."

"What did you do?" the therapist asked.

"I ate mine . . . and Wang's."

"How did you feel after what your dad said?"

Angie shrugged. *"Hungry."*

"I was going to wait for your brother," said Angie's father, reaching into the gift bag. "I've got something I think you'll be excited to have."

He held out a brand-new, on-trend cell phone with accompanying shatterproof case.

"We're paying for the service, so your mom has no reason to take it from you."

"So Mom doesn't know about it?" Angie asked.

He picked up his fork. "She doesn't need to."

Angie stared at the contraband cell phone. A phone she was expected to keep from her mother because her father didn't have the courage to meet Connie somewhere in the middle of their fighting.

"Wang," her dad called out.

Wang jogged up, popping his earbuds around his neck, stopping just short of the table. "Is that an earring, Dad?"

"Yeah," his dad said, self-consciously tugging at it. "Cool, huh?"

"No," said Wang.

"You have one."

"I'm seventeen," Wang said. "I have an active sex life and a deep collection of quality playlists. You're, like, almost fifty, yo. It just looks silly." Wang motioned for Angie to move over. "What did I miss?"

Angie rubbed her eye while sliding her plate toward him. "Dad wants to know why I put Nat in the Ohio River."

"Huh," Wang said, dumping chili-garlic sauce by the spoonful over the food. "Why didn't you tell us she was in the urn, Dad?"

"We did that part too," Angie said quietly.

"What did he say?" Wang asked.

"Okay, enough," their couldn't-be-accountable father said. "And that's too much chili sauce, Wang."

"I don't need you to tell me how to eat," Wang said.

Angie leaned in, whispering, "You'll likely die or wish you had."

Wang now clanged the fork against the plate. Apparently, it was a night of clanging forks.

"Seriously, Dad," Wang said. "Why didn't you tell us?"

Their father looked to Sharon, who could do little more than hold his hand beneath the table, an action that didn't sit well with Wang.

"Your mother," their dad began. "She needed it to be . . . it was easier to let her have it. She said she'd tell you when she was ready."

Wang looked to Angie. Angie, who seemed to lack the latitude that Wang was giving their dad.

"Look," said their dad. "This meal isn't about the urn, though I see how it was . . . hurtful."

He in no way understood how hurtful lying about the location of their sister's remains had been. That much Angie could surmise from the tone of his voice, which was a kind of tell. It was an inflection reserved for avoiding conflict.

"I have something for both of you." He reached into the sparkly gift bag.

He handed each of them a narrow gray envelope. Wang swigged a gulp of Angie's soda while Angie ripped open the side of her envelope. She shook the contents onto the table.

Two concert tickets and a hundred-dollar bill. Angie looked blankly at her brother.

"It's concert tickets. I thought it was something you could do together. Get out of the house. Take a couple of friends. There's four in total."

Angie slid the tickets and money back into the envelope. This was not the thing she wanted from her couldn't-be-accountable father. She knew this feeling. Like when he bought her a computer and cell phone and candy after she was released from the Yellow Ridge treatment facility post–attempted suicide. This wasn't a gift. It was a payoff.

"So, that's what this is about?" Wang said. "Tonight? Yo, I thought you were here to help with what's going on with Mom. She's like Bell and Jar."

"It's *The Bell Jar,* actually," Angie corrected.

"I know what it is," Wang snapped.

"I am," their dad said. "We're here. We plan to talk to her. If she'll talk."

Wang glared at Sharon. She was the enemy as far as he was concerned. The enemy who had no place—

"But why is *she* here?" Wang asked.

This was not a line even Angie felt safe to cross with her father.

"Because she's my wife," their father said.

"Right," Wang said. "And because you can't spend a second alone with us."

"That's not true," his father said.

"Yeah, then tell me," Wang said. "Tell me the last time you spent any time with Angie and me? Are you even going to this concert?"

"Like I said . . . look. Sharon and I, we . . . Wang, I get you've struggled here with your mom. And Sharon and I have talked it over, and we'd like you to come live with us. On a trial basis. Assuming there wouldn't be any . . . assuming you could adjust. Which I know you can."

Wang's eyes ping-ponged between them, and then to Angie. Angie, who was now staring at a scuff on the tabletop.

"What about Angie?" Wang said.

A new kind of quiet divided them. It was a distinct quiet that Angie had heard when she had asked to go with her dad when he first moved out. An ask that was returned with the label of *special*. It was a no then. It was a no now.

Angie shook her head. "It's not a package deal, Wang."

"We could," said her father, "talk about that as an option. Definitely a visit at Christmas break. It's really up to your mother."

"Screw Mom. I want to talk about it now," Wang said.

"He doesn't want me," Angie said. "That's what the phone was about, right, Dad? Consolation prize. For being the least favorite of the three, or the most messed up."

The waitress came by, setting down water glasses.

"Get you something, hon?" she asked Wang.

He shook his head, staring at his dad. The dad he had wanted more than anything to want him—to take him away from Dryfalls.

The waitress was barely out of earshot when Angie said to Wang, "It's okay. You can go with them."

"Bullshit," Wang said, turning to his dad. "What's wrong with you? Earring, new motorcycle, a wardrobe of wannabe cool. Do you even got a clue what Angie has been through? What *I* been through, Dad? Do you even read the fucking texts I send you or is it just newish Sharon that does?"

"Watch it," their dad said.

Wang shook his head and leaned against the booth.

This was not the Wang Angie knew from their post-missing-sister-in-the-Iraq-War time. It wasn't even the Wang she knew when Nat had still lived with them. Wang was standing up to their dad—for her? It was an aberration that would be marked in mere moments by frogs falling from the sky.

"I believed you," Wang said, holding up the envelope. "I believed you when you said you'd help us. You don't give a shit."

"It's more complicated than that, son," their dad said. "We have a family, and we are trying . . ."

"A family?" Wang said.

"Jesse," said Sharon.

"No, they need to listen," their dad said, turning to Wang. "Your sister has specific needs—"

"Wow," Wang said. "You really gonna do her like that? You have no idea what Angie needs. Yeah, she's weird. She's hella weird, but don't think her problems make her, like, defective, because she isn't, Dad. Being hurt isn't being broken."

"That isn't what I meant," said their dad. "I don't mean she's broken or special in that particular way."

"What particular way is it then?" asked Wang. "You know, don't even. You lied to me about why you were coming tonight. You lied about why you stayed so long. Why you split. You know what? This is bullshit. This whole thing is bullshit."

Wang slid out of the booth.

"If you could just sit down and hear what I have to say," said their father.

"Nah, I'm good," Wang said. "See, it actually is a package deal, Dad. Me and Angie. You don't get to pick whichever one you think is easier or looks best in your holiday card with your *new* family." Wang turned to Angie. "You coming?"

The answer was absolutely, unquestionably yes. Angie scooted out from the grips of the ill-fitting table as Wang blew out the door.

"Angie," her dad said.

"Don't promise him anything anymore," Angie said. "Don't tell him you'll visit or that you'll call. Just don't."

"You think you can understand, but you can't, honey," he said.

"Maybe not. But I know that you're full of shit if you think an all-you-can-eat buffet and tickets to a concert that don't even include you showing up, *again*, is going to make anything better for us."

Angie was halfway to the door when she walked back to the booth.

"Also, taking the family dog?" Angie said. "Really messed up, Dad."

"Your mother hates Lester."

"But *we* didn't. He meant everything to Wang."

It was true.

Wang loved Lester.

Lester loved Wang.

These were indisputable facts.

Angie reached across the table and grabbed the phone. Practically speaking, she still needed one. She opened the door, the bell jangling as she left. She was well on her way to Wang's Jeep, engine running, Tupac bass beating, when the clicking of heels tapped behind her.

"Angie," Sharon called out.

Angie stopped. "Sharon, don't—"

"I'm not going to defend him," she said. "I can't defend or explain how he has avoided being there for you and your brother."

It was in that moment that Sharon had fully captured Angie's attention. In a way that wasn't muddled in quasi-resentment for being the one her dad loved more than her and Wang.

"I'm just sorry," Sharon said. "It's harder for some reason with you and Wang without your sister for him. Again, I'm not excusing it."

"She was kind of the Gorilla Glue."

Sharon half smiled. It was layered in compassion and uncertainty. "It's funny, because I always thought of you as the glue."

It was a thought Angie had never considered.

Not one single time.

"You know," Sharon said. "I would have screamed if someone had put food on my plate when I was your age. I really *struggled* with my weight."

"The thing is, I'm not struggling with my weight. Everyone else is."

The loudness of Wang revving the engine swelled as he shouted, "Angie!"

"I gotta go," Angie said.

She climbed into Wang's Jeep. The wheels squealed out of the parking lot. Sharon still stood where Angie had left her. Angie's father came out of the restaurant, watching them pull away.

There was no specific soundtrack in Angie's mind. Just the sound of the distance growing between her and her father.

Chapter 5

Angie watched from the magazine aisle as Wang flirted with Lori Ochoa, a high-school senior working the Dryfalls IGA register. It wasn't that Wang had been dishonest about wanting to grab cheeseburgers and marshmallow shakes from Dee's Diner with Angie. They were both starving post–hellish dinner fail with their couldn't-be-accountable dad. It wasn't as though Wang had been dishonest about running into the grocery for a charging cable for his phone. Where fiction and fact had collided was when he'd omitted that Lori was working. Lori, the girl he'd privately pined for all summer and into the fall because she had been dating his buddy Winter. But with their recent breakup and Winter out, Wang saw an in. All of which seemed like poor decision-making on his part, but Wang specialized in the art of poor decision-making.

A Moderate List of Wang's Bad Decisions

1. Putting Monistat in Angie's toothpaste only to have his mother borrow it.
2. Eating an excessively large portion of wasabi to spite John/Rick and getting unbelievably sick to his stomach.
3. Insulting a girl holding a full can of Coke and consequently having it thrown at his head.
4. Gluing the individual pages of the school library's Twilight series together while in detention.
5. TP'ing his ex-girlfriend's house without disabling the security camera.
6. Cheating on his last three girlfriends.
7. Ordering twenty-nine pizzas with Connie's credit card and having them delivered to the principal's house.
8. Eating five live leeches on a dare and getting a bacterial infection.

Bored with her options of *Field and Stream, Bowhunter, J-14,* and a host of fitness, cooking, and home decorating magazines, Angie wandered the store. From one processed food aisle to the next, her stomach howled. She hadn't eaten since lunch, which felt like last week right then. She grabbed a can of Sour Cream and Onion Pringles and stopped.

"You can eat whatever you want," her therapist had said. *"Just choose it. Know why you're choosing it."*

"That's hard," Angie had said. *"I'm hungry. I just want to eat."*

"And you get to eat," said her therapist. *"I'm not telling you not to eat. I just want to encourage you to be conscious of what you eat. Is it what you want, or is it a reaction to something else? If you want ice cream, have some ice cream."*

It was then that Angie reshelved the canister because ice cream was exactly what she wanted. Though she was sure that wasn't the intended takeaway from her session.

Angie perused the seven freezer doors housing local favorite Jeni's Brown Butter Almond Brittle, Sweet Corn and Black Raspberry, and Darkest Chocolate. She stepped two freezer doors to her right, and the suction of the door exhaled as she opened it. The dense, cool air splashed against her face, sending a shiver across her shoulders. Her fingers tapped the tops of three ice cream pints before landing on Graeter's Buckeye Blitz. She closed the fogged glass door to see . . . Lucas Waite?

By some randomness of the universe, there in the ice cream section of the IGA, Angie stood with a quart of Graeter's and the winner of *Undiscovered*. Dryfalls' most famous breakout musician. Named by *Rolling Stone* as the "front man to watch," Rancid Reign's Lucas Waite was legend. The small-town singer had filled stadiums, teen magazines' trifold posters, and the hearts of women world-wide. At one point, he had his own brand of deodorant. He was a mystery, a phantom—an enigma of the highest gossip proportions. Because Rancid Reign had collapsed under scandal—under the pressure, many had said, and Lucas's star seemed to have burned out with them.

He had been in Dryfalls for months but rarely left his father's abandoned factory. But there he was in the IGA on the longest Thursday maybe ever. Wearing dusty, paint-speckled work boots, rockabilly rolled jeans, and a flannel shirt with a tear at the elbow. His clothes would have been irrelevant had they not said everything about him. He was a man in fray, or so Angie had decided.

Lucas Waite was waiting for—

"You good?" he said, glancing up from texting.

"Uh, um. Yeah."

He reached for the edge of the door, leaning toward the freezer. "It's a quandary, isn't it?"

"I'm sorry?" Angie said.

"Ice cream. I never know which one to pick when I come here. I grew up on UDF, Häagen-Dazs, and Velvet. Then there was that hard-core Phish Food phase. I put it in my root-beer floats, Sunday sundaes after church or a Rocket Club meeting."

"Some people remember moments by the song that was playing," Angie said. "But I usually remember it by ice cream."

"Exactly." He looked directly at her. "Like if you get . . ."

He walked two freezers to the left, swaying between both while dipping down to see what was inside. "Take this. Okay, here is an unassuming choice. Blue Bunny Mint Chocolate Chip. To me, this says breakup, not romance."

"Absolutely," Angie said.

"In my opinion," Lucas added, "ice cream is one of the most important personal dessert decisions you can make."

"I couldn't agree more," Angie said.

He chuckled, holding out his hand. "I'm Lucas."

"Uh, yeah, I know. Everyone knows."

"Right. You didn't ask for my autograph or a selfie, so I just thought . . ."

"I'm not really a selfie person."

"Me neither, but my manager said I need to be," he said. "Sometimes I like to pretend no one knows me."

"Maybe in Belgium?" Angie offered.

"No, I'm pretty big in Belgium. Now, parts of Africa and Norway? Definitely more invisible. And there's Antarctica."

"I hear they have a raging metal scene," Angie said.

He laughed.

"I don't know that to be true," Angie said. "It was just something weird to say."

"What did you pick?" he said. "If it's okay to ask."

She held up the now-sweating pint of ice cream.

"Good choice," he said. "Does it ever seem a little sweet to you, though?"

Angie considered the question. "Maybe. It's a lot of peanut butter. A lot of chocolate. Which I guess is a lot of sweet."

"I like peanut butter on pancakes. On toast. Apples. I don't know if I like it with chocolate, though. After the whole Reese's Pieces fake-chocolate scandal, I think my trust in the combo was broken."

"Right? I went through the *same* thing when I realized there was no actual chocolate in Reese's. Obviously, I've recovered . . . as evidenced by my choice."

"Well, there's hope for me, then," he said.

Quiet.

Awkward now-what quiet.

Lucas turned on his boot heels, facing the freezer doors. "I think . . . I'm gonna get . . . Yes." He reached for the top shelf. "Ben & Jerry's Dublin Mudslide, or as I like to call it, the Jilted Lover."

"What?" Angie laughed. "Why?"

Lucas closed the cooler door. "Because it was what I was eating when my girlfriend said she had cheated on me . . . with my best friend. I ate it for breakfast, lunch, and dinner for something like a week."

It was no secret that Lucas's last girlfriend had broken up with him in a very public, online way. Broadcasting what she deemed the shortcomings of the relationship, she had found herself in a new relationship in New York City. SoHo, so the rumor went.

"If you ever get your heart broken, look no further than this," he said.

The all-brother band Hanson's '90s chart-topping hit "MMMBop" echoed from the canned intercom above them.

"Have you ever realized that you can't hear 'MMMBop' and not be happy?" Lucas said.

Angie laughed. "I guess I hadn't thought about it. It is happy-making. Unless maybe . . . you were Clockwork Oranged with your eyes pried open and made to watch videos of war and slaughterhouse procedures for twenty-four consecutive hours while the song played on repeat."

Lucas looked flatly at her.

"Or maybe it just makes you feel happy." Angie turned the toes of her boots inward.

"I keep thinking you look familiar," he said.

"You probably knew my sister," Angie said. "Everyone does."

He thought about it for a moment. An unusually long moment. "Nope."

"Statue in the park?" Angie said.

"I guess I didn't notice."

"It's kind of impossible," Angie continued, "not to notice. She's sort of the fulcrum of the town. Except for you."

"I guess I should look at it, then," he said. "The statue."

Quiet.

More bizarre quiet.

"Anyway," she said. "I should . . . go look for my brother, who has likely been fully rejected by a girl way beyond his cool grade."

"Well," Lucas said, holding out his hand. "It was good to talk with an ice cream aficionado. A rarity."

Angie shook Lucas's hand. It wasn't a magical hand that sparked and glowed upon contact. Even if he had shaken the hands of hordes of famous people, of fans, of the Dalai Lama. Yup, Lucas Waite had met the Dalai Lama. It was just a hand with a scar above the left knuckle.

Lucas walked in one direction. Angie the other. As she turned the corner, she paused. She paused because an idea flashed in her mind.

"Lucas," she called out a little too loud.

"Yup."

"My brother and I are going to get some burgers from Dee's. You wanna . . . come with us?"

No sooner was the invite out there like a fish flopping onshore, gasping for air, did Angie race through ways to walk it back, so Lucas wouldn't have to say no. So he wouldn't have to embarrass her for thinking he'd want to grab a burger with a couple of—

"Sure," he said.

Angie's response was on a three-second delay. Somewhere floating on the International Space Station. Possibly.

"Um, okay," she finally said.

And then . . . in an Angie-imagined music video of what happened next, she and Lucas would round the freezer section, the rules of gravity largely suspended as organic squash, avocados, and romaine lettuce took flight behind them. Angie's hair would lift off her husky shoulders and spray back from some unseen wind source. Their confident stride would be met with gobsmacked shoppers while swirling cans of soda, unsealed barrels of Utz Cheese Balls, open magazines, somersaulting protein bars—entire rotisserie chickens would all be free-floating in the air. The roof of the store would rip from its frame. Even the walls would soar up, as Angie and Lucas stepped onto a concert stage and—

"Dude," Wang said, snapping Angie back to reality, where Lucas was at the register, paying for his ice cream. "Are you seriously not getting Phish Food?"

Angie and Wang watched from the counter at Dee's Diner as Lucas faced a minimob of moms and teenagers and twenty-something college girls in the parking lot.

"Wild," Wang said, gnawing on his soda straw.

"I can't even imagine," Angie said, sipping her shake.

"Well, you kinda can."

Angie chuckled. "Not like that. Not like I was literally the sun."

Wang's eyes cut past Angie to a girl sitting in a booth by the jukebox. His grin unfurled. Angie was midturn when he kicked her shin.

"Really?" She rubbed her leg. "Guess your heartbreaking rejection from Lori quickly mended."

"We're going out tomorrow."

"No way," Angie said.

"Is this the face of a liar?" he asked.

The question was clearly rhetorical because Wang had an innate ability to lie in nearly any circumstance.

"Okay," he said. "The face of a liar lying right now?"

"Don't you think it's kind of bad form? Hooking up with your best friend's ex?"

"Winter's a tool," Wang said. "He's all dick jokes and hypermasculine insecurity. What? My shit's evolved, yo."

"Evolved, huh? So, that's why you're hiding your love for ABBA and all things culinary curious from your hypermasculine friends."

"Just say what you really mean, Ang."

"I did," she said.

He spun back and forth on the stool. "Nah, you think I can't be cool with Lori."

"You were just making flirt-eyes with a girl two booths from the restroom," Angie said. "So, yeah, I question your level of, um, coolness with her."

"You ask Jamboree out?" Wang asked.

Angie looked away.

"See, this is why I didn't tell you about KC," Wang said. "She literally decimates you—stomps you into the ground—then zooms in on two wheels with a fresh tat, and you bail on Jamboree. Who's, like, smoking and decent."

"I didn't *bail* on anything," Angie said. "I'm going over to her place tonight."

"Uh-huh."

Two greasy paper bags were set in front of Angie, who reached for her wallet.

"I am," Angie said to Wang. "I'm going over there, and I'm . . . going to ask her out."

He annoyingly slurped his empty Vanilla Coke. "Uh-huh."

"Hey," Lucas said. "Sorry about that."

"Wang, give me a ten," Angie said.

"I got this," Lucas said.

"Cool." Wang swept up the bags and headed for the door.

"He was raised by wolves," Angie defended. "Human wolves, but wolves all the same."

"It's fine, really." Lucas took his change.

As they were walking out, Courtney Jones and her flock of female followers were coming in. With Stacy Ann Sloan no longer leading the pack of the I Hate Angie clique, Courtney had gladly picked up the reins.

"Mr. Waite," Courtney said, fawning. "Can I get a selfie?"

"Sure," he said.

Courtney raised her phone. She did a quick teeth check, only to realize Angie was in the shot. "Moo . . . move, Fat Angie."

Angie stepped to the side, but photobombed the pic at the last minute.

"Loser," Courtney said to her.

Angie followed Lucas out of the restaurant.

"Friend of yours?" he said.

"Oh yeah. All my friends call me loser."

He grinned.

"I had some of those friends in high school," he said.

"Yeah, right."

"Seriously," he said. "You think the president of the William Anders High Rocket Club was scoring digits?"

It was true that Lucas had been known more for his brain than his brawn in high school. His sophomore yearbook photo had been featured in a cover story of *Men's Fitness*, a magazine that frequently appeared in Angie's house because of her mother's ex, John/Rick.

"Anyway," Lucas said. "Thanks for understanding about not wanting to eat in there. Sometimes it's a lot. All the people. I've kind of been keeping a low profile."

They stepped out into a field overlooking the interstate. Lucas dropped the tailgate. Wang sprang into the truck bed, then turned to help Angie. Graceful she was not as she crawled in.

Wang peered inside the cab from the back window. "'73 Chevy?"

"Actually, '71." Lucas reached into a cooler, moving the ice cream aside to pull out a Frostop root beer.

"Man, it's cherry in there," Wang said. "This ride must've set you back. Not that you can't afford it, right?"

"Wang," Angie said.

"What?" he said.

"No, it's okay," Lucas said, unwrapping his hamburger. "It was a gift. From my grandmother."

"Cool-ass, GM." Wang grabbed his burger, propping himself against the back of the cab.

Lucas tore one of the bags open. A huge pile of Cajun-seasoned wedge fries spread to the edges of the paper.

"She owns her own collision and body shop," Lucas said. "Tells the best raunchy jokes. Definitely used to make my dad squirm."

Wang and Angie were noticeably quiet. Which was surprising given Wang's usual tactless ways.

"Anyway," Lucas said. "She found this Chevy in a salvage yard. Fully rebuilt the engine herself. Four-fifty-four big block V8."

Lucas could have literally spoken in Mandarin to Angie.

"I'm not car-ish," she said.

"It's got some pull and a purr," Wang said, grabbing a handful of fries.

"Sort of." Lucas took a bite of his burger, audibly savoring it. "Wow. I haven't had one of these since I got back."

"It's about the cheese skirt for me," Angie said.

"Oh yeah." Lucas nodded.

"Ang tell you about her video?" Wang said.

"No."

"Stop," Angie said to Wang, because the last thing Angie wanted Lucas Waite to see was her singing.

Wang slipped his phone from his jeans pocket and scooted beside Lucas, propping his cell on his knee. Angie nervously chewed while watching every small and big reaction on Lucas's face.

"Minute I saw it," Wang said, sipping from Angie's shake, "I was like—Lucas Waite on *Undiscovered*. When you did that mash up with Sex Pistols and—"

"Amy Winehouse," Lucas said.

"Dude, I was like, what?" Wang jacked the volume.

Angie could not have the video end fast enough. It was so embarrassing to have someone like Lucas watch someone like her.

"It's good," Lucas said to Angie when it finished. "Really."

"I fell off pitch a few times," Angie said. "I'd never sung outside of my shower before."

"You'd never performed live with a band?" Lucas said.

She shook her head. "Wrote the lyrics the same day. It was kind of a have-to, why-not moment."

"Wow," Lucas said. "The good thing about punk is it's forgiving. But what you did mixing vocal range and those runs? How many rehearsals?"

"None," she said. "I'd never even met the band."

Wang slapped Lucas across the shoulder. "She's legit, right? Like Mozart."

"Wang," Angie said. "I'm dying in front of you. Can you not see it?"

"He's proud of you," Lucas said.

Wang smirked, savoring the support from Lucas. It was a truly annoying trait of his.

"How old are you?" Angie asked her brother.

"Yo," Wang said. "Bring it in for a selfie."

They scooted in as Wang's flash blinded them.

"Why?" Angie said, seeing spots.

Before Wang could answer, his phone rang. He hopped off the side of the truck and headed toward his Jeep.

"I'm sorry about the video thing," Angie said.

"Why?" Lucas asked.

"Because . . ." Angie said. "I don't know. It's nothing compared to what you've done. I mean, Rancid Reign—you redefined how we listen to genre-bending-and-blending alternative-pop-ska-rock. You're synonymous with chords that don't adhere to musical theory, yet construct an emotional arc. What you did with 'Heather, I Hear You' and 'Magnify' disjointed everything people thought about solid vocals matched against orchestration and rock instrumentation."

"Huh," he said, eating a fry.

"You took what could have been a branding nightmare from the competition you won and made your own music," Angie said. "Plus, the cover of *NME* and *Rolling Stone* the same week. That's really making it."

Lucas cleared his throat. "We were on the cover of *Rolling Stone* the same night our drummer got wasted, and our guitarist wrecked our hotel suite and punched two security guards . . . hours before we were nominated for an MTV Music Award for a song we hated and a video we were forced to do by the label. That's not making it, Angie. That's getting lost."

Lucas tossed his napkin into the paper bag. Angie had obviously struck a nerve, which she hadn't meant to do.

"The competition had this residual effect," he said. "I just kept trying to prove that I was more than this massively marketed idea."

"But you did prove it," Angie said. "I mean, except for the part where it all . . . seemed to . . ."

"Dismantle?" he said. "Yeah. I just wish someone had told me . . . not to start a band just to win a competition, not to be less of who you are. You start a band because you have something to say. Because you want to do or be something better than who you are without it . . ." Lucas paused. "Otherwise, why you doing it?"

"Wang would say for the ladies," Angie said.

Lucas chuckled.

"Lot of people do. It's a solid song. What you wrote. Really. Ear worm in a good way. It lingers."

Angie grinned. "Thanks. I think?"

"I gotta get going." He fished her ice cream out of his ice chest.

"Keep it," she said. "Maybe it can repair your trust. Post–Reese's Pieces scandal."

He laughed. "You sure?"

She nodded. "Yeah."

He hopped off the tailgate, then held his hand out to help her down.

"Thanks for the burger," Angie said. "And the conversation. I never thought I'd be talking to Lucas Waite about music. It's nice knowing you're just—"

"A person."

"Yeah."

"Rocket Club president," he said. "Always and forever."

Angie laughed. "My friend Darius is going to love that. Anyway. See you."

Angie was halfway to Wang's Jeep when Lucas called out, "Angie."

"Yeah?"

"Keep writing," Lucas said. "Singing. You got something to say."

"You too," Angie said. "I mean, if you want to. Not that you have to or . . . you know what I mean. Bye."

Angie walked toward Wang's Jeep, her mind reeling over the reality that she and Lucas Waite had bonded over ice cream and cheese skirts on burgers. Over music and motivation. It was a moment Angie wouldn't have believed had Wang not been there to witness it. Well, as much as Wang witnessed anything with his phone pressed to his ear.

She climbed into the Jeep. Her excitement to tell Jamboree about the good, the bad, and the ugly of her evening was eclipsed only by her elation to finally and officially ask her out. No hints of what they were or could be. No looks of unanswered longing or lips almost kissing and—Angie could not wait!

Wang hopped into the Jeep.

"Hey, can you drop me off at Jamboree's?" Angie asked.

"Negatory." He pocketed his phone. "Dad's been to the house. Shit went sideways."

"How sideways?" Angie asked.

"Don't know," he said. "He said Mom wants us home. He's already on the way to Cleveland. Surprise. Shit gets hard, and he's out. We deal with the fallout."

Their dad had not historically been as categorically "out" as Wang portrayed him. He had tried, for many years, to be in. In with Angie and Wang and, of course, their sister. It was their dad who took the kids to concerts in the city, movies at Cinema Duplex, Putt-Putt, and laser tag. He, unlike Connie, was invested in each of their interests, not just Nat's. When their dad began to be less present, Wang and Angie felt, well, abandoned. Wang the most. A truth not unrealized by Angie, especially right then.

"Hey," Angie said. "You okay?"

He shook his head. "Let's just go."

Wang turned over the engine, blasting a poser playlist as they headed home. The last place Angie wanted to be.

Chapter 6

Angie stood over her shattered Sony Walkman. It had been thrown from her bedroom window and landed on the driveway. This theory of its demise was solely based on the fact that Angie's bedroom window was now open, light on.

She knelt, picking up the pieces of plastic, cradling them ever so carefully.

Wang glared up at the window, his rage spiking. "What the fuck?"

He marched toward the front door.

"Wang." Angie followed him. "Don't."

He skipped every other stair as he ascended to the second floor of the house. Angie raced behind him. They passed the Wall of Grand Sisterdom, as they called it. A series of framed photos of their sister at various stages of athletic, academic, and armed-forces prowess.

Wang paused at his open door. Angie nearly ran into him. He flicked on the light. Clothes, comic books, Blu-rays, several pornographic magazines all spilled from a pile on his bed.

"What. The. Actual. Fuck!" he said.

Angie switched her attention to her bedroom. Door ajar. Light licking the doorjamb and floor. She carefully nudged the door farther open with the toe of her boot. It creaked ever so quietly as Angie's mouth dropped open. The slightest of gasps trickled out. Her room had been upended. The nightstand and desk drawers emptied and tossed. The bookcase bare—books scattered across the floor—spilling out from her trash can. Clothes ripped from their hangers and piled into the center of the room. Shoeboxes, binders, cassette tapes, dresser drawers—nothing had not been touched.

Angie stood there, Walkman still cradled in her arms, cautiously watching her mother sitting on the edge of Angie's disheveled bed. Nat's basketball jersey lay limply across her lap. The jersey given to Angie for making varsity basketball . . . for not giving up.

"Mom?" Angie said, softly.

Wang stormed in. "What the fuck, Mom?"

"Go to your room," Connie said, so softly that it was frightening.

"You can't go through my stuff," he said. "That's my space. It belongs to me."

"This is my house," she snapped. "Nothing belongs to you. Nothing. Now go to your room, Wang."

"You just said it wasn't my room!" Wang shouted.

"Go!" she said, now standing.

"You're crazy," he said. "Crazy! Fucking hate you."

"Wang," Angie said as he rushed out, leaving her, of course, with a Wang-diagnosed crazy person. While an unofficial diagnosis, as Wang was not a licensed psychotherapist, Connie's behavior was certainly questionable from a mental health standpoint. Though the term *crazy* did not sit well with Angie. Not well at all.

Wang's sneakers pounded down the stairs. The front door literally slammed behind him.

Connie returned to her spot on Angie's tiny twin bed, rubbing a scab along her elbow. Her mother seemed surprised to realize that it was there.

"Mom?" Angie carefully said. "Are you . . . what happened?"

"It was always easier with your sister," Connie said.

"What?"

"Your sister." Connie abandoned the scab. Her hand rested along the jersey. "She practically flew out of me. The midwife had one glove on, and here she comes, barreling out. She couldn't wait to be in this world. Could. Not. Wait."

Connie laughed to herself. She had been drinking.

Angie could tell by the way her eyes seemed to almost float from one part of the room to the next.

"She was three when she started playing basketball." Connie paused, unsure. "No, was it four? Four. That seems right. I didn't want her to play, but your father convinced me. He said she was *special*. She was extraordinary. Nothing was ever hard with her—hard for her. School, friends. I wasn't like that. I had to work for things. Work really hard. It was just different for me. Your sister, she made it all seem so effortless."

Angie shifted her stance. Notebook paper crinkled beneath her boot. Connie noticed none of it.

"I just keep thinking how much she wanted to be in this world." Connie traced the numbers along the jersey. "The midwife only had one glove on. That's funny, isn't it?"

Connie tipped her head toward Angie's bedroom window. A faint echo of wind chimes carried from Jake's front porch across the street. The wind gathered from a distance, shaking the leaves of the black oak tree outside Angie's window. Everything seemed as it should be except that moment. There. With her mother—

"It was different with you." Connie cleared her throat. "The morning sickness. Which is a lie because it was all day. Some mornings I'd pull the car over three times on the way to work, vomiting. Your father." Connie chuckled. "He said it would pass. He always had something unhelpful to say."

Connie reminisced, rubbing the scab on her elbow again.

"I was in labor with you for thirty-five hours," Connie said. "The doctor, your father, the midwife, everyone standing around me saying, 'Push. Push.' No matter how much I did, you just wouldn't come out. Finally, I gave up. I was exhausted. I was sweaty and tired and hungry, and I just couldn't do it anymore." Connie looked at Angie. "Even then you were hard."

Angie's cheeks flushed—angry, ashamed. A collision of emotions raced through her chest, her head—none of them pleasant. Angie very much preferred pleasant feelings.

"Your sister convinced your dad to name you Angelica. I wanted to name you Ellen after my great aunt. She said you weren't an Ellen. I was tired. I was exhausted. It was two against one. Her and your father. I just wanted it to be over." Connie considered what she'd said. "That's not how it's supposed to be. You're supposed to want to take on the world after having a child. The way I had with Nat. The endorphins . . . the hormones . . . with you, I just wanted it . . . to stop."

Angie's stomach soured.

Her heart sank.

She would have preferred to be almost anywhere but in that moment with her drunken mother.

"It only got worse when we brought you home. You would just cry and cry," Connie said. "I'd pick you up. I'd feed you. Nothing satisfied you except your sister. No matter what I did."

Connie shook her head, swallowing what seemed to be tears—a reaction largely reserved for Angie's sister.

"Mom, I . . ." Angie paused. "I think that—"

"I can only imagine the level of disgust and disappointment she'd feel if she saw you now." Connie looked directly at Angie.

Connie. The mother who quit anger-management therapy because she said she had no anger to manage. Clearly that was an inaccurate self-assessment, Angie had decided, because she was angry.

"That's not true," Angie said.

"True?" Connie nodded. "Let's talk about truth."

Connie reached beneath the jersey and held up Angie's therapeutic journal. Angie's mouth opened. No gasp. Not even a breath.

"You wrote down our private lives and shared them with who?" Connie asked. "That woo-woo therapist? Your friends? Did you post *this* online?"

"You read my therapeutic journal?" Angie said.

"Of course I read it," Connie said. "I went through your entire room. I don't know who you are, Angie. You are a *stranger* to me. You get into fights—"

"I didn't get into—"

"With that boy, Gary Klein—" Connie started.

"He attacked me, Mom. Gary attacked me because

he's a misogynistic homophobe. He was the one who was expelled. He was the one who—"

"It's always someone else's fault, Angie," said Connie.

"No, it isn't. I mean, unless it is."

"You left this house when you were grounded and went to Cincinnati?" Connie said. "Seriously, Angie?"

Flustered, Angie scrambled with what to say but had nothing.

"Joan called me tonight," Connie continued. "Worried about how I was doing because of you in some video. I mean, did you think I wouldn't find out?"

Angie sighed. "No. I knew you would."

"Of course you did. That's why you posted it."

"I didn't post it."

"I want you to take it down," Connie demanded.

"Mom . . . no."

Connie sprang off the bed. Angie stumbled back into the door, clutching the pieces of her Walkman, arms instinctively raised to block her face.

"Take down the video, Angie," Connie ordered.

"Mom, please," Angie pleaded. "Please . . . just . . . stop."

The earthy, chocolaty-tobacco smell of Connie's prized bottle of Pappy Van Winkle steeped in the air between them. A three-thousand-dollar whiskey rarity given to Connie by her boss after winning a multimillion-dollar case, it was an accolade "to be admired, not consumed," Connie had said. However, Wang had not-so-cleverly swiped a finger's worth to sample with Angie and Jake. Angie, of course, was a hard no because drinking under the age of twenty-one was illegal, and she believed they would get caught.

"We're not going to get caught," Wang had insisted.

Wang did get caught because he had estimated incorrectly and taken far more than a finger's worth. The fallout had been cataclysmic, and after a series of punishments, Connie hid the bottle in her bedroom with some "personal" items. So personal that even Wang would not go in there.

Ever!

Connie stepped away from Angie, seeming to try to center herself. Regain control.

"I didn't . . . do anything wrong." Angie's arms cautiously lowered. "I mean, yes, I left when I was grounded. That part was wrong. But singing—that wasn't wrong, Mom. I'm really good at it."

"You think I don't know that song was meant for me?" Connie asked.

"What?"

"I'm the bad mother, right?" Connie looked at Angie. "That's the role you want to cast me in? For the town? For anyone who will listen?"

Historically, Connie had been a bad mother to Angie and Wang; however, Angie had surmised this was not the time for such truths. Nor was it the time for Angie to express how much she wished Connie would choose to do better, drink less, and basically get it together. Sharing such hopes would likely be perceived as attacking, and Angie just wanted the whole moment to be over.

"It's because I sold the movie rights, isn't it?" Connie said. "Because I didn't tell you. Because it's not about—"

"The video of me singing has nothing to do with any of that."

"Doesn't it? You have to have all the attention. It doesn't matter what *kind* of attention, so long as it is yours."

"Don't you have that in reverse?" Angie asked.

"I'm not the one who ran away—across Ohio and where else? Where did you—"

"I didn't run away—"

"Posting videos—" Connie said.

"One video—and I didn't post it. I—"

"I know you've been sneaking food. When I've specifically told you—"

"I don't sneak—I eat," Angie said. "I eat food. It's normal to eat food, Mom."

"You're fat, Angie," said Connie.

And there it was. Every heated argument returned to the most basic perceived problem with Angie. She was fat.

And so what?

It had been a "so what" for Angie the past few weeks. At school, around town, and especially in therapy. She was Angie, and she was fat and she was okay with that. Only when Connie said it right then, it somehow reduced her to rubble because Connie's fat wasn't Angie's reclamation of the word. Connie's version made Angie hungrier—smaller—bigger—uglier—it made her so . . . mad!

"I know what I am," Angie said, pushing back at the almost unbearable weight of her mother's disgust.

Connie shook her head in what seemed a moment of surrender. At least, Angie hoped it would be.

"I don't know what else to do with you," Connie said. "I don't know what works."

"I guess I'm grounded," Angie said. "Again."

"No. But you're not getting your phone back. Or your computer or the iPad. I don't care what your father says." Connie paused. "People are laughing at you. You understand that, right?"

Angie kept her head down; her chin doubled. Maybe it tripled. She couldn't be certain. She just felt so sick inside.

Connie tossed Angie's therapeutic journal onto a mound of books and clothes. "Clean up your room and go to bed."

Angie's muscles tightened as Connie walked past her, fearing her in a way so specific. She listened as her mother's footsteps disappeared down the hallway and into her bedroom. The room that was the farthest from Angie's, closest to Nat's.

It was in hearing her mother's door finally close that Angie exhaled, not realizing she had been holding her breath.

Angie stepped through the wreckage of her room. The last letter from her sister had sheltered in place inside a copy of *The Miseducation of Cameron Post,* but the WHY NOT? postcard had not fared as well. It lay wadded up in a half ball near the trash can. Angie dropped to her knees, attempting to smooth out the deep creases. Tears swelled, her anxiety screaming. She looked up from the crinkled postcard, staring at her teary-eyed reflection in her full-length mirror.

"Sometimes I look in the mirror," Angie had confessed. *"And I see this thin girl. Inside the fat girl that's me. And I hate her."*

"Why?" the therapist had asked.

"Because I think she's the only one my mother could ever love."

Angie curled up onto her bed, clothes and DVDs sliding onto the floor. She clutched the letter from her sister, trying to understand why everything had to be so hard.

Chapter 7

Angie had slept through her alarm and, consequently, two classes. Rather than attempting to forge a written excuse, as Wang always did, she simply told the truth. The you-poor-girl look on the school secretary's face as she marked her excused. Riding on the coattails of her tragically deceased sister and her own suicide attempt was low, but it was a low Angie accepted.

The bell rang. Kids fanned out of class, filling the halls. Angie clasped her pass as she made her way toward her locker.

"Hey," Jake said, falling in step beside her. "Where were you this morning?"

"I overslept," she said, spinning her locker combination.

"I thought that was a physical impossibility," he said. "Something about your internal clock and the Earth's axis points."

"It was a weird night," she said.

"How'd it go yesterday?" he said, shoulder against a locker.

Angie didn't follow.

"Jamboree?" he said.

"Yeah, um . . . it ended up being a *different* kind of day."

"What up, Jake!" A football player high-fived him in passing. "It's all us tonight!"

Jake turned back to Angie. "Because of KC?"

The answer was no.

The answer was yes-ish.

The answer was that Angie didn't entirely know the answer.

"KC blew you off," Jake said, tucking in his football jersey. "The way KC does when things don't work for her."

"I know what happened," Angie said. "I was there."

"So, you're not getting back with her?" Jake asked.

"Why would you just assume that?"

"Because where KC is concerned, you seem to lose . . . you."

Before Angie could respond, Courtney Jones pivoted between them, her flock of followers in tow.

"It's One-Hit Wonder, everyone," Courtney said, mocking Angie.

"Go away, Courtney," said Jake.

"If you want to use up your homecoming-king currency to keep helping the hapless, that's on you, Jake," she said, then turned to Angie. "You get that was a pity burger with Lucas last night. Right?"

Angie clenched her jaw.

"Because no one would ever be interested in watching another video of you," she said. "Unless you slit your wrists again."

A resounding "OOooooo," erupted from the flock.

Angie's cheeks flushed. She was undeniably—

"Leave, Courtney," Jake said, stepping between her and Angie.

Courtney sauntered away, waving her index finger like a straight razor across her wrist.

"You okay?" he asked Angie.

"No," she said. "I don't need you to step in all Captain America. I'm able to—defend myself. I'm not the same girl my sister needed you to rescue."

"Whoa," Jake said. "I just . . . wow. Okay."

They stood in the loud quiet of the emptying hall.

"You're right. It's your life," Jake said, backing away. "See you after the pep rally maybe."

Jake peeled off toward the library, leaving Angie at her locker to stew. To boil. To feel herself spinning out of control. She slammed her locker shut.

"Hey, Angie," said a pudgy freshman girl.

Angie walked past the pudgy freshman girl and past her Algebra II class. She pushed through the double doors that led to a set of vending machines. She dug out several dollar bills from her jeans pocket and frantically fed them into the machine. The thud of junk food echoed as a Butterfinger, Hershey's bar, Kit Kat, Almond Joy, Payday, and two bags of Cheetos pressed against the plexiglass and descended.

Angie stuffed her high-in-fat, empty-calorie panic buy into her backpack and headed for the girls' bathroom. She pushed on the third stall, her preferred choice, but it was locked.

She looked left, then right. All but the first stall were occupied.

It would have to do.

She slid the lock closed with the tail of her T-shirt. Her mind was racing. Her emotions felt so big—so loud—as she fought with her jammed backpack zipper. After a concerted effort, it unzipped. She stared, wild-eyed, at the treasure trove of sugar and carbs. At the things that made her feel—

"Good," her therapist had said. *"Tell me what happens when you feel overwhelmed?"*

"I crave . . . something. Anything. No. Sugar. Candy. Junk food. I just—I needed it . . . to make it stop."

"Does it?"

"I don't understand," Angie said.

"Does it make it stop?"

Angie pondered the question for a considerable amount of time. Well over eleven seconds.

"Yeah," she said, pausing.

"What?" her therapist asked.

"No," Angie said. *"It doesn't."*

The bathroom stalls emptied, girls hurrying out as the tardy bell rang. Angie stared hopelessly at the junk food. This was not going to work.

Angie used the bottom of her shirt to unlatch the stall lock. Handful by the handful, she threw the Butterfinger, the Hershey's bar, the Kit Kat, the Almond Joy, the Payday, two bags of Cheetos, and three rogue half-eaten rolls of Life Savers into the trash. She stepped out of the restroom and into the quiet of everyone in class. That's when she heard the faint sound of dribbling.

She walked toward the gym. The drumming echo of basketballs bouncing calming her. Angie paused at the trophy case featuring her ever-overachieving sister before heading to the gymnasium floor. She stood in the spot where her whole life had changed. Where she had collapsed, wrists bleeding, screaming, during the pep rally.

Angie knelt, looking for a hint of the stain that had somehow never washed away in her mind.

"Angie?" Coach Laden said, walking across the basketball court. "Not who I expected in here."

"I'm kind of avoiding my life and a pop quiz," Angie

said, standing up. "Which I guess is not really a pop quiz if you know about it."

"Typically, no," Coach Laden said, noticing where Angie was standing.

Coach Laden had been the first person to get to Angie that day just a year earlier. She had held Angie down, trying to stop the bleeding. Telling her all the while, "Hold on, Angie. You have to hold on for me." Coach Laden had been the person to ride in the ambulance with Angie because Wang was out smoking with his friends. Connie had been closing a deal on the West Coast. It was Coach Laden who was there, talking Angie down from the cliff she couldn't seem to step away from.

"You okay?" she asked Angie.

Angie shrugged.

"Wanna shoot a few?" Coach nodded toward the court.

Angie grinned. "Sure."

Coach Laden grabbed a ball off the caddie and dribbled onto the court.

"So," she said, aiming for a free throw. "Why you avoiding your life?"

The shot went off with the whisper of nothing but net. Angie rebounded the ball.

"It's mostly good," Angie said. "I have friends."

"Can I say how glad I am to hear that?"

Angie stepped to the free-throw line. "And . . . Wang and I get along better. A lot better. It's . . . bizarre."

Angie bent her knees, and with the Linda Laden technique, sank it for two.

"How's it going with your mom?" Coach asked.

Angie sighed, passing the ball. "She sold the rights to my sister's story."

"Yeah," said Coach Laden. "She called about filming here."

"Of course she did," Angie said.

Coach dribbled to the three-point line. "Things aren't any better? At home?"

Angie shrugged. "The barometer of better is . . . questionable."

The shot went off. Backboard and three!

"I could talk to her," Coach Laden offered.

"Please don't," Angie said, rebounding. "She just is . . ."

An abusive, myopic alcoholic who can't see beyond her own pain and—

"Having a hard time?" Angie said, the ball pressed between her palms. Her eyes cut to her sister's oversized basketball jersey hanging from the rafters. "Sometimes it's like Nat's been gone for years. But other times. I don't know. It feels so . . . close. Weird, huh?"

"No," Coach Laden said. "I miss her. She was so hard on herself. Harder than I could ever be."

That was saying something, given Coach Laden's relentless basketball drills.

"The level of perfection that she wanted," Coach said.

"The way she would fight for every single second of a game."

"Yup," Angie said. "She was pretty perfect."

"No," Coach Laden said. "She wanted to be. For your mom."

Angie rested the ball on her chest.

"I miss you on my team," Coach Laden said.

"I wasn't really that special of a player," Angie said.

"No, you were an *exceptional* player with an incredibly difficult loss. A loss that none of us can understand in the way you do."

Angie smiled-not-smiled.

"You know, there's a spot for you," Coach said, holding her hands out for the ball. "If you want it."

Angie passed the ball. "I don't think it's my thing."

Coach Laden dribbled and went up, flawless form, nothing-but-net jump shot. "What about music? That video everyone's talking about."

"It's been, like, a day. How do you even know?"

"A basketball team of hopefuls who couldn't stop talking about it," said Coach Laden. "And Stacy Ann might have shown it to me. Nice to see the two of you are—"

"Not engaged in the art of hand-to-hand combat anymore?" Angie said.

"That's not exactly how I would've put it," Coach said, "but sure."

"We're not BFF smiley-emojis or anything, but it's

mostly okay," Angie said. "She's dating Jake. Jake is happy. And she seems to be less . . ."

"Angry?"

"Mean, vindictive, cruel," Angie said. "And yeah, angry."

Coach bounce-passed the ball to Angie.

"As for the music," Angie said. "I don't know. My mom wants me to take the video down. With this whole movie thing, she just wants to pretend I'm not real. You should see the headshot for the actor playing me."

Angie dribbled and was set to shoot when Coach Laden asked, "What do you want?"

Angie paused. "It doesn't matter."

"Angie, what do you want?" she asked again.

"I . . ." Angie started, but paused. "I want to stop doing things . . . for other people. Playing basketball was for Nat. It wasn't about me. But singing? It's like this secret I've carried around because girls like me—girls who are . . . you know."

Coach Laden's brow furrowed. "I don't."

"I'm different." Angie shot the basketball.

It ricocheted into Coach Laden's hands. "And? Music is full of different kinds of people."

"I'm fat," Angie said. "I'm a joke."

Coach Laden shook her head. "To who?"

And there it was. The question that had plowed through the noise in Angie's brilliant and beautiful mind. Coach

Laden waited and waited and when it seemed that Angie might free-fall into a panic, there was . . . clarity.

"I'm not a joke," Angie said, the confused reality stretched across her face. "I'm not."

"No," Coach Laden said. "You are not a joke."

Angie's grin expanded. "I'm Fat Angie."

"Wait, what?"

"No, it's a good thing," Angie said, shouldering her backpack. "It's a really good thing. I need to—can you write me a pass?"

"Sure, but—are you sure you're okay?"

"I don't think I've ever been more okay," she said. "I know exactly what I want."

Chapter 8

Through the thinning herd of students, Angie spotted Jamboree, eating lunch in the quad. Her head flooded with an endless array of musical selections, but it was her own "Rebel Girl Revolution" that she strutted to. Well, an Angie kind of strut.

Then, as if cinematically cued, the wind whipped her hair back. Her strawberry ChapStick lips parted. She adjusted her jeans creeping dangerously toward a cameltoe. Her boots drummed against the blue-and-white letters spelling *Go! Fight! WIN!* chalked along the sidewalk. This was her work-it, big, beautiful girl-woman moment. Her declaration long in the making. This was when Angie would, without hesitation—

"I have something to tell you," Angie announced to Jamboree.

Jamboree paused, cheek full of sandwich. "Hey."

"Sorry," Angie said. "You probably wanna finish chewing."

"I'm good," Jamboree said, swallowing. "What's up?"

Angie straddled the bench beside Jamboree. "I'm sorry I didn't text you. Last night."

"It's okay," Jamboree said. "I had a feeling when you didn't come by that maybe dinner wasn't so great."

"Yeah, it was . . . bad." Angie hoisted her backpack onto the table, pulling out her therapeutic journal. "I've been thinking . . . about my life. A lot. Lately."

"Okay," Jamboree said.

"About," Angie said, clearing her throat, "how things have been changing so fast. You and me. Friends again. Me having friends. Like, what?"

Angie fidgeted with the worn edge of her journal.

"Is everything okay?" Jamboree said.

"Yeah," Angie said. "No, it's great. It's just . . . I keep thinking about the video and . . . me singing. People liking it."

"When you sing, there's an . . . energy. An intimacy. You pull people in. All the way. Close."

Angie gulped. The frenetic surge—urge to reveal everything in her head and heart and—

"There's something I have to tell you," Angie said. "I think I've known, but I couldn't admit it. I didn't know how to say it."

"Just say it."

Angie took a deep breath. "I'm so nervous."

"You don't have to be nervous," Jamboree said.

"I just . . . I've never felt so . . . sure," Angie said.

"Yeah," Jamboree said. "I get it."

"Yeah." Angie exhaled. "Okay. I . . ."

Jamboree leaned forward ever so slightly. Anticipating—

"I want to start a band," Angie said.

"Um . . . what?" Jamboree said.

"An all-girl band," Angie continued. "I want to start one."

Jamboree leaned back.

"What—you think it's a bad idea?" Angie asked. "Stupid?"

"No," Jamboree said. "I think it's great. Really. I just thought . . . yeah."

"I was thinking," Angie said, flipping through her journal. "These are songs I started a while back. I mean, most of them are gonna suck. Really terribly suck, but I feel like . . . like here."

Angie spun her notebook toward Jamboree. Barely able to contain her excitement as Jamboree read the lyrics.

"It's just a draft," Angie said apologetically. "I was playing with it last period."

"It's good," Jamboree said. "I can hear the rhythm."

"Right?" Angie said. "You know how you talk about music or traveling. That feeling of . . . belonging. Of being right where you should be. I was talking to Coach Laden, and I knew. Where I should be."

"I love it," Jamboree said.

"Yeah?" Angie said.

"Yeah. Of course. Why not?"

"Exactly," Angie said. "I couldn't wait to tell you. I knew you'd get it. I mean I hoped."

Jamboree put her hand over Angie's. An ordinary gesture between friends, had it not been filled full with an unmet desire for something more.

"I love this for you," Jamboree said. "I love all the good things for you."

Angie's heart had returned to the pounding bundle of nerves it had been the morning before, when she had failed to ask Jamboree out. As right as everything felt, something kept Angie's declaration of a romantic next step corralled.

"I . . . was wondering . . . I wanted to ask you if . . ."

"What?" Jamboree asked.

But Angie just couldn't do it. "I, uh. There's this comp—"

"Two million hits!" Zeke shouted, thrusting their phone across the table. "Look."

Angie leaned over the screen.

"Two freaking million, plus-sized, beautiful, robust, 'Rebel Girl Revolution' views!" Zeke said. "Girl, what did I tell you?"

"You tell me a lot of things," Angie said, distracted by Jamboree's hair brushing against her cheek. Her—

"I told you that you had something to say." Zeke adjusted their Pokémon-duct-taped ostomy bag. "The proof is in the clicks. Plus, get this. I got a message from BuzzFeed. They wanna talk to you—to us."

"Seriously?" Angie asked.

"For real," Zeke said.

"Did you know about this?" Angie asked Jamboree.

Jamboree was about to answer when Zeke said, "Angie, even Selena, may the goddess rest her infinite soul, is listening to that song from heaven."

Angie chuckled.

"I'm telling you, chica." Zeke rotated the phone back toward them. "This is just the beginning."

"Exactly. I was just telling Jamboree I want to start a band because—"

"Yes!" Zeke hopped on the bench. "I knew it when I saw you with Lucas Waite on Instagram and Snapchat. I grabbed my 8-Ball off the floor this morning and was like, 'Is Angie going to start a band?' and the 8-Ball was like, 'You may rely on it.' The 8-Ball never lies before breakfast tacos."

"Lucas Waite?" Jamboree said.

"It was completely random," Angie said. "I met him after dinner last night."

"She and Wang literally had burgers on his tailgate," Zeke reported.

"That's on Instagram?" Angie asked Zeke.

"It's on TMZ too," said Zeke. "Even washed up, he's still a celebrity."

"He's not washed up," Angie said.

"Lyrical genius, okay, I'll give you that," Zeke said, texting. "But he walked out on a three-album, multimillion-dollar deal."

"Wait," Jamboree said to Angie. "So, that's why you couldn't stop by last night?"

"No," Angie said. "That wasn't the reason. I—"

"I know *just* who to ask," Zeke interrupted again. "My girl Jenny is killer on bass, but kind of hates punk. I can have her and a few other people meet up at The Slice tonight. Around nine."

"Running into Lucas Waite wasn't why," Angie assured Jamboree. "Things just got really—"

Loud in Angie's mind right then. A series of fast movie jump cuts. A montage starting with her overloaded buffet plate, her dad's earring, Sharon chewing, Lori playfully shoving Wang, Lucas surrounded by women, Courtney posing, Angie's bedroom—her sister's postcard—her mom . . . Connie gutted by the loss of—

"Angie," Zeke said. "The sound?"

"What?" Angie said, snapping out of her own head.

"Punk? Pop? Rock? Alternative?" Zeke said.

"Right, um . . . so I was just going to tell Jamboree." Angie slipped her phone from her back pocket.

"Nice upgrade," Zeke said, checking it out.

"Guilt gift from my dad," Angie said, clicking on a website.

Zeke and Jamboree hovered over the phone screen.

"Rock Riot?" Jamboree read out loud.

"It's an online competition," Angie said. "For unsigned bands. Female bands. And look. Ms. Joan Jett is one of the judges. *The* Ms. Joan Jett. Rebel of rock 'n' roll."

"Where did you hear about this?" Jamboree asked.

"I . . . just . . . found it."

That was a canard—an outright blatant deception. It was a lie.

Lie (v): The act of bending or distorting a statement in an effort to deceive. Famous liars include but are not limited to former president Richard Nixon, P. T. Barnum, James W. Johnston, eight members of the 1919 White Sox team, and Gatsby in the novel *The Great Gatsby.*

Angie had been well educated on the act of lying by her corporate, not-currently-employed attorney mother, her couldn't-be-accountable father, and of course, Wang. She loathed lying in theory and in practice, yet there she was deep in said lie because KC had been the one to tell her about the competition. A detail best omitted, Angie had decided. Though she wasn't entirely sure why.

"A twenty-five-thousand-dollar purse!" Zeke said. "A

possible label deal and a feature in *Rolling Stone* online and print. Ang! This is . . ."

"Cool, right?" Angie said.

"Absolutely," Jamboree said. "When's the deadline?"

"It's a little tight." Angie sighed.

"Four weeks," Zeke said.

"Three-ish," Angie said.

"More than enough time," said Zeke.

"What?" said Jamboree.

"Angie blew Cincinnati out without a single rehearsal," Zeke contested. "No reason she couldn't win this."

"It's not just about winning," Angie said. "It's about—"

"No, but you want to win and—" Zeke said.

"Stop pushing," Jamboree said. "You're always pushing her."

"I don't feel particularly pushed," Angie voiced. "I—"

"She doesn't feel pushed." Zeke glared at Jamboree.

"Why are you fighting like you're my parents?" Angie said.

"Because ever since she got back from Belgium—" Zeke said.

"Really?" Jamboree asked. "We're doing Belgium again? I thought we left that on the side of the road on the way to Cincinnati."

"It's because you're always trying to limit me," Zeke said. "Like you're trying to limit Angie right now."

"That's so not true," Jamboree said. "Did you even look at the rules? All the things she'd have to do just to qualify?"

"See," Zeke said. "Limits. The rules are a suggestion."

"The deadline is in three weeks," Jamboree said.

"Two million views," Zeke argued.

"You're right. I'm wrong," Jamboree said. "Feel better? Because I don't want to fight with you."

"Whatever," Zeke said, getting up from the table. "Text me if you wanna do this, Angie."

Zeke took off.

Quiet.

More quiet.

"That was weird," Angie finally said. "I mean, it was weird, right?"

Jamboree shrugged. "Yeah. They just can't slow anything down. That's why they're on Darius's couch."

"What?"

"They got kicked out," Jamboree said. "A week ago."

"They didn't say anything."

"I only know because Darius told me," Jamboree said.

A leaf fluttered, doing this little slow dance before hitting the bench between them. Jamboree traced the outline of its screaming-fire-orange body.

"You know," Jamboree said. "I've been in bands, and my friends have been in bands. And it's not like everyone gets together and it just works. It takes a lot of practice. And sometimes it still doesn't come together."

Angie nodded. "You think what happened in Cincinnati was random."

"I don't."

Angie sighed. "Yeah. You kind of do."

Angie swung her leg over the bench, hoisting her backpack across her shoulders.

"Angie . . ." Jamboree reached for her wrist.

"You know," Angie said, "everyone gets to have their thing. Zeke and their documentary and film school next year. Darius . . . who I don't really see because of Rocket Club, AP classes, and planning to enlist. And you. You want to do another semester abroad."

"I haven't decided."

"But you're excited," Angie said. "No one says you can't or you shouldn't. My whole life has been a can't—but this? Music? This is my thing."

"I want you to . . . I want . . . you . . . to have this," Jamboree said. "I just don't want you to get . . ."

Jamboree's thumb rubbed across the scars on Angie's right wrist. The raised skin that was a constant reminder of Angie's desperate step into the void.

Angie nodded. "I'm not that fragile anymore. I thought you knew that."

Angie backed away from Jamboree, the leaves clattering, rapping in her ears as she walked away.

Chapter 9

Angie left school just before the final bell. Because of her "incident" in the gymnasium, she had a lifetime pass to not attend pep rallies. She was halfway down Main Street when amped-up students blaring music from their cars ripped past her. The possibility of the Hornets continuing their undefeated season blared with them.

Angie paused outside the storefront window of Uncivilized Ink, KC's mom's tattoo studio. Peeking past the neon shop sign, Angie watched a guy flash his rib cage to Esther. His hand cupping the length of where he wanted to get inked. Esther nodding in that way of "that's gonna hurt," but Rib Guy wasn't having it.

Angie hadn't seen Esther since KC left. Seeing her brought back all the things that made Esther more than the tattoo/music-loving, new-feminism, best maker of burgers on the grill. She had all the answers and none of them and wasn't afraid to admit it. She gave the best hugs and told the best stories.

The. Absolute. Best!

Esther had never criticized what Angie ate or didn't. She'd even baked Angie a cake for her birthday when Connie had insisted she abstain from sweets. Esther was kind in a way Angie's mom had never been and—

"Hey," KC said, startling Angie.

As always, KC's look was both iconic and hypnotic. From style to stance, KC lunged at any opportunity to avoid assimilating to small-town, Midwestern norms.

"Planning on some ink?" KC said, tucking her helmet under her arm. "Maybe a broken heart?"

KC offered a playful smile. A smile that historically would've sent Angie into a near-absentminded forgiveness about whatever was wrong between them, but she was in no mood to be charmed. To be misled. To be gamed.

KC leaned on the heels of her cowboy boots. "Over two million hits on your vid. Definitely beyond ultra-even."

It was her spouting of *ultra-even* or *essential dough* or other KCisms that Angie had adored when they were together because it was so different from anyone in Dryfalls—a signature of creativity. But right then, the KCisms felt false and distancing.

"Didn't see you at the pep rally," KC said.

Angie stared at the toes of her boots.

"Not that I blame you," KC continued. "It's all a bunch of pomp and circumstance. Silly skits and rah-rah to a season no one will remember in twenty years."

"Unless they win State," Angie said.

KC chuckled. "Unless."

Quiet.

Super awkward I'm-standing-across-from-my-ex-who-shattered-my-heart-and-now-what quiet. Which technically wasn't that quiet in Angie's mind.

"So . . . what are you doing right now?" KC asked.

"Going home."

The roar of dueling motorcycle engines rattled past them.

"Let me give you a ride." KC stepped toward her scooter.

Angie laughed to herself.

"What?" KC asked. "Too cool?"

"More like too heavy. Scooters have weight limits. Even a Ruckus with a custom build."

"So, you Scoobied my ride," KC said, a flirty edge returning to her silky voice.

The truth was Angie had Scoobied the Ruckus. She had also scrolled through KC's Instagram, where her Dallas party/concert pics had been deleted. Pics that had included—

"So, no ride," KC said. "Any Friday night plans? Maybe something with the spicy redhead you dashed after yesterday when we were midconvo?"

"I wasn't mid anything with you," Angie said. "You were talking. I didn't wanna talk."

"I was opening my heart to you," KC said.

"No, you were absolving yourself."

"Wow," KC said. "Did you lace that dart in poison, or just heartache?"

Angie shook her head, kicking the toe of her boot in a crack in the sidewalk. "I don't know what you want me to say."

"Is she your girlfriend?" KC asked. "Ms. Spicy?"

Jamboree was supposed to be—she should have been. Until the day before, all signs pointed in neon yellow to yes. But after lunch, all Angie could think about was how Jamboree had touched her wrists—how she had seemed to believe that was all that Angie was—could be.

"Look, you're here," KC said, stepping toward the shop. "At least say hi to Esther before you bail. She asks about you on the regular. It's kind of on drip at our house."

Angie grimaced.

"What?" KC asked.

"We broke up," Angie said.

"Yeah, but you didn't break up with my mom," KC said. "I'm willing to time-share her. Besides. She loves you . . . you know that."

KC swung the door open. Janis Joplin's "Piece of My Heart" flooded out. Esther looked up from tattooing Rib

Cage Dude, face in absolute angst. "Angie!"

Angie did not like this scenario.

Angie did not like KC baiting her with Esther, and it felt very bait-y.

Angie did not like this moment, so she walked away.

KC's boots beat against the sidewalk as she followed.

"You can't stay mad at me," KC said. "It's cosmically impossible."

"Stop."

"What?" KC asked.

"Stop acting like nothing is wrong," Angie said.

"Why can't we just resume our regularly scheduled knowing of each other?"

"Because life isn't one of your mom's vintage VHS movies," Angie said. "In real life, bad things happen. People leave and die and sometimes what happens after feels even worse than the dying part. Sometimes there's so much wrong and hard that no one believes you or sees you, and when they finally do, they just bail. You bailed, KC."

"So . . . we're just gonna act like we don't know each other? That's the plan?"

"We don't."

KC stepped in front of Angie. "Your favorite word is *heliophile*. You like the sky thirteen minutes before it rains. Not twelve. Not fourteen. Thirteen. You hate the sound of silence. And you wish there were a truly feminist version of *Charlie's Angels*."

Angie adjusted her backpack as KC leaned into her sightline.

"Your mom's a nightmare. Your dad's checked out. And Wang? I don't know. The jury's undecided."

"That doesn't mean you know me," Angie said. "And I definitely don't know you like I thought I did."

"I've only been gone for a few months—"

"A lot has happened," Angie insisted.

"Tell me," said KC. "Tell me what happened—with you and Gary Klein. Tell me why you didn't press charges after that homophobic asshole attacked you. Tell me why you let him just ride off into the Montana sunset?"

"It's complicated," Angie said.

"You hate that word."

It was true. Angie hated the word.

"See. I know you," KC said.

Angie also hated talking, thinking, or in any way being reminded about what Gary Klein had done. The way he had attacked her. How her mother had dissuaded her from pressing charges. How Connie, even when presented with the facts, could not fully accept that Angie was not at fault. Which seemed super screwed up to Angie because mothers were supposed to believe their daughters.

"C'mon," KC said. "Look, I messed up. Okay?"

"No, it's not okay."

"Then how can I make it okay?" KC asked.

"You can't just *okay* this," Angie said. "Me—us."

"So, we are an us?" KC said.

"No."

A line of women began to spill out of the yoga studio. Incense, perfume, and BO trailing behind them.

"Look, I'm not asking you to be my girlfriend because I already had that, and I messed it up," KC said, an unexpected sincerity in her voice. "Can't we be friends?"

"Friends?" Angie said.

"Yeah," she said.

"I don't know what that means."

"It means," KC said, rocking on the back of her boot heels again, "Esther and I are going to Betty's for a Muy Ensalada plate and bean-and-cheese pupusas. Kind of a welcome-back-to-Dryfalls thing. Come with. No strings. I promise."

A stringless dinner with KC? It wasn't a situation Angie had imagined herself in, yet there was something oddly comforting at the thought of cheese pupusas with KC and Esther. All of which made absolutely no sense.

"Look, it's . . . it's cool," KC said, walking toward the tattoo shop.

Let her walk away, Angie thought. *Let her go. Let her—*

"They've started serving complimentary mango jalapeño salsa on Fridays now," Angie said.

KC paused, shyly grinning. "I love mangoes. They're the best fruit ever. Next to watermelon and jalapeños. Despite the ongoing debate about the classification of peppers."

"Botanists see them as a fruit" Angie said matter-of-factly. "Jalapeños."

KC smiled.

Angie mostly smiled.

It was an official, somewhat awkward, but genuine smilefest. Angie's trepidation and hurt began to thaw ever so slightly.

KC swung the door open. Elastica's "Connection" clawed its way out of the shop speakers.

"After you," KC said to Angie. "Platonically."

Angie walked toward KC, and just like that, she had officially let KC back into her life. Platonically speaking, of course.

Chapter 10

High on her Betty's Muy Mexican Casa Caliente Enchilada Special and surprisingly fun, like-nothing-had-ever-happened dinner with KC and Esther, Angie rushed upstairs to change before meeting Zeke and her possible future bandmates at The Slice.

Two steps from the top, she paused. Her sister's bedroom door was open. It was a matter of undisputed fact that Connie had all but caution-taped Nat's room off to anyone without a news camera or a direct line to a movie producer.

Angie rounded the banister and saw Wang, defying the rules of their mother, sitting on the floor in the middle of the room.

"Hey," Angie said.

Wang threw her a nod, popping out his earbuds. "You can come in. She's not here."

Angie stepped inside, feeling the weight of the room she had seen only from the doorway or news reports in the last two years. A space that, at first, seemed largely unchanged since her sister's deployment to the Middle East. Every book—every trophy had its place, but something was off. Something wasn't right.

Angie sat across from Wang, placing a Styrofoam container between them.

"Super wet burrito," she said. "Extra jalapeño sauce."

"Thanks," he said.

"I was just going to stick it in your minifridge," Angie said. "I thought you'd be out with Lori."

"Yeah, I wasn't feelin' it."

"It's all you were feeling all summer—"

"I just wasn't feeling it, okay?" he said.

"Yeah."

Quiet.

More awkward quiet.

"Sorry about last night," he said. "Taking off. Leaving you here."

Angie shrugged. "I get it. It was a take-off-and-leave kind of moment."

Wang ran his palm along the carpet fibers. "I guess."

"Do you know where she is?" Angie asked.

He dug a wadded-up napkin out of his pocket and tossed it at Angie.

"The city," he said as she read the note. "With Joan, of course. Shopping for the interview. Such bullshit."

Angie looked at him.

"A poignant look at the real family behind an American hero," Wang mocked. "Like a phoenix rising from the ashes." He shook his head. "Like who watches that shit?"

It was a matter of common knowledge that Angie did. Often wondering if other families went through loss the way hers had. As imposters, donning forced smiles but real tears that Connie had told them not to shed. As a family with so many pieces and parts never truly examined under the bright lights and long lenses, they were an idea of a family in grief. A family of candid-not-so-candid interviews edited with B-roll of posed shots. Shots of them sitting on a weathered bench along Legacy Lake or walking the sidewalks of their upper-middle-class neighborhood. Showing the world the heart and heartbreak of their largely staged experience. Even if the feelings Angie and Wang had about Nat's capture and later death had been real on camera, the sequence of them had been edited for entertainment.

"I keep trying to pretend it's not gonna happen," Angie said. "The movie. The book deal. The interview."

"I'm not doing that interview." Wang shook his head.

"We have to do it."

"We don't have to do shit," he said.

"What's going on? Really?"

Wang slipped a coin out of his cargo pocket, holding it between his thumb and index finger.

"The double-headed beast," Angie said.

"You were *so* pissed when you realized Nat had been calling heads all those years because—"

"Both sides were heads," Angie said.

"You couldn't believe she'd lie." Wang admired the coin. "I loved knowing that she did. It made her more like us. You know?"

"She was always like us," Angie said.

Wang shook his head, looking at the coin. "She was never like us."

It was true, and it wasn't. Nat was like everyone in Dryfalls. She had fears, strengths, darkness, yet she was only allowed to show one version of herself: Connie's. It was that pressure for perfection, that demand to excel, that sent Angie's sister into a war even more dangerous than the one in their own home.

"Remember why she didn't take it with her?" he asked Angie.

Angie shook her head.

"She said she couldn't rig this next part," he said. "Told me exactly where she left it. It's like she knew she wasn't coming back."

"I don't think that's true," Angie said.

He slid the coin back into his pocket. "Yeah. Maybe."

Beat.

A much longer beat.

"So, school today?" Angie said.

"I felt sick."

"So . . . you weren't doing anything illegal, maybe with someone like Criminal Cody?" Angie asked.

"Yo, I told you my shit's legit."

"So, you were legitimately sick?" Angie asked.

"Yes, I was legitimately sick of Mom's shit and Dad's shit and I needed a breather."

"I get it, but it's your senior year," Angie said. "Graduation."

"You don't have to degree up to degree up."

"That makes no sense," Angie said.

"Diploma is a piece of paper," he said. "It means what you assign it. I assign it nothing."

"It means you graduated," Angie said. "Besides, you always said it was the best kind of f-you to Mom."

"Just say the word, Angie."

"I don't need to say the f-word. You know the word. It's permanently emblazoned on your vocal cords."

"*Fuck* Mom," Wang said. "The diploma means nothing to her. You. Me. We're in competition with a dead person, yo. Like, how grim is that? I could legit cure cancer, and she'd be like 'Well, Nat could've done that and built a colony on Mars.' Whatever."

It wasn't that Wang was wrong. Nat had achieved a sort of nirvana by dying in captivity. She was a hero—an

American hero, and Connie had deliberately been cast as the wounded mother of said hero. Leaving little room for Angie or Wang.

"Maybe you should go live with Dad," Angie offered.

Wang rocked back and forth. "That's not going to happen."

"He wants you to," Angie said.

"I don't care what he wants," Wang snapped. "Okay? I'm not ditching you."

Angie shrugged. "Okay."

Quiet.

More believable but uncomfortable quiet.

"It's weird," Wang said. "I came in here because I thought it would smell like her, you know? It used to. When Mom would take off on her business trips or her long weekends to New Orleans or Vegas or wherever, I'd come in here sometimes. Everything smelled like Nat still. The sheets. The clothes. Her Jordans. Man, did they reek. Like damn, yo. She needed to Febreze that shit."

Angie laughed halfheartedly.

"It's different now," he said. "It's like the funeral." He swallowed hard, his jaw visibly clenching. "Like dry cleaning or . . . salty tears or whatever the smell Mom can't bleach out, paint over . . . regrout. Instead it just smells—"

"Empty," Angie finished.

"Yeah," he said. "There's no dust even. Anywhere. That's weird, right?"

Of course it was weird. But like everything else in Angie's life, the definition of weird had expanded its perimeters in the fallout of her sister's death. The expansion of weird had become the confusing new normal. A new normal Angie was surprised to see Wang questioning.

"I just thought there would be dust," he said. "A cobweb. A piece of trash in the trash can. It was always overflowing. Gum foils shaped like paper airplanes. Wadded-up college-ruled paper. It's the only thing she liked to write on."

Angie looked away from the empty, dustless mesh trash can to her sister's desk chair. The back of it was wrapped with Nat's letterman, sleeves covered in patches. Along the walls, posters of astronomy, defunct boy bands, and basketball icons had been perfectly repositioned. Obsessively so. Even the custom five-shelf bookcase full of trophies, ribbons, medals, and plaques had been rearranged. That's when Angie realized what had been off when she came in. It had been staged. All of it.

Wang slid the closet door open. "She used to ball her jeans up on the floor in the back. Remember?"

"Yeah."

"That's how it was," Wang said. "They were still there. All balled up."

Nat's clothes were now hung in order by color on black wooden IKEA hangers. All facing the same direction. It was so contrary to her sister in every way. That much order. Where was the chaos—the energy—the messiness?

Wang crawled inside the closet, ran his fingers along the baseboards. He faced his palm toward Angie.

"Nothing," he said. "How is there nothing, Ang?"

Angie crawled into the closet and sat beside him.

"It's all hers, but it's not *her*," he said. "Why would Mom do that? Why would she take her away from us?"

Angie held Wang's hand; tears streaked his cheeks, dripping off the edge of his chin.

"I wasn't like you," Wang said. "I always knew Nat wasn't gonna come back, and I could be cool with it because I could come in here, and it was like . . . she was still here. I didn't have to . . . let her go."

Unlike Angie, Wang hadn't poured their sister's ashes in the river. He hadn't ever really been able to say good-bye. Like everything in his life, even grieving his sister had been taken from him.

"Wang, maybe—"

"Forget it," he said. "It doesn't matter."

"You don't have to do that," she said. "You don't have to be all fake-tough."

"It's not going to change anything." He wiped his face with the collar of his T-shirt. "Crying and shit. She's gone."

Wang's phone chimed. Annoyed, he flashed the screen to Angie. It was Jamboree.

"Your girl is burnin' up my phone," he said, biting on the collar of his T-shirt.

"She's not my anything."

"Hmm." He sniffed. "She's something, 'cause this is message number seven."

"We had a fight-not-fight. Kind of," Angie said. "I don't know."

"About a band," he said. "A competition? I read the first six texts."

She nodded. "You probably think it's stupid. Me. In a band."

"Why would you think that?" he asked. "Dude—"

"Not a dude," she corrected.

"Your video has more hits than that guy who farted and lit his ass on fire, and people really liked that."

"That was a compliment in some way, right?" she asked.

"Yeah," he said. "Besides, I would be willing to offer my services as manager. For a nominal fee."

"Nominal, huh?" she said.

"Yo, don't hate the player, hate—"

"The game," Angie recited. "Really? At an IQ of 147?"

Wang laughed. "It hurts, don't it?"

Angie crawled out of the closet, standing up.

"C'mon, Nominal Fee," she said.

"Where we going?"

"The Slice." She grinned. "To start a band."

Chapter 11

Wang whipped his Jeep into the side parking lot of The Slice. He and Angie stepped out in a seemingly cued motion, splitting through the Friday night, post-football-game crowd. A musical cocktail of rock and hip-hop pounded the lukewarm air. Everywhere was excitement—a Hornets' Nest game-winning frenzy.

"Wang!" Winter shouted, cruising by in a truck. "What up, faggot bitch?"

Wang grimaced.

"Guess he knows about Lori," Angie said to him.

"Ang," Zeke shouted, pushing through the crowd. "I'm so glad you didn't let Jam talk you out of this. This band is gonna be criminal."

The notion of Wang as manager made Zeke's suggestion all the more likely.

"Hey, um . . . I want to talk to you about something," Angie said. "Why didn't you tell me you were sleeping at Darius's? What happened? I know it's been bad, but—"

"Pinche primo can't keep his mouth shut about anything," Zeke said.

"We're friends," Angie said. "All of us."

"I'm not friends with everyone," Wang said, eyes glued to a girl pressing her hips against her boyfriend's—

Angie turned back to Zeke. "Jamboree said you got kicked out—"

"I don't care what she had to say."

"Look, I'm not too thrilled with her either, but—"

"For real," Zeke said. "I just need space from all that. So can we just not? For now?"

Angie reluctantly conceded.

"So look," Zeke said. "I had to do a sub for Jenny because she broke her finger, but don't worry. I asked for a favor and got—"

A car horn honked.

The trio looked up in unison as a cool-crush-blue Pontiac LeMans roared into the parking lot, twisting through the crowd, swinging around a caravan of squealing teens. The car's entrance was amplified by Girlschool's mischievous metal/rock "C'mon, Let's Go" rioting from its speakers.

The engine growled as the freshly detailed LeMans came to a stop.

The headlights exhaled.

The driver's door ached as it opened. It was—

"Finster Kahlo Ortiz," Zeke said, pulling their camera out of their messenger bag.

One half of the infamous Ortiz sisters, nineteen-year-old Finster Kahlo Ortiz and her killer pompadour—classically short along the sides, tall up top—stepped out of the car. Her steel-toed black boots clapped along the asphalt. Enigmatic, climactic—she was a brooding mystery in flannel and fitted jeans. An encore of soft and hard often reserved for bad-boy teen-movie leads, Finster was a thing of gossip, of innuendo, of actual rebellion. Refusing to be bullied, to be made invisible, Finster had been the kind of woman Angie historically didn't know how to be: fearless.

Finster opened her trunk, pulling out a bass case, a small amp, and a crate of cables. As she passed the back seat, driver's side, she leaned into the open window and shouted, "We're here!"

Annoyed, the younger half of the Ortiz sisters, Chloe, popped up, earbuds dangling while she played a 3DS. She poured out of the car, back-kicked the door shut, and immediately hopped onto a skateboard, somehow managing to maneuver through the crowd while gaming.

"Perfect, right?" Zeke said.

"Finster is already in a band," Angie said. "A really good one."

"Not anymore," Wang said, reading a statement on the

band's website. "The band 'transitioned' from alternative to alternative Christian midtour in a 'newly awakened understanding of our purpose. We continue to welcome everyone.' I'm guessing not everyone."

"What up, Fin?" Zeke threw a nod and a fist bump.

"What's up is where's your cousin?" Finster said. "That vato owes me fifty."

"Woman, you'll never see that money," Zeke said. "Puto owes me seventy-five."

They laughed.

"So, this is her," Zeke said. "This is Angie."

"Fat Angie," Angie added, hand awkwardly outstretched. "It's my band name. Like a pen name, but you know, for a singer."

Finster knelt along the side of the building, popping open her bass case. "Is that like P-H-A-T or just the *F*?"

"Just the *F*," Angie said.

"Cool," Finster said, setting up her gear. "Loved the song, by the way. Kind of Bikini Kill meets Adele with a little Leslie and the Ly's on performance."

"Thanks," said Angie.

"So, that was really the first time you performed?" Finster asked.

"I'd never even met the band," Angie said.

"Wow. I threw up twice the first time I got on an actual stage. Like, chilaquiles and rice and beans. Everywhere."

It was at the imagining of this that Angie began to gag.

"Anyway, it won't take us long to set up," Finster said, spotting her sister. "Chloe! Get your gear. I got work in thirty."

Chloe threw Finster the bird as she skated toward the trunk, video game still in play.

Angie pulled Zeke and Wang to the side. "Why are they setting up?"

"It's an audition," Zeke said.

"Here—now?" Angie asked. "I said let's meet. Let's talk. Let's—"

"Ang, we don't got a lot of time," Zeke said. "Plus, it's the Ortiz sisters."

"Why would they want to be in a band with me?" Angie said.

"For the competition," Zeke said.

"Well, yeah, but also to be in a band, right? Beyond the two weeks?"

"As manager—" Wang began.

"Stop talking," Zeke said to Wang before looking at Angie. "This is who we got if we wanna make it happen. And I know you wanna make it happen. The momentum is now. This is your moment, girl."

"They're really good," Wang said. "I think—"

"Chloe, hurry up," Finster shouted, shouldering her bass.

"Just a sec," Chloe shouted back.

"My sister is kind of pissed," Finster told Angie, tuning her bass. "Her boyfriend broke up with her because she wouldn't let him feel her up. She's in seventh grade. Like, shit. Save a little of that for high school."

"Totally shit," Angie said awkwardly.

"She wanted to sit and sulk, but I'm on sister-sitting duty, so she had to come."

Chloe stepped up with her guitar slung at her side, two hands holding her amp.

"Sucks about the breakup," Zeke said to Chloe. "Pues, don't worry. The heart is a titan. You will survive."

Chloe looked at Angie. "So you're the suicide queen?"

"Cállate," said Finster.

"What?" Chloe said to her sister. "You asked Zeke earlier."

Finster took Chloe's gear. "Not in the same way."

Angie saw this as a moment not to wall up or be defensive. She simply needed to share her truth. Angie leaned down to Chloe, who was several inches shorter. "My sister was captured, well, um, killed in Iraq. My parents are just . . . we had a dog, his name was Lester, but my dad took him in the divorce. I don't know what they call him now because he wouldn't respond to his name. And yeah, there were dark times. Times where I felt like I couldn't—"

"I didn't need all that," Chloe said. "I just wanted to know if you were that girl."

"Oh," Angie said. "Yeah. I guess."

Chloe turned to Finster. "I want a pizza *and* a cherry Pepsi for this. Plus ten bucks for the arcade."

"Ay, you're bleeding me, Mexican," Finster said. "Whatever. Just finish setting up."

"Chloe," Zeke said, camera pointed at her. "What are you feeling right now?"

Chloe gnashed her teeth, plugging her guitar in. "I feel like I hate my sister."

"I'm gonna die someday and you're gonna regret that shit," Finster said.

"Maybe," Chloe said, kicking her effects box. "Maybe not."

Finster began slapping the bass. Rudimentary samplings soon evolved as she slid into the Red Hot Chili Peppers' "Get Up and Jump." Angie was transfixed by the left-handed bassist blasting through chords, picking up changes. Christian rock Finster was not. She played with her whole body, and it wasn't a body picking for Jesus.

"Wonder if she does everything left-handed," Angie said.

"I hope so," Zeke said, filming.

A loose circle of onlookers began to form as Finster nodded for Chloe to join in. Chloe, clearly not one to be shepherded, took her time before shaking the whammy bar in a chord collision of squealing sequences, then skidding into—

"Caprice Five," Zeke said.

Paganini's Caprice no. 5 (n): One of twenty-four pieces composed for violin. Niccolo Paganini's no. 5 is a technical beast. It has been transcribed for various instruments; electric guitarist Steve Vai's "Eugene's Trick Bag" in the box-office flop *Crossroads* showcased its level of difficulty, which is extreme. Very, very extreme!

Chloe had become famous for mastering Caprice 5 at the age of nine. A video gone viral led to invitations to perform on several notable television talk shows. But unlike Lucas Waite, Chloe wasn't given a key to the City of Dryfalls. She was Mexican American with a lesbian sister and two dads. Dryfalls just wasn't that kind of progressive yet. Maybe not ever.

The parking lot chatter and car music had been vanquished by Chloe, who shredded the guitar with a near boredom—blowing a big purple bubble-gum bubble while doing it, her fingers firing up and down the neck of the guitar. It was a wild thing to witness up close.

People watched from their booths inside The Slice. Even the dude who had been making out with his girlfriend was now watching.

When Chloe was done, she yawned.

"Paganini?" Finster said. "Kind of a crutch."

"Let's see you do it," Chloe challenged.

Finster looked at Angie. "You ready?"

Angie looked around the crowd. Everyone watching—waiting.

"Just do your thing," Zeke said. "Besides, the video will be killer. Trust me."

Angie walked up to the mic, standing uncomfortably behind it.

"What do you want to try?" Finster asked.

"Um—"

"I'm not doing the Killers or Fall Out Boy," Chloe said.

"The boyfriend's favorites," Finster said to Angie. "You know the Donnas?"

"'Take It Off,'" Angie said.

Finster looked at Chloe.

"I guess." Chloe pushed off the wall, setting her 3DS on the ground. "But the irony of the song isn't lost on me."

Angie took a deep breath. Her fingers curled around the dented microphone. This was an *it* moment. The universe had bequeathed her the rarest of opportunities. Performing with the Ortiz sisters. Albeit in a parking lot. A parking lot packed with high schoolers. Many with their cell phones already vertical. Waiting for Angie to—

"Go." Finster nodded to Chloe.

Chloe started the song, followed by Finster, supplementing for the missing percussion. Zeke watched from the pop-out viewfinder on her camera. The red RECORD button blinked at Angie. And blinked and—

Angie hit her opening cue but rushed the lyrics. She fought to recover, though her window for staying in tempo was closing. When they hit the bridge, she began to find some footing only to forget a set of lyrics she'd sung privately dozens of times. More phones were now filming. The weight of their cameras, the awkward confusion on some of their faces about everything Angie was doing wrong . . . Her throat tightened—she sang out of key.

Angie backed off the mic. Chloe and Finster stopped playing.

"Sorry," Angie said to Finster. "I'm just . . ." Her eyes trailed through the crowd. "Maybe I didn't warm up enough."

"It's not the warm-up," Chloe said, picking up her 3DS.

Finster leaned in to Angie. "You know—"

"Pretend they're not there?"

Finster chuckled. "I was going to say fuck what they think. This is your revolution. Right?"

"Yeah," Angie said, not entirely convinced as she watched the crowd's interest begin to wane.

A crowd that had only recently allowed her to emerge from the role of loser, wacko, fatso outcast to officially coronate her with popularity. Well, mostly. And while Angie's newfound popularity might have been a misshapen crown, she wasn't ready to rescind it. But there she was, standing in the parking lot of The Slice with real musicians at her side, feeling like a fraud. Feeling the shadow of her perfectly perfect sister closing in.

"Look, if you want—" Finster started.

"Let's go again," Angie said.

Finster nodded to Chloe, who stood there, guitar hanging across her, shaking her head.

"Today," Finster said to her.

"You're not the boss of me," Chloe said.

"You're the one that starts the song."

"Fine, I'll start it," she said.

Only this time Chloe added an unwritten guitar solo. Swinging her arm out wide, throwing Finster the bird between chords. She did this several times before transitioning into the song as written.

Angie leaned into the mic. Her timing was moderately better, but she was still off. She couldn't shake it—those who were still watching. Looking at her—through her. This wasn't Cincinnati. Monday she'd have to go back to school and face them and anyone else who saw her on Instagram or Facebook. She didn't want to fail and—she couldn't go backward. She couldn't—

Angie walked away from the mic, breaking through a group of girls.

"Ang," Zeke called out.

Wang cut through the crowd, catching up to her. "Yo."

"Something's wrong," Angie said, anxiety spiking.

"What?" he said.

"This was a bad idea. Let's just go."

"No," he said, stepping in front of her.

"Wang, don't—"

"*Karate Kid Part III*," he blurted out.

"What?" she asked.

"Part three," he said. "Like, it was crap, right?"

Frustrated, she huff-shrugged.

"But that part where Daniel's getting his ass kicked in the tournament?" he continued. "He's there all weak-ass on the side of the mat. Clutching his ribs and panting. What did Mr. Miyagi tell him?"

"Wang, please."

"Mr. Miyagi's like, 'It's cool to lose to the douche you're fighting, but don't lose to your punk-ass fear.' Right?"

That wasn't exactly how the message was presented in the film.

"You're just afraid, yo," he said. "I get it. Fear's a bitch. Just kick it in the taco."

Inspirational movies were filled with inspirational speeches. Well-written, thought-out, emotional speeches often accompanied by sweeping orchestration. Shots of honey-rich cracks of light expanding from a window, dawn stretching across a lonesome landscape, the world somehow born anew.

This was not an inspirational movie, and Wang refused to live as though it were, as evidenced by—

"Go do the crane version of singing," he continued, exhausting the metaphor.

"The crane is in part one," she said.

"After all of that, that's all you have to say?" he asked.

Angie watched Finster and Zeke talking. Chloe leaned against the building, playing her game.

"As your manager—" Wang started.

"Technically, there wasn't a legally binding agreement—"

"Shut up," he said. "Beyoncé you are not. Yet. But you're never gonna be if you don't commit. Mistakes and all."

Somewhere in Wang's version of a pep talk, a logic manifested and reached into Angie. She walked back toward Finster and Chloe.

"Hey. I'm just not audience ready yet," Angie said. "But I will be."

"It's cool," Finster said. "We probably should've met up more private, but I gotta work until one before picking up a shift at Dee's."

All of which Angie felt was Finster's way of saying this wasn't going to work out.

"You know," Finster said, "the pressure is different when it's your people."

"I don't know how much they're my people, but yeah," Angie said. "I guess."

"So, rehearse tomorrow night?" Finster said. "Seven thirty?"

"Wait. You still want to band—be in a band—with me?" Angie said.

Finster grinned. "Look, I'm over dude bands and their dude bullshit. Their lateness. Their egos. Their juvenile attempts to use the band to basically score dates. I like your vibe. What you're about. So, if you're down for some low-ego collaboration, I'm in."

"Yeah," Angie said, overly shaking Finster's hand. "Definitely."

"Besides," Finster said, "if it takes a competition to bring women together to make massively unapologetic music in Dryfalls, then hell yes."

"Yes!" Angie said. "So, we're a band."

"Nobody asked me," Chloe said, playing her 3DS. "Nobody asks me shit."

Angie looked at Chloe. "Want to be in a band with the suicide queen?"

Chloe looked her up and down before saying, "Whatever. It's not like I have a boyfriend anymore. Thanks a lot for freaking him out, Fin."

Angie turned back to Finster. "Guess we're a band."

"Cool," Finster said. "I can ask around about a drummer. I know we're pinched for time."

"I'm on it," Wang announced, introducing himself to Finster. "Wang. Band manager."

"He's my brother," Angie said. "He's mostly harmless."

Zeke shook their head, looking at Angie. "You trust him?"

Angie looked at Wang.

Wang looked at Angie.

This appeared to be a pivotal moment in their relationship as siblings. Of course she didn't trust him. Not with anything big like truth, justice, or a reliable analysis of her emotional landscape. She did, however, recognize that Wang could be more than his criminal, mischief-prone self. He had, after all, stood up to their couldn't-be-accountable father in defense of Angie. And only an hour earlier, he had shared some of his deepest hurt about the loss of their sister. Perhaps Wang was ready to turn over a new leaf—an old leaf—some leaf that didn't have him in court-appointed therapy or being randomly drug-tested.

"Yeah," Angie said.

Zeke stepped to Wang. "Dude, don't mess this up."

"Relax," Wang said. "I got this."

Zeke broke away, helping Finster and Chloe pack up. Wang wandered toward The Slice, tapping texts, bumping into people as he did.

And Angie . . . she stood there, basking in the brilliance of band euphoria. Realizing that as excited as she was to start, she was equally afraid to fail. To choke. To forget lyrics—to write lyrics for original songs, because there had to be original songs. Songs that didn't suck.

That's when Rancid Reign's "Thrill Ride" roller-coastered out of a weak set of van speakers. Shaking Angie out of her fear and into an idea. A truly fantastic idea. Because there was one person who could help her—help all of them.

And she couldn't wait to ask.

Chapter 12

Angie pounded on the factory door of the now defunct Waite, Inc. Its five-story brick facade loomed against the stormy, midmorning sky. Its walls were tagged with uninspired graffiti. A trio of dumpsters bulged with garbage bags, two-by-fours, metal piping, and several stained mattresses. Tufts of weeds sprouted from the massive to hairline cracks along the asphalt parking lot. It was a lonely place with only the sound of the wind and the interstate lashing against it.

A gust of wind blew Angie's hair back. She shivered, zipping up her hoodie. The sky moments from a downpour, and of course she didn't have an umbrella. She was about to knock again when the hinges of the door squealed. A driving, moody music spilled from inside.

"Hey," Lucas said, wiping his hands on a shop rag.

"Hey," she said.

He dipped his head out the door.

"It's just me," Angie said.

"You here to reclaim your half-eaten pint of ice cream?" he asked.

"You liked it," she said.

"You have officially restored my faith in the combination of chocolate and peanut butter," he said.

A rogue raindrop smacked Angie in the eye.

"Uh, you wanna . . . come in?" he said.

She slid between him and the door. The powerhouse vocals and driving drumbeat swirling around her.

"What is that?" she said.

He lowered the volume. "Just something I was playing with."

Her eyes wandered from the cement floor to the expansive ceilings. From the steel beams to the massive aluminum-framed windows. A mattress on the floor with milk-crate nightstands full of vinyl. The place smelled like sawdust, paint, and coffee.

"This is a cool place to live," she said, tripping over an extension cable. "You live here, right?"

"For now. Have a seat," he said, offering a tattered bar stool in a makeshift kitchen.

Angie's eyes tracked up a series of stairs to an office. The mystery of what had happened to Lucas's dad up there had been hung out for half the town to gossip about.

Lucas swung open the top of two stacked minifridges.

"I got cold pizza. Uh . . . questionable leftover Chinese." He popped open the lid and sniffed. "Very questionable. Let's see. A bag of mini carrots and filtered water that tastes unfiltered. And ice cream."

"Water. Thanks."

"So," he said, pouring. "I guess everybody knows I'm out here."

"I don't know," Angie said. "I went to your mom's house and asked."

"How'd that go?" He set the water in front of her.

"She told me she was sorry for my loss," Angie said. "Which is what people say to me when they don't know what else to say. Because of my sister. How she didn't . . . how she died."

Lucas nodded. "Yeah, I didn't get that was your sister the other night."

"It's really okay," Angie said. "Sometimes I just wish people would forget." A pang of guilt throbbed. "Not forever, just . . ."

"For a while," he said.

"Yeah," she said.

"Well, if people don't remember, the Internet does," he said, throwing the cold pizza in a microwave. "I'm sorry if it was weird. With my mom. We're not exactly talking right now."

"I get that feeling more than you could know," Angie

said, noticing the edge of some scaffolding behind a black tarp.

"Is that the stage from the *Heather Runs* tour?" she asked, hopping off the stool.

"Sort of," he said.

She reached for the tarp. "Can I?"

"Sure," he said. "Just be careful. It's kind of a mess back there."

Angie pulled the tarp back, her eyes widening as she walked toward the stage. "Whoa . . . Why is this here?"

"Some people like puzzles. I like rockets and stages. The way things build. Come together. I always thought it could be better. Big but still intimate. The idea of taking something commercial and consumable and making it still mean something, you know?"

Angie did not know. It was not something she had ever had to think about, but there she was in an abandoned factory thinking about big but still intimate. Thinking about . . .

"Forty-two cities in forty-six days," Angie said, admiring the set. "Sold-out arenas. Pop-up club performances—roving concerts in moving trucks. That might have been my favorite."

He smiled. "Mine too."

"Everyone said you were the next . . ." Angie paused.

"Yeah," he said. "They did."

"I didn't mean that you aren't . . ."

"It's good," he said. "It was a choice. One of the few I actually made. Except for keeping this place."

"Is that why you're fighting with your mom?" Angie asked. "For keeping it?"

"We're fighting about a lot of things," he said. "Which is strange. It wasn't always like that. Us fighting. We used to really get along."

Lucas picked up a piece of lumber and threw it in a wheelbarrow. The clunk-drop echoed.

"Wanna check it out?" he asked.

"Really?"

"Watch your step," he said, climbing a set of stairs to the stage.

"A friend of mine asked if he could have his annual fundraiser here in a couple of weeks," Lucas said, walking past fanned sheets of music written by hand. "So I got some guys coming to help me finish up the stage. Haul out some trash."

Angie kneeled, picking up a sheet of music. "What is all this?"

"Just some of that stuff I told you I was playing with," he said. "You read music?"

"Kind of," she said. "I wouldn't call it my superpower."

He shuffled through a few pages.

"Check this out," he said, sitting beside her. "It's a louder version of 'Martha, May I,' but with a glitter-rock vibe. Producers wouldn't record it. Said it didn't 'fit' our sound."

"What about the band?" Angie asked.

"Jordi was cool about it," he said. "The others were just into making the label happy. So . . . we never recorded it."

"But you wrote it, right?" she asked. "You could record it."

He laughed to himself. "I guess. Maybe."

Angie walked around the stage, standing behind the microphone. Imagining beyond the factory. Imagining—the small venue amassing into a stadium. And before she could fully fall into the fantasy—

"You gonna tell me what's up?" he said. "I have this feeling there's an up."

"I've been thinking. About what you said."

"Which part?" he said, wrangling a cable.

"About how I had something to say." She took a deep, steady breath. "I do. And . . . I'm starting a band."

"That's great," he said. "You should."

"See, the thing is, um . . . I kind of need your help."

"You don't need me to start a band," he said. "Just put the call out. Get together. Write songs. Bad, shitty, I-can't-believe-I-thought-that songs. Then write some good ones. Fun ones. Practice. Fight. Make up. It's a lot like any other relationship. When it works, you'll know. And if it doesn't, you'll move on."

"I can't decide if that sounds exciting or terrifying," she said.

"Maybe it's both."

"Last night I tried to sing in front of people, and I choked," Angie said. "There was so much—I just—my throat tightened and my mind . . . everyone was looking and . . ."

Angie's phone chimed, but she ignored it.

"Makes sense." He tossed the cable into a milk crate.

"It does?"

"Sure," he said. "It's different after someone sees what you can do. That video. People see you now."

"Yeah." She sighed.

"It's not a bad thing," he said. "You just gotta put more tricks in the mind. The way you look at the audience. Who you're singing to—why you're singing. You'll get there."

"I kind of need to get there quicker than usual," she said. "There's a competition—Rock Riot. And it's this—"

"I know what it is," he said, hopping off the stage.

"I get how you feel about competitions, but—"

"Then why are you here asking me to help you with one?" he said. "Angie, those things are stacked. Look, you want to start a band? Do it because you love music. Because it's fun. Because . . . you're lost without it."

"I have been lost," Angie said. "I've been lost my whole life. Trying to be something for my ex-girlfriend or my dad or my mom . . . my sister. None of it was ever about me—what I wanted." Angie paused. "The only time I've ever felt right about something—as scared as I was to fail, and I was scared—was singing on that stage in Cincinnati. I felt so alive, Lucas. Being behind that mic. And ever since, I've felt like there was something bigger in me. Something—I didn't want to admit even to myself because I thought . . . because I thought a girl like me couldn't. I don't believe that anymore. I won't believe it anymore."

"And you shouldn't," he said. "But when you sang in Cincinnati, that performance was pure. It was flawed. It was rich. It was loud and emotional and . . . don't mess that up with a competition. Learn the craft. Love it. Figure out who are before you try to make yourself into something for someone else."

Lucas began to walk away.

Angie sighed. This was not the response she had wanted, and it would not be the response she would settle for. No more settling. No more accepting anyone else's limits for her.

"Heather . . ." soulfully ached from her voice.

Lucas continued to walk.

And Angie continued to sing, but rather than sing in the expected major key, she continued in minor.

"Heather, this was the worst kind of day.
The way they didn't say your name right
on the nightly news."

Lucas stopped at the edge of the tarp.

"Heather, they had you hide your face.
Erase the thing that made you unique.
I can't pretend I didn't notice
when your eyes went dark.

I can't pretend I didn't notice.
I can't pretend I didn't—

Heather . . .

They told you to wait.
Not to dream in color.
They padded your mind
like they padded each other.
Let me breathe.
Exhale and scream . . .

Heather . . .

I hear you now.
My voice is hoarse.
Your lips are numb.
Dumb how this all happened.

Heather . . . run.

Just run."

Angie waited. The quiet hung heavy across her beautiful, plump shoulders.

"I never heard it like that," Lucas said.

"Me neither," Angie said, equally surprised.

"The chorus," Lucas said, walking toward her. "You changed it."

"It needed to be darker," she considered. "Mournful?"

"Yeah," he said. "It did. I like the run you added. Can you do it again?"

"I think?"

And she did. Again and again and on her third effort, he offered her a tweak.

"No training, huh?" he asked.

"No," she said. "I just thought I sounded like Adele in the shower because everyone does."

He laughed. "Not everyone. There's a richness to your voice. A versatility. How you can go from smooth to round and raspy. And those runs. But you're losing some air."

"Can you help me?" Angie said. "I don't have a chance at this competition without you. I mean, I'd have a chance. Like, you know, one in a trillion."

Lucas grinned. "How many songs?"

"Is that a yes?" she asked. "Two. But we need a gig. Like

a real gig, not just playing at someone's picnic."

"So, two songs and a real gig?" he said.

"Oh, and a video intro. Who we are. What makes us us."

Lucas slowly paced. His boots echoed against the floor.

"You really wanna do this?" he asked.

"I really want to do this," Angie said, her phone chiming. She ignored it.

"Okay," he said.

"Really?" She jumped off the stage and not with a lot of grace.

"If I can help, I will," he said.

"You absolutely can," Angie said. "I'm so excited. I can't wait to tell everyone!"

This time when Angie's phone chimed she read the text from Wang: She's being weird. Where r u?

"Uh, I have to go," she said. "But we'll be back at seven thirty. If that's okay?"

"Sure," he said.

Angie bumped into the tarp on the way out, popping back through it. "Lucas?"

"Yeah?"

"Thanks . . . sincerely," she said, her phone chiming. "Uh! Bye! Bye."

"Go."

Angie rushed out of the warehouse and into the shivering sprinkle of rain, literally springing off the ground in uncontrollable glee.

She had a band.

She had Lucas Waite as a mentor.

Now she just had to get through a birthday party . . . with her mother.

Chapter 13

Angie stood in the corner of her aunt Megan's living room, batting a bobbing Mylar Minion balloon away from her face. She tugged at the itchy, too-tight dress she had worn to avoid any potential feud with her hungover mother. Her mother who had surprisingly said nothing about the viral music video. It was as if the entire ransack-Angie's-room thing had never happened. Connie had simply given Angie and Wang her tired speech about the necessity of attending family gatherings even if they felt absolutely unbearable.

This was definitely that kind of gathering.

The half-birthday party for Angie's six-month-old cousin could only be described as bizarre. A celebration with people eating off half plates, consuming catered half hot dogs and half hamburgers on half buns, Angie watched as a half dozen women gathered around the birthday cake: a realistically sculpted monstrosity of her cousin in crawl pose. All of which would have been fine had it not looked as if she'd been sawed in half. No butt. No legs. No toes. Only a torso with arms and a head. Her right pinky missing because a nephew had sampled it. The women raised their cell phones and took selfies with the cake all the same.

Angie stared down at her half plate with its lone triangle of an egg-salad sandwich spotted with black olives, crust removed. She had been manipulated into the food choice by the mere presence of her couldn't-get-it-together mother, who had served herself a sizeable slice of deep-dish pepperoni pizza.

Angie's couldn't-get-it-together mother stood at the opposite side of the living room, farthest from the crowd of partygoers and the pop-music playlist. She clutched her second cup of Baby Bubbly, a mixture of champagne and ginger ale, to her chest. Listless, she stared out a streaky pane inset on the French double doors, at the excessively landscaped backyard. The backyard packed with parents and children and a circus of activities such as Jenga Giant, cornhole, and pin the tail on the half donkey. Kids clawed and jumped inside a fifteen-foot superhero bounce house. A boy yanked the mane of a miniature horse fitted with a lamé unicorn horn while an aging, skinny clown constructed balloon animals of questionable shape.

The Minion balloon floated back into Angie's airspace, staring at her with its goggled Minion eyes before drifting away.

Angie had agreed to come to the party because she mostly had to.

Angie had agreed to come to the party because Wang had said he'd be her wingman.

Angie had not seen Wang since they came in the front door, of course.

The Pinterest-inspired party had been pushed on Angie's aunt Megan by her mother-in-law, Ruth, who was standing in the backyard, seeming to flirt with a waiter likely twenty years her junior.

"They give you a discount if you buy more than forty," said Mrs. O'Connor, eyeing the army of forty-eight swaying Minion balloons.

"A discount off a dollar balloon?" said Ms. Johnson. "That's not true."

"Megan said that's why Ruth bought so many," Mrs. O'Connor asserted.

Mrs. O'Connor was the neighborhood knower of things. Of affairs. Of divorces. Of late mortgages. Of deliveries of mail or lack thereof. When she could, she would expand this knowing at school-board meetings, the PTA, and pretty much wherever her opinion could be heard. She had been relegated to such an existence of her own volition, as relayed to Angie by her aunt on more than a dozen occasions.

Mrs. O'Connor noticed Angie attempting to hide behind one of the dreaded balloons. "You're Connie's other daughter, aren't you?"

Connie's "other daughter" was a demarcation of the nicest order. Better than her "fat daughter" or "special daughter" or "troubled daughter" or "disappointing daughter" or even, and this was no joke, as one woman had said, Connie's "possessed daughter."

Angie forced herself to smile and nod.

"Such a shame what happened to your family," said Mrs. O'Connor, who could leave no scab unpicked. "We prayed so hard every single night that your beautiful sister would come home."

Angie was not sure what the proper response was for the donation of nightly prayer. She knew there must be one, as both of the women seemed to be waiting for it.

"I guess the Lord had other plans," Mrs. O'Connor offered.

Angie cringed silently.

Ms. Johnson pointed to a picture-book display, and the two meandered toward it.

Angie let out the biggest exhale. She couldn't wait for the cake to be cut, hoping it wasn't red velvet, and their exit to be swift because everything about the party made her uncomfortable. The too-tight, itchy dress, the crust-free triangle egg-salad sandwich, the questionable pop-music playlist, and Wang ditching her for the last fourteen minutes. Something had to give.

The Mylar had to go.

Angie set her plate on an end table. Covertly-not-incredibly-covertly, she wrangled several of the balloons. She faded farther into the background of the party, standing near the realistic-looking-but-fake ficus tree. She scooped up a pin from the cloth diaper display and carefully and precisely punctured one of the balloons. A quiet exhale-hiss of helium seeped out.

Her eyes shifted left, then right as she pressed the balloon to her chest until it flattened. Then she pierced another one and then another, and in the frenzy of Mylar extinction—

"What are you doing?" Wang said, startling her.

She hid the still-leaking balloon behind her. It was a ridiculous effort to conceal her crime. The panicked mind does what it will when in a state of, well, panic.

"Shh . . ." she said to him.

"Why you killing the balloons?" he asked.

"They're terrible for the environment," she whispered.

"Yo, I'm the one that told you. Mylar's like herpes. It's forever. But you're not saving anything executing them. Besides there's like a hundred latex ones in the garage. They're gonna have everyone release them after the cake."

He tipped his drink toward her. She took a sip. Her face immediately wrenched in disgust.

"What is that?" she said.

"Jack and ginger," he said. "No way am I getting through this sober."

"You're breaking the law," Angie said. "Uncle Gabe is a police officer. The law is kind of important."

"He works desk and hates his life," said Wang. "He doesn't care what I do."

Angie grabbed the cup and poured it into the fake ficus.

"What the fuck, Afterschool Special?" Wang said.

"What the f, DUI Wannabe? You can't get into any more trouble. You're like—two strikes in or something."

"Angie, nobody gets busted for drinking at a half-birthday party. It's just not a thing."

"And this is from your extensive experience attending half-birthday parties?" she asked.

Wang nodded toward Connie. "Mom's on her fourth."

"Second," Angie corrected.

"Fourth," he said. "I've been counting. Also, I walked in on Aunt Megan, hiding in the laundry room. I think she hates this shit as much as we do. I'm never getting married. You just end up giving in to shit you don't want."

"I don't think you have to be married to do that," Angie said.

"Huh?" He considered it, then said, "Let's eat."

They wove through the cornucopia of halfness. Of things that should have been whole. Wang piled a mountain of half sliders and fries, bowing his half plate.

"Get something," he said.

Angie shook her head.

"Why?" he asked.

"I'm not hungry," she said.

That was a lie. Angie was very hungry. Hungry for gourmet sliders, but Connie's proximity was an appetite suppressant. Angie didn't want to endure the possibility of passive-aggressive commentary—of judgmental eyes and verbal digs about how thin Angie's cousins were. How fatness was from Angie's father's side of the family, and what an absolute loser he was and no wonder he'd had a stroke—a mild stroke, but a stroke all the same—before fifty.

Wang plunked three sliders and a generous handful of fries onto a plate, holding it out to her. "Tell her you're holding them for me if she says something."

"Thanks," she said.

The two of them plopped onto the sofa.

"You excited," he said, mouthful of burger, "about rehearsal tonight?"

"I can't wait," she said.

"Told you Lucas would go for it," Wang said. "A band manager knows shit."

"Uh-huh," she said, eating. "Does a band manager know how to manifest a drummer before rehearsal?"

"I got leads."

"You know, Zeke and Finster know people."

"Did Luke Skywalker ever doubt the wisdom of Obi-Wan Kenobi?" he asked.

Angie had never been a fan of the Star Wars franchise and consequently was not familiar with the character narrative.

"No," Wang answered for her.

That's when the unexpected happened.

Connie tapped Angie on the shoulder, motioned for her to scoot toward Wang so she could sit down . . . with them?

There they were. The three of them sitting side by what-was-happening side. Wang jammed his earbuds in, leaving Angie essentially alone as her mother seemed to survey the room.

"This is the most ridiculous waste of time and money," Connie said. "Pinterest."

Had the universe turned upside down? Would frogs, salamanders, or some other form of amphibian plummet from the sky, smacking partygoers in their happy faces? Had Angie and Connie somehow been on a similar page about the party?

"Why would anyone do this?" Connie said, holding up half of a birthday hat. "Why would you want a half of anything?" Connie looked directly at Angie. "It's stupid to you, isn't it?"

Angie looked to Wang, who was eating and texting. She turned back toward her mother.

"Yeah," Angie said.

Connie tossed the hat on the coffee table. She finished her drink and wiped the edges of her mouth clean. Her back straightened, her body tightened, winding itself into some form of—

"Connie, how are you?" asked Mrs. O'Connor.

Was there literally no one else for this woman to bother?

Connie labored a smile. "I'm good, Karen. How are you?"

"You know," she said. "Our sons both graduated from Harvard last year. They're working in New York. Place in the Hamptons."

Angie rolled-not-rolled her eyes.

"We heard about the movie," said Mrs. O'Connor. "That they'll be filming here during homecoming."

"Just a few scenes," said Connie, looking at the bottom of her empty drink cup. "The director has a very cinema verité approach."

Not that Connie had known what cinema verité was until her friend Joan googled it.

"And a family interview," Connie said. "A little documentary they're making."

"Well, you must be so excited. I mean . . . not excited, but . . ."

Intentionally or otherwise, Mrs. O'Connor had done

something worse than bragging about her sons' collective Harvard/Hamptons success. She had essentially congratulated Angie's mother on selling her dead daughter's story to the highest bidder.

Angie watched her mother, the master of believable phony charm, struggle to stretch into a polite smile.

This was a first.

Wang leaned forward and said, "You got hummus on your shoe," to Mrs. O'Connor.

She did, in fact, have a splotch of hummus on her shoe, and now she had a viable out. "Well, it was good to see you, Connie. You look . . ."

Connie waited.

"Well, you know," Mrs. O'Connor said, leaving.

Connie shut her eyes, stretching her neck to one side, and then the other. Angie gulped and began to perspire. Being that close to her mother always made her feel so disgustingly hulking, yet so—

"Small," Angie had said to her therapist. *"She makes me feel small. Just being near me."*

"Can you imagine yourself sharing that with your mother?" said her therapist.

"She'd tell me to change my shirt. My mother doesn't do hard. She just . . . explodes. As long as no one can see."

"See what?" asked her therapist. *"Angie? See—"*

"Connie." Aunt Megan kneeled in front of her. "I didn't see you all come in. Hey, Wang. Angie."

Wang did not respond, so Connie reached across Angie and yanked an earbud out.

"Ouch! What the hell?" Wang snapped.

"Say hi to your aunt," Connie directed.

"What up?" he said, irritated as he jammed his earbud back in.

"Thank you for coming," Aunt Megan said, resting her hand on Connie's knee. "Ruth has been . . . anyway. It's good to see you out of the house. It's good for you, don't you think?"

Fact #6,239: In the rules of party etiquette, as in life, never ask a question you truly don't want an answer to.

Connie remained quiet.

"Are you okay?" Angie cautiously asked her mom.

"What?" Connie asked, as if caught daydreaming.

"Where's Rick?" Aunt Megan asked.

Had Aunt Megan missed the breakup memo? Mentioning John/Rick was specifically off the menu of items to discuss.

"He texted that he had a soufflé recipe that I'd—"

"Why are you texting my boyfriend, Megan?" Connie asked.

"We don't text," Aunt Megan said. "It was just . . . I mean, God, Connie."

And that was when the half of everything came into a whole lot of tension.

"God, Connie," Angie's mother repeated sarcastically, a

mock-puzzled look on her face. "It's not strange that I have had some level of inappropriate behavior with all of your boyfriends since high school. Most recently, getting drunk at your daughter's statue dedication ceremony and flirting with your then-boyfriend, Rick. Is that the 'God, Connie' you meant, Megan?"

Angie knew this tone—this texture in her mother's voice. It was all war and no mercy.

"Okay, I didn't—" Aunt Megan offered.

"God, Connie," her mother interrupted. "Despite all of that, thank you for coming to this ridiculous party after your own daughter came back in pieces."

"Connie." Aunt Megan was shell-shocked by the cruelty of her sister.

"No, what you meant was, Thank you, Connie for coming here after I banged on your front door this morning, guilting you to show up because I made you the godmother of a child I didn't want. Because, of course, Megan, you needed support for this unbelievably vapid celebration orchestrated by Gabe's overbearing mother."

"Stop," Megan said to her sister.

And it seemed as if it were over, but a thought came to Connie. "You know, your daughter has never worn the same outfit twice."

Aunt Megan was uniquely confused by the segue per the furrowing of her appropriately sculpted eyebrows.

"You post selfies with Amber like she's a—a doll?"

Connie said. "Beginning every single post with 'My perfect, sweet angel.' Yet you complain incessantly to me about how much trouble she is—how you don't know if you can be a good mother, yet here we all are in a room full of half food and half hats, and . . . I don't even know what this is." Connie held up a mutilated—

"Noisemaker," Megan said.

Connie chuckled. "You cut out the part that makes the noise."

Angie's mouth was agape, her eyes ping-ponging between her mother and her aunt. Even Wang had slipped out both earbuds.

"I think—" But before Aunt Megan could finish, Connie stood up and went into the kitchen.

Angie and Wang looked at Aunt Megan. To Angie's surprise, her aunt followed Connie.

"Dude," Wang said to Angie.

She was so stunned she didn't even correct him.

Soon the battle between sisters slit through the pop playlist and party chatter.

"It is not my fault that you're miserable and make everyone around you that way," Aunt Megan said from the kitchen.

And that was when the glass started breaking . . . and breaking and breaking.

Angie and Wang raced to the kitchen, pushing past the people who had already begun to gather in the doorway.

Connie threw a platter onto the floor. Pieces shattered as far as the toe of Angie's shoe.

"Connie, stop it," Aunt Megan said, a granite kitchen island between them.

Uncle Gabe pushed between Angie and Wang. "Connie, you need to calm down."

"Don't try to de-escalate me, Gabe."

"Gabe," said Aunt Megan, signaling him to leave.

"No," he said.

"Just give me a second," she asked calmly. "Please."

Reluctantly, he stepped back, convincing many of those watching to do the same.

Connie paced back and forth, glass crackling under the soles of her pumps. The sound amplified in Angie's ears. It grated and pierced—it deepened and—

"Connie," said Aunt Megan. "I understand that you're grieving, but the drinking and the—"

"What do you understand? I mean, really understand, Megan? Because don't talk to me, again, like you have a *fucking* clue what it's like to lose the most important thing in your life."

Aunt Megan looked at Angie and Wang, standing in the doorway. Then to her sister. "You are not the only person who lost Nat—"

"She was *my* daughter—mine," Connie said. "And Angie pours what's left of her down the Ohio River?"

"She explained to you—"

"Don't defend her, Megan," Connie warned.

"You have two other children, Connie. Two living and breathing children who are trying to understand—understand why they're an absolute afterthought to you unless there's a camera around."

Angie's eyes widened at her aunt's bluntness—the unfettered boldness to go metaphorical horn-to-horn with Connie.

"You're proud of yourself, aren't you?" Connie said. "This is like your victory lap."

"What?"

"You get to see me lose and be some pathetic version of my seventeen-year-old self all over again. Where you were—"

"Fifteen and flawed and stupid and selfish?" Aunt Megan said. "That version? The version where the boys liked me more than you? Is that what you're holding on to, because I don't care about that stuff anymore, Connie. But I am trying to figure out how to be a better parent than you, so I don't someday push my daughter so hard that she has to enlist into a war just to escape my expectations."

"Why were you texting Rick?" Connie said.

"Forget it," said Aunt Megan. "You're drunk. Break all the dishes if it makes you feel better."

"You're screwing him, aren't you?" Connie asked.

Megan pressed her palms against the island separating the two of them.

"You need help, Connie," said Aunt Megan. "Real. Help."

With the reality of the few people who had continued to watch standing there, Connie desperately tried to muster the facade she used for news specials, magazine photo spreads, and the Christmas cards they used to send out before Nat didn't come home.

It simply wasn't working.

Aunt Megan stepped over broken glass and china as she left the kitchen, taking Wang with her. After a moment, Connie went to the pantry and pulled out a broom and dustpan.

"Mom?" Angie said faintly.

Connie looked at Angie.

Angie looked at Connie.

It was an unexpected moment. The two of them seeing each other with George Michael's "Father Figure" playing in the background.

The glass crackled beneath Angie's shoes as she slowly stepped toward her mother. "I could . . . help you."

Connie leaned against the island. Some part of her seemed to soften.

Angie reached for the dustpan. "I can—" but Connie pulled it away.

"I've got it," she said, quietly.

Angie watched as her mother swept up the pieces of glass and china, until every last shard was removed. As if nothing had ever been broken at all.

Chapter 14

Chloe skateboarded through the warehouse popping ollies and other tricks as Angie and Finster stood on the stage, heads back, admiring the enormity of it. Trusses and tracks, lights and elevating platforms. Dual-projection screens on each side of the stage.

"I've been on stages," Finster said, head still back. "But not like this. This is some money. The gear alone. That's at least a five-K drum set. Wild, huh?"

"Fin," Angie said.

Finster turned to her.

"Um, I, uh"—Angie cleared her throat—"wanted to say thanks. For giving me a chance . . . after last night. The whole parking-lot-freak-out thing."

"Maybe you're giving it to me," Finster said. "I finally get to be in a band that has something to say."

Angie sighed. "I hope so."

"Don't you think?" Finster asked. "What you did in Cincy? Never rehearsing with the band—any band. Getting up there, and that was . . . and look." Finster splayed her arms wide, taking in all the space. "You got Lucas Waite to wanna help us."

Angie considered it.

"Fortune is favoring you, woman," Finster said. "Trust it. Don't let last night get you in your head. Nothing stunts a woman's revolution like fear. I've been playing that card a lot lately. I'm over it."

Finster, the would-be love child of James Dean and Salma Hayek, if such a conception could have been possible, had endured the gossip mill and thrill people got out of running someone different through the mud. But there she was, head up, confidence on.

"Those lyrics you texted," Finster said. "You show them to Lucas?"

Angie shook her head.

"Show 'em to him," Finster said. "I know the guy's kind of a mystery, but lyrics? He's a solid."

"Damn!" Zeke shouted.

Angie and Finster turned as Zeke lumbered in, tripods slung over both shoulders, duct-taped light-kit case dragging behind them. Wang trailed Zeke, texting, carrying their camera bag while sipping from a Big Gulp.

"I thought this place was a squatter's den," Zeke said.

"It was," Angie said. "I think."

"This is gonna look so good in the footage," Zeke said, putting everything down. "I can already see where I want to put the smoke machine."

"Smoke machine?" Wang said.

"Don't crush my creativity," Zeke said, forming a frame with their fingers.

Chloe popped the tail of her board and jogged up the stage steps, then immediately dropped her board and skated across the stage.

"Where's Lucas?" Zeke asked, looking around. "I'm actually kind of excited to meet him."

"He's on his way," Angie said.

Chloe cut around Finster, who was opening her bass case.

"Maybe he died on the side of the road?" Chloe said, kickflipping her board like a boss. "That's what happened to his dad, right?"

Everyone got quiet.

It wasn't at all what happened to his dad. Mr. Waite had—

"No," Lucas said, stepping through the tarp. "My dad died by suicide."

Chloe leaned on the tail of her board.

"Here," Lucas said. "Upstairs."

Everyone stayed quiet. Everyone but Chloe, who turned

to Finster and said, "You brought me to a haunted place? You're *such* a bad sister. I'm telling Mom."

Frustrated, Chloe pushed off her board, speeding toward the end of the stage. She flicked her right leg up and out, her board spinning a fast three-sixty before she sail-landed on the warehouse floor. She skated up to Lucas, popped the tail of her board, and stared him down.

"So," Chloe said, unimpressed. "You're Lucas Waite. Weird."

"Three-sixty inward heel is pretty impressive," he said.

"Not really," she said, skating away.

"Um, hey," said Finster, hopping off the stage. "Sorry about my sister. She's going through . . . being my sister. I'm Finster."

They shook hands.

"Finster plays bass," Angie said. "And Chloe over there . . ."

Chloe half waved while skateboarding.

"She plays guitar," Angie said. "And um, Zeke is filming everything."

Zeke pointed the camera at Lucas. He was unquestionably uncomfortable as they began to circle him.

"I'm making a movie about everything in my life," Zeke said. "My shitty parents. My amazing abuela. My primo Darius, who is mostly okay. His moods. They swing."

"His moods?" Angie said.

"This warehouse," Zeke said, still filming. "Man, it's perfect. Mystery. Story. Heartache."

"Thanks," he said, looking confused as he turned to Angie. "Drummer?"

As if cued, Angie and Zeke looked at Wang.

"Relax," he said. "Would I let you down?"

Angie waited to see if this was a rhetorical question because Wang had let his sister down on a number of occasions. So many, in fact, that Angie was about to list the number of ways he had let her down when the warehouse door bang-closed. Chloe's skateboard rolled to a stop. The sound of footsteps echoed. Everyone watched as a hand pulled the tarp back . . . and Jamboree stepped through.

Angie's heart leaped.

"Told you I had a drummer," Wang said, quite proud of himself.

"Jamboree!" Chloe said. "Thank God! At least there'll be one good person in this band."

Jamboree laughed. "Hey, Chloe," she said, her eyes cutting to Angie, whose heart was still doing that leaping thing.

"What up, Jam?" Finster said.

The two hugged. Hugged in that way where their butts didn't push out—where their hips pushed in. It was an action worth noting, Angie thought.

Zeke turned their camera off. They were definitely the least thrilled to see Jamboree.

"Sorry I'm late." Jamboree awkwardly shook hands with Lucas. "I'm Jamboree. Drummer."

"You played on a drum set much?" he asked.

"It's where I started."

"She's amazing," Angie blurted out. "Um, on drums. Set. Thingy."

What had Angie actually meant to say?

"All right," Lucas said. "Drum. Set thingy. So . . ."

Everyone waited as Lucas stood there in silence for approximately four and one-half seconds.

Chloe, now sitting on her board, stared at him seeming, well, bored.

"Um. Yeah. Okay." He scratched the back of his head. "So, I've never done this before, but . . . I guess—"

Chloe raised her hand.

"Yeah," Lucas said.

"Is it true that you slept with Lady Gaga?" she asked.

"Uh, no. So . . ."

Chloe's hand went up once again. Lucas sighed, nodding to her.

"Why did you quit Rancid Reign?" Chloe asked.

Quiet.

Extended duration of immensely weighted quiet because it was the question everyone likely wanted to ask, but didn't have the Chloe-hones to.

"Because . . . I didn't have anything to say anymore," Lucas said.

Chloe raised her hand a third time.

"Baja la mano," Finster said to Chloe.

"No me jodes," Chloe said to her sister.

"It's fine," Lucas said. "Although I don't know what the hell you said. I took Latin, not Spanish. I should've taken both. Anyway. Go ahead."

"So, why all this?" Chloe said. "Stage. Gear. Us?"

Lucas looked down at his boots. "It was my dad's. This place. And he always wanted to do something different with it. He just didn't think he could. This is my different. Concert rehearsal space. Recording studio, maybe. I don't know. I'm sort of working it all out." Lucas paused. "As for you, Angie . . . made an impression. So, you know, why not?"

Everyone waited to see if Chloe would raise her hand again.

She did not.

"Here's what I'm thinking," Lucas said. "Let's see where you all are. Music-wise. Then we can kind of map it from there. And feel free to use whatever gear you want."

"Hey, Lucas," Finster said. "Before we get going and all. I just came from a band where a bunch of guys tried to shut me down. And I think I'm speaking for everyone in saying, while we're super grateful to work with you, we're not interested in being a typical girl band. Skirts and cleavage shirts. Well, at least not me. We gotta be us, or this doesn't work."

"Good," Lucas said. "Because I'm not into all that shit anymore."

Finster seemed surprised. Pleasantly so.

"But you gotta figure out what 'us' is, right?" said Lucas.

Finster nodded.

"Okay," he said. "So let's do that."

Finster and Chloe began to set up as Jamboree and Angie met along the side stairs of the stage. They both started to say something, then—

"I'm sorry," they said in unison.

Their collective smile was soft and full of apology.

"I'm sorry about yesterday," Jamboree said.

"Same." Angie nodded.

"You have to know I don't think Cincinnati was an accident," Jamboree said. "I think it was everything. What happened onstage. Along the river. Us. Friends, again." Jamboree paused then. "And I don't think of you as fragile. You're one of the strongest people I've ever known. Since we were kids, you know?"

Angie's shy-and-awkward ramped up.

"That's why . . ." Jamboree climbed to the step just below Angie. "Why . . ."

In the movies, Jamboree would have pulled Angie toward her. Then, after a snippet of trailerworthy dialogue, they would have—

"I'm here," Jamboree said. "Because I believe in the music. Your music."

"Same," Angie said. "I mean. Sorry. I got . . . in my head. Words, blah."

Jamboree grinned.

Angie grinned.

It was the sweetest grinfest possibly ever when Zeke stepped closer to the stage and said to Jamboree, "So, you're officially Team Fat Angie?"

"I've always been Team Angie," Jamboree said to Zeke. "I'm also Team Zeke, so maybe you could try talking to me instead of fighting with me."

"So *I'm* the problem?" Zeke said.

"That's not what I meant," Jamboree said.

"Zeke, c'mon," Angie said.

"This isn't about you, Ang," Zeke said.

"If we're all about this band, then it is about me," she challenged.

Zeke looked between Angie and Jamboree. And in that moment of time suspended in silence, Angie knew now was the time to say something. To ask why Zeke was so mad all the time. Why were they sleeping at Darius's and not at home. Why they wouldn't talk about breaking up with Raquel. For all of the whys that mattered, Angie didn't know how to ask about any of them. Because somewhere in the blackness of the top and bottom of the sixteen-by-nine letterbox frame of Zeke's world lived all the things Zeke didn't want to face.

"Angie," Lucas said.

"I'm going to go set up," Jamboree said to Angie.

"Hey," Angie said to Jamboree. "I'm really glad you're here."

"Me too."

Angie jogged offstage to meet up with Lucas.

"You warm up?" he asked.

"Um . . . kind of. I mean, I watched a YouTube video."

"Let's go try it live," he said.

They walked side by side away from the rehearsal space.

Zeke threw Angie a nod.

Angie threw Zeke a nod back.

And that was the gist of it. Nods that said everything and kind of nothing.

"Okay," Lucas said from the warehouse floor. "Let's try something everyone knows."

Angie nervously stood behind the microphone.

"Yeah, we talked ahead of time." Finster handed Lucas a list of songs they could cover.

He read over the songs, nodding. Then he looked up at Angie.

"Which one do you want to try?" he asked.

Chloe's bubble-gum bubble burst.

"Um . . ." Angie said, clearing her throat.

She wanted to do all of them. Every single one. It wasn't that she couldn't. It was that she was—

"What's wrong?" he asked.

"She's freaked she'll choke," Chloe said, fingering chords on her guitar.

Sadly, it was true. Very true.

Lucas looked at Angie. "Just pick one," he said, holding the list out to her.

"Um, let's, uh . . ." Angie scanned the list again. "'U + Ur Hand.'"

"Okay," Lucas said. "Let's try it as it's written. Then we can see about mixing it up. Add some grit. Maybe even play around with it in a minor key."

"Minor?" Chloe said, hopping off a stool.

"To see range," Lucas said to her.

Chloe laughed, launching into a solo of her own creation. Fingers flying down the electric guitar neck. Jamming on the whammy bar. Then blasting, squealing uninhibited metal to punk that slunk into rock finally topped with classical. It was a radical exhibition of her talent.

"Damn . . ." Wang said under his breath.

Lucas grabbed a sheet of music from a box and walked it to Chloe. "Play this."

He held the music out to her.

"I've never seen that," she said.

"So you can't?" he asked.

"I can *play* it. I just need to see it."

"She can sing it," Lucas said, pointing to Angie. "She just needs to practice it."

Chloe stood with her arms crossed.

Lucas walked away from Chloe. "Okay," Lucas said. "Let's start."

Jamboree played the lead-in, followed by Chloe and Finster. Angie squeezed the microphone and began to sing, her heart racing, her nerves no longer in waiting but absolutely to the forefront. Her throat was tightening. Why? Why was this happening? Her voice cracked. She stepped back. The band quit playing.

"I'm sorry," Angie said.

"Let's go again," Lucas said.

Angie exhaled a shaky breath and saw Wang mouth "You got this," as she headed back to the mic.

The band started again. Angie's entrance was worse than the first time. Her mind filling up with a litany of noise. Her mom sweeping up the shards of glass. *Mrs. O'Connor and her condescending condolences. Helicopters. Machine guns. Basketballs dribbling. Gary Klein—straddling her. Punching. His rage. War. The gym floor where she collapsed.* The tempo of her mind overwhelming the tempo of the song. Everything was wrong. She just wanted it to—

"Stop," Lucas said.

Angie looked away from him.

"Girl, you got this," Zeke said from behind a camera.

Angie did not have this, though she very much wanted—needed to.

Lucas climbed onto the stage. "What's in your head?"

"What?" she said.

"In your head," he said. "What's distracting you?"

Angie shrugged, panic punching its petulant way through. "Um . . . everything," she said.

"Stop. Thinking."

Angie didn't understand. "That's a physical impossibility," she said.

"Were you thinking in Cincinnati that night?"

Angie considered his question. Then said, "No. I was . . . mad. Then I was just . . ."

"Being," he said. "Come back to the mic."

She sighed and reluctantly walked back.

"Closer," he said. "When you're singing, you're practically eating the mic. Okay? Shut your eyes."

Angie shifted uncomfortably. He motioned for her to close her eyes.

"What's in your head?" he said.

She didn't know how to answer.

"Don't think," he said. "Respond."

"Timing—um, tempo—"

Her sister's casket. Wang crying. Jake and his dog Ryan and Lester who hated his name and running in the snow and . . . the road trip and the RV and Zeke laughing and Darius laughing and Jamboree and . . . Angie. Angie—

"What's in your head?" he said.

Angie standing on the stage in Cincinnati, screaming.

Angie squeezed the microphone and screamed. It was guttural. It was primal. It was full of fat, fabulous revolution.

Lucas signaled the band to start playing. They began. Angie started to open her eyes, but he covered them with his hand. She moved into the mic, her entrance smoother. Her body feeling the music. Not thinking about it.

She stumbled over a lyric.

"Keep going," he said, hand still over her eyes. "Recover."

She came back in, and when they hit the bridge, she was on fire! Metaphorically speaking, of course.

When Jamboree finally whipped across the drums, closing out the song, everyone stood in silence.

"What's in your head?" Lucas said.

Angie smiled. "Music."

Lucas pulled his hand away.

Angie opened her eyes.

Wang clapped, walking toward the stage. "Now that was some straight-up, do-the-crane, Mr. Miyagi singing shit." He howled.

Zeke joined him.

Angie laughed and looked back at Jamboree beaming at her.

"Let's go again," Lucas said, jumping off the stage.

Angie had done it. Now, she just had to do it with her eyes open. She was ready to try.

Chapter 15

Early the next morning, they were all back at the warehouse. Lucas was outside, finishing up a phone call as the band sat on the stage, sharing song lyrics. Zeke roamed among them, filming.

"Free food!" Wang announced, walking toward the stage. "Courtesy of Amy's Cozy Kitchen."

He flung a breakfast sandwich toward Angie.

"How free?" she said, fumbling it.

"Relax," Wang said, tossing one to Finster. "I just mentioned the band and you and Lucas and the competition all in the same sentence. I didn't even have to milk it too much."

Chloe unwrapped hers. Her face wrenched in disgust. "I don't do meat."

"Of course you don't," said Wang. "It's a free sandwich."

"I don't do free meat either." She flung the sandwich back at him. "And don't mock my dedication to a meatless society."

"Here, take mine." Jamboree tossed her sandwich to Chloe. No meat, just egg.

Chloe fake-smiled as Wang threw her sandwich to Jamboree. Jamboree reached across Angie to catch it, spilling into Angie's lap as she did.

"Sorry," Jamboree said. "Who knew breakfast was a full-contact sport?"

It was a contact that sent Angie's nerves aflutter.

"Thanks, Jam," Finster said. "She's been hard-core about the meat thing. Which I can respect."

"I just remember her eating your dad's ribs by the pound," Jamboree said.

"Yeah, now she won't even walk past the meat aisle at the grocery unless she's making a video about abolishing it."

Jamboree laughed.

"Oh, hey." Finster reached into her bag. "Grabbed this for you when we stopped at the gas station."

Like the hip-to-hip hug the day before, Angie watched the handoff of Jamboree's favorite drink with curious anticipation. Only someone who really knew Jamboree would know about her longstanding love for Raspberry Zing Tea.

"Thank you," Jamboree said, clutching the sweaty bottle of moderately sugary goodness.

"I didn't know you could still buy that," Angie said to Jamboree.

"There's a gas station between here and Hamilton," Finster said. "They stock like three of them at a time every couple of months."

Angie smiled, eating her sandwich. Eating her sandwich and thinking why did Finster know about the stocking habits of Jamboree's favorite drink?

"Want a sip?" Jamboree offered.

A sip? From the gift of the would-be love child of Salma Hayek and James Dean, if such a conception could have been possible? No, Angie did not want a sip of that. Not that Angie had any right to be ruffled in the emotional feathers over such a gift. She had no overt stake in the game of Jamboree's affection. She hadn't even—

"Can I ask you something?" Angie said.

And the nervousness upticked.

"Always." Jamboree grinned.

"You and Finster—and, um, Chloe," Angie said. "You all seem to know each other—pretty well."

"Yeah, well," Jamboree said, "Finster and I met my freshman year at band camp. Trumpet and trombone. That's what she was playing."

"Oh, well, sure. Yeah," Angie said, but had no idea why.

"Yeah," Jamboree said. "We hung out a lot after football games. Both of us were in Jazz Band. We actually ended up playing in a pretty terrible guy band that year. Basically, we'd show up to practice on time while Marc, Ronnie, and DeShaun showed up whenever. Because they were in it for girls and garage gigs, they didn't really care what we had to say about music. So Fin and I spent a lot of time playing music in her basement. Chloe was always there, so she'd play with us. She was only moderately less jaded than she is now."

Angie laughed.

"Anyway," Jamboree said. "I got busy with stuff. Finster ended up joining Omnibus, and that was kind of it."

"Why didn't you just have a band of your own?"

Jamboree shrugged. "Just wasn't a . . . good fit then."

"And now?"

Jamboree smiled, and it lit every wick in Angie's body. "Now I think it's going to be amazing."

They smiled at each other, pushed and pulled into a quiet almost-longing—until Jamboree's phone pinged. She picked it up and immediately planted it facedown on the stage.

"Everything . . . okay?" Angie asked.

Jamboree sighed. "Yeah. Troy's been texting."

Troy? As in *the* Troy? As in the unofficial Mr. Perfect of Mr. Perfects? The body, the clothes, the eyes, the nose—the everything that women who wanted men would likely weep in passion for? That Troy?

"He invited me to his homecoming," Jamboree said.

"Oh," Angie said, a surprised inflection in her voice.

"I'm not going," Jamboree said. "I'm not . . . interested. In going. You know."

Jamboree looked at Angie.

Angie looked at Jamboree.

It was in this elongated look layered in teenage ache and vulnerability that the door to ask Jamboree out sprang wide open. The door Angie had wanted to walk through Thursday morning but let close was now unlocked. Angie simply had to say . . .

"Homecoming," Angie said. "Is just . . . you know. Yeah."

What had she just said?

"Right," Jamboree said, tearing off a piece of bread from her sandwich.

Awkward.

Sooooo . . . awkward.

"So, I guess you're not interested," Jamboree said.

"Interested?"

"Homecoming."

"Oh . . . um," Angie said. "You know, it's a . . . largely archaic, heteronormative kind of event meant to promote school spirit and premarital sex."

What had Angie just said, again?

Then Jamboree laughed. "It's good that you haven't thought too much about it."

Angie laughed.

And somehow the weighty tension broke.

"Yeah, I don't know about it either," Jamboree said. "It's not really fun. If you can't go with the person you want to be with."

Angie cleared her throat, and before she could respond—

"Hey, I'm sorry I had to step out," Lucas said. "I've got a delivery coming from Cleveland."

"No worries," Wang said, throwing him a breakfast sandwich. "It's probably cold."

"Thanks," Lucas said. "Okay, so where are we now?"

Chloe raised her hand.

"Yes, Chloe," he said.

"We need a band name."

"We need a sound first," he said.

Chloe raised her hand. Resigned, he pointed to her.

"Up with the female. Down with the patriarchy," she said.

Finster grinned and knuckle-bumped her.

"Okay, so what is that?" Lucas asked.

"You should really show that song to Lucas," Jamboree whispered to Angie. "The one Finster liked."

"Oh, yeah," Angie said, turning to Lucas. "We have one that we all kind of liked. Finster plucked out a bass line for it after practice. Chloe added some guitar riffs. And Jamboree and I tweaked the lyrics. It's rough but . . ."

Zeke hung over Lucas's shoulder, filming.

"I thought we were going to do 'Bleached,'" Zeke said.

"I'm not saying we're not," Angie said.

"It's just something we all played around with," Finster said.

Zeke looked at Jamboree.

"So, you're writing songs now?" Zeke challenged.

Jamboree shook her head.

"Hey," Finster said. "This is a collective. Everyone gets a voice."

"Angie and I already wrote a song that works, Fin," said Zeke. "Something that's commercial."

"Yeah, but that was before this," Angie said. "Before we kind of knew what we wanted to do. Approach it."

"So you got a problem with how we write songs?" Zeke said.

"No," Angie said. "I have a problem with—"

Chloe singsonged, "Cat fight."

"Hey," Lucas said. "Finster's right. Everyone agreed yesterday that the ideas were free flow."

Zeke shook their head and stormed off past Wang, who was texting, his feet propped on a chair.

"This isn't good bandmateship," Wang said.

"Shut up, Wang," Zeke said, slapping the tarp out of their way.

Angie got up and followed after them.

Zeke shoved the warehouse door open.

"Hey," Angie said, chasing after Zeke.

"Look," Zeke said. "I'm just saying that we've got a notebook full of songs."

"Yeah, and we need to pick the best from those or anything else the band believes in," said Angie. "Because we're not doing this like the bands Jamboree and Fin have been in. We're being our own different."

"Girl, we don't have time for that," Zeke said. "It's already crunched on time to get all this together. Go with what works."

"How do we know?" Angie asked.

"'Rebel Girl Revolution'—"

"Isn't the only kind of song to do," Angie said.

Zeke stayed quiet, shaking their head.

"Why are you at Darius's?" Angie asked.

Zeke glared.

"Why are you mad—all the time?" Angie said. "I'm so scared to ask you because I'm afraid you'll do to me what you do to Jamboree. And I don't wanna not be friends with you."

Zeke began to soften. In as much as Zeke could allow themselves.

"My brother started it," Zeke said. "Telling my dad. My mom. How I wanted to be a boy, and I was like, that's not what I'm saying. My parents don't get they/them. They get she/her, he/him. I don't feel like a she/her or a he/him. I don't check those freaking boxes, you know?" Zeke shook their head. "My dad was like 'Patricia, you be a girl or get out of my house.' So I did. I've been at Darius's ever since. His dad tried talking to my dad. His mom tried to be all appealing to my mom. Nada. My mom was like 'God gave me a daughter. The devil wants to give me a son.' You believe that? I'm like some black stain. Something they can't—ay . . ."

Angie walked toward Zeke. "I'm going to hug you. Can I?"

Zeke half laughed. "Sure."

Angie put her arms around Zeke. It took a while, but Zeke finally hugged Angie back.

"I hate it, Ang," Zeke said. "My parents. Who I am. And I *hate* this fucking bag. I just . . . I don't know."

"Well, you can't hate yourself," Angie said. "It will mess with your whole chingona-empire thing."

Zeke laughed.

"We got each other, you know?" Angie said, looking at Zeke. "This thing . . . we're all doing. This is our revolution."

Zeke nodded.

"Wanna go back in?" Angie said.

"What am I supposed to say?" Zeke asked.

Angie sighed. "I don't know. Sorry?"

Zeke chuckled.

Angie chuckled.

The moment had officially been defused. Like in movies where stone-faced heroes clipped the wires of a bomb, Angie had managed to stop the world of Zeke from exploding. At least for now. And now was a start. Angie liked starts very much.

"C'mon," Angie said.

The two of them walked back into the warehouse together. Closer than ever before.

After rehearsal, the band piled into a booth at Dee's Diner. Angie keyed in the number 173 on the multicolor bubble-tube jukebox. Soon "I Love Rock 'n' Roll" blasted from the speakers. Angie scooted into the booth beside Wang, who was still involved in a text fight with Winter. Winter, who had been his best bro but was now calling Wang a punk-ass ho. It was clearly not intended as a term of endearment. It was a—

"Great song," Finster said to Angie. "Classic glam-rock anthem. First girl I ever kissed had this playing in her bedroom. A bag of tortilla chips, Rotel cheese dip, and 'I Love Rock 'n' Roll.' Wild, huh?"

"I love Rotel," Angie said.

Finster laughed. "Me too, now."

Chloe sighed, playing her 3DS.

"Ms. Joan Jett," Angie said. "Can you believe she's going to actually see us perform?"

"You get that the use of the word *Ms.* is a kind of wasted bridge between the Miss and Mrs.?" Chloe said, setting her game down.

Angie had never considered the meaning of Ms., Miss,

or Mrs. before. She simply saw them as a acknowledgments of respect.

"Words matter," Chloe said, slurping her soda empty. "I'm in seventh grade, and I know that."

Zeke laughed, reaching into a basket of fries, bathing a few in a combination of mayo and ketchup. "You can call Joan Jett whatever you want, girl."

Jamboree came out of the restroom and slid in beside Angie.

"Hey," Jamboree said.

"Hey," Angie said back.

They were swimming in a nonverbal pool of cutesy hellos and unspoken gay-girl-gay-crush energy when Zeke said, "Okay." Camera recording. "Ruin a band name with one letter. Go Chloe."

"Tickelback," Chloe said.

Everyone looked blankly at her except Wang who said, "Nickelback, yo."

"Oh," everyone else said.

"I got one," Finster said. "Food Fighters."

"Nice," Jamboree said. "Um . . . Six Pistols."

"Oh, I know, I know," Angie said. "Bed Hot Chili Peppers."

"Queef," Wang said, slamming his phone facedown on the table.

Zeke threw a fry at him.

"It was legit," he said, throwing it back at them.

"Yeah, if you're a gross boy," Zeke said.

"Good thing I'm one hundred percent man then," he said, proud of his response.

Angie rolled-not-rolled-but-mostly-rolled her eyes at him.

"We need a band name," Chloe blurted.

The waitress balanced a shelf of plates on each of her arms, setting one in front of each of them.

"Maybe we could call the band—"

But before Zeke could finish, Chloe said, "Trust Bucket."

"I think it already exists," Finster said, drizzling ketchup on her fries.

"I know," Wang said. "Lady Mullet. And you could wear these wigs and . . ."

Everyone stared blankly at him.

"What?" he said. "Bands have gimmicks."

"Uh, not necessarily," said Finster. "Plus, I like my hair. I'm not wigging it."

"Okay," Jamboree said, pouring ranch dressing on her chicken sandwich. "So we're female. We're political. We're anti–male gaze. We are—"

"Anti-appropriation and forced heteronormative values," Angie said.

"The Tampons. No, no, wait. Toxic Utters," Wang said enthusiastically.

"Where do you come up with these?" Zeke said.

"He watches a lot of bad films," Angie said.

Zeke nodded understandingly.

"Okay, what about, um," Finster said, "Mercury in Retrograde? We could shorten it to M.I.R."

"Fancy Chanclas," Chloe said.

The general silent-but-seemingly-loud consensus was no.

"What?" Chloe said. "It's a good name."

"It doesn't really capture the spirit of what we want to do," Angie said.

"Whatever," Chloe said.

Finster bit into her burger, grease oozing along the cheese skirt and onto the plate, Chloe giving her overt side-eye.

"I respect your meatless society, but I'm not there yet," Finster said, wiping her mouth with her napkin. "Angie? Any band names?"

Angie rested her hand on her cheek. Thinking. And thinking. Then—

"What I like about us is the way we're writing our songs," she said. "How we're all part of it. How Chloe could play bass on one if she wanted to and Finster could play guitar."

"Not that she should," Chloe said, stabbing a leaf of lettuce.

"There's a wildness to us," Jamboree said. "Even the way Lucas talks about music."

"Who is *so* weird," Chloe said.

Angie stayed quiet, then said, "It's kind of like we're wild. Like we're . . . feral."

"Go Feral," Jamboree said. "That's it."

Everyone sat quiet for approximately four and one-third seconds.

"I like it," Finster said.

"Me too," Zeke said, much to Jamboree's surprise. "It's good, Jam."

Angie looked at Chloe, who continued eating. "It's not Fancy Chanclas, but it's all right, I guess."

With that, Angie proudly announced, "Go Feral. It's—"

"Wait," Wang said, adjusting in his seat. "As band manager, I get the final say."

"Aren't you, like, the mascot?" Chloe said. "Managers *do* things."

"Who brought you free breakfast this morning?" he said to her.

"With *meat,*" she said back to him.

Finster laughed as Wang's eyes clicked outside the window to the parking lot. Angie's followed, and she saw Winter pile out of a truck, carrying a can of . . .

"Son of—" Wang started.

Spray paint! Winter had a can of spray paint and was heading for Wang's Jeep. Wang climbed out of the booth by stepping on the table, planting his sneaker into a dish of lemon meringue pie. He slid to the floor and stumbled out the door. The band followed.

"Wang!" Angie shouted as he grabbed Winter by the shirt.

The word *FAG* was spray-painted across the side of Wang's Jeep. Finster ran to her car and popped the trunk. Angie—in the state of the panicked mind—ran toward her brother. The other guys now piled out of the truck. They started punching Wang in the face—in the back. Fists were flying. Angie tried to pry Wang and Winter apart. Jamboree wedged somewhere inside it all. But it was Finster who broke between everyone with a baseball bat. She shoved everyone apart—back.

"I know you fucking hit on Lori this summer, Wang," Winter said. "Fucking best friend backstabber."

Wang spit at Winter. Blood splattered on the asphalt. "I didn't do shit with Lori," Wang said. "But your mother was good last night—"

Winter charged at Wang. Finster and Zeke were now in between.

"Go," Finster said, bat pointing at Winter. "Now!"

"Fuck you, dyke," Winter said.

"Not even if you were a woman," she said.

Winter waited. Jaw clenched as tight as his fists. Angie's heart raced as she pressed her hand to Wang's chest.

Winter and the guys who had once been "Wang's Boys" finally climbed back in the truck. Trying to menace them with a look, Finster and Zeke stood strong in front of Wang. The guys revved up the engine, poser rap blasting as they peeled out. It was an overtly testosterone exit as they steered into traffic, horns honking all around them.

Angie exhaled, shaking her head. "What were you thinking?"

"He spray-painted my fucking Jeep!

"You want to get arrested?" Angie said. "You want to end up in jail—juvie?"

"No," he snapped.

Angie looked at Wang. His lip was bleeding, his eye starting to bruise. His face looked like hers when—

"My uncle works at a body shop," Finster said to Wang. "He could probably help you out. He's had to do it for me twice."

Wang swallowed and sighed. Angie knew this wasn't Wang. It seemed like he might know it too.

Everyone continued to stand there in silence until Chloe walked up to Wang.

"What?" he said.

"Come back and eat your cow," she said, pulling his wrist toward the restaurant. She led him inside, saying, "You're buying me another piece of pie."

Finster chuckled, blowing out a big breath. She patted Angie's shoulder as she followed them inside. Zeke was a clip behind Finster, but Angie stayed still. Still looking at the specks of blood Wang had spit on the ground, her mind filling up with flashes of—

Angie's hands shook.

"Hey," Jamboree said, reaching for Angie's hands. "You're okay. He's okay."

"I just . . ." Angie said, moving back—trying to not see—feel—

Gary Klein—straddling—punching her. Blood flinging from his nose. His face filled with hate and rage and fear and—she couldn't get him to—

"Just . . ." She cleared her throat. "Gary . . ."

"Is gone," Jamboree said.

"Yeah," Angie said.

Angie looked into the diner window. Wang sat there with ice in a paper napkin pressed against his eye.

"He can't mess up, Jamboree," Angie said. "He's toast if he does."

Jamboree nodded. "Come back in. C'mon."

Jamboree took Angie's hand. They walked inside. Together.

Chapter 16

This was what life was supposed to be for Angie. A series of largely upbeat montage sequences. Of songwriting sessions, rehearsals, dinners at The Slice or Dee's. Of Zeke setting up random scenes to film. Throwing smoke bombs for them to walk through, lighting sparklers, and generating other bizarre effects for the competition band intro video. Being on camera remained hard for Angie, but she tried to go with it. Most of the time.

Over that next week, Angie strutted through the halls of William Anders High chin up, chest out, and with a smile that could only be described as truly triumphant. She had friends. She had the band. She had viral fame. All she had to do was keep on keepin' on, as the tired cliché went. But

Angie didn't care about tired clichés because this? This life was exponentially good because even KC had seemed to turn over several new leaves. Listening. Sharing. Genuinely excited about the band, KC had become the kind of friend Angie had always hoped for. Maybe they had been destined for friendship all along.

As the band practiced during the day and into the night, something truly magical began to happen. The music was coming together. And with the passing of each day, Angie seemed to inch a little closer to finally asking Jamboree to be more than friends.

Zeke was in full multicamera setup mode, having erected an arsenal of lights, silk diffusers, and various other gear around a lone chair onstage as the band arrived Saturday afternoon.

"What's all this?" Finster said, looking up at the stage.

"For the interviews," Zeke said, tightening a C-stand. "The intro vid?"

Finster was about to respond when Lucas said, "Hey. Sorry I'm late."

Chloe dropped the nose of her board down, skating along the front edge of the stage. Arms crossed, electric guitar slung on her back as she glared at him.

"No more skateboarding onstage," Lucas said. "I'm not insured for it yet."

"The revolution doesn't need insurance," Chloe said, steering her board back onto the main part of the stage.

"Don't make me sound like someone's parent," Lucas said to Chloe. "I'm still in my twenties and struggle with the basics of laundry."

Angie laughed.

"All right, I have an announcement," Lucas said.

"I know we've been struggling to find a gig," Lucas said, "so I asked for a favor. A friend of mine is having an event here next Saturday. He said you could play it."

"Wait," Finster said. "Doesn't it have to be a paid thing? Like a legit gig?"

Angie looked from Finster to Lucas as Jamboree stepped up beside Angie.

"It's . . . legit," Lucas said. "It's a fundraiser he does every year. Showed him a few rehearsal clips. He liked your sound. Your energy."

Chloe rocked back and forth on her board. "So we're gonna play for a bunch of old people, eating mini meat products on noncompostable plates."

Lucas waited a moment, then said, "You're going to play for Plymouth Montreal."

And a pin could have LITERALLY dropped.

Two pins, in fact!

Angie finally broke the silence. "Plymouth. Montreal?"

Lucas nodded, grinning.

"Yeah, right," Chloe said.

"I'm serious," Lucas said to Chloe.

Everyone remained suspended, stunned into silence,

because Plymouth Montreal was one of the most prominent artists/producers in the music industry. With producing instincts compared to the formidable Quincy Jones, Timbaland, and Dr. Dre, Plymouth Montreal's approach to his music and the bands he produced was personal, provocative, and positioned new voices for longevity in the industry.

"There will be several other bands playing," Lucas said. "But we'll need to play a longer set. At least five songs."

"Five?" Angie said.

"You can do it," Lucas said. "Or I wouldn't have asked for the favor. Okay?"

Zeke's mouth had managed to stay open.

"What up?" Wang slapped the tarp back, texting while toting a few bags of food. "I've got Sonic cheesy tots, burgers, dogs, and yes, a meatless option."

"Lucas booked us to play for Plymouth Montreal next Saturday," Angie blurted out.

Wang stopped midstep. He even quit texting.

Beat.

Longer beat then—

"Shut up!" Wang said.

Angie laughed, nodding.

"Shut! Up!" Wang's excitement was uncontainable.

Finster and Jamboree laughed.

Even Chloe, the queen of stone-cold chingona, smiled.

"Dude!" Wang rushed up on Lucas, grabbing him and shaking him up and down.

Zeke spun one of the cameras around and started filming, continuing even after Wang finally let Lucas go.

"Okay," Lucas said, attention back on the band. "So. Basically, it's like you get two shots. Playing for Plymouth. Footage for the competition."

Angie looked at Jamboree, excitement sparring between them.

"I know we need to go over the new music," Lucas continued. "But Zeke's set up for the promo video. Which I know we're not all in agreement about, but the video is equally important to the music you play."

"I still don't agree," Finster said to Lucas.

"About which part?" he asked.

"I mean, I get we need to be . . . open, but it feels—like we're just doing it to manipulate people. Like all these cameras and angles. It doesn't feel real."

Lucas walked toward Finster. "I'm not asking you to be fake. I'm asking for the opposite. I'm asking you to be real."

"Girl, I'm with Lucas," Zeke said to Finster. "A lot of the bands that already submitted posted a lot of crap promo intros that don't really say anything. Usually their music doesn't either. We got something to say, you know?"

"Exactly," Lucas said. "The video needs to be emotional, but not fabricated. Show them your heart, but don't wear it.

Be it. This is a chance to build an audience before they ever click on your song. People connect to stories. Your story. Why each of you is here—what makes you deserving of this shot. Out of thousands of bands."

Chloe raised her hand.

"Yes . . . Chloe," Lucas said.

"I'm in it for the pizza," she said. "Fin promised me free pizza until Christmas."

"Ay, Mexican," Finster said to her sister. "Take this seriously."

"What? He said honest," Chloe said.

Lucas walked closer to the stage, looking up at Chloe. "I've seen you practice. Listened to your ideas. You're not just in it for the pizza."

Chloe held her tough-girl pose, but Lucas had found a small yet real way inside. He stepped back, talking to the band. "Your story is everything. It belongs to you. No one else. That's what will set you apart in this competition. In life."

"Man," Wang said. "You just got all, like, *woo*."

Lucas half laughed, shaking his head.

"So . . . we just pour our hearts out?" Finster said.

"Yeah," Angie said, resigned to the reality of what had to come next. "I'll go."

Everyone watched Angie climb the stage steps, knowing how hard it was for her to be in front of a camera, let alone several. The amount of discomfort and shame and history of lenses thrust in her face, exploiting her pain when her sister went missing. When she came home . . . in pieces. In parts.

Angie continued across the stage, sighing as she stepped through the barrage of lights, cameras, microphones.

Her nervousness upticked as she sat down.

Zeke clicked a light toggle. The brightness exhaled onto Angie. She squinted.

"Sorry," Zeke said, dimming the light some. "Better?"

She nodded, peering through the chipped metal stands and cables at Jamboree. Jamboree, who smiled reassuringly at Angie. Angie forced a smile back.

"So, you don't want to look into the lens, Ang," Zeke said. "Just put your eyes here on my fist."

Lucas stood to the side of Zeke.

Angie struggled to steady her attention.

"Just tell your story," Lucas said. "Who Angie is. What Go Feral is for you."

Lucas stepped back.

Angie gulped.

"And rolling," Zeke said, watching Angie on a camera monitor.

Angie adjusted her seat.

She cleared her throat, inhaling a deep breath and then . . .

"What is it?" her therapist had asked her.

"I don't know how to be me," Angie said. *"Which is funny,*

right? Because . . . everyone knows how to be themselves. They just . . . be it. I don't know how to do that."

The therapist leaned forward and said, *"What do you think it means to be you? Not comparing yourself to anyone else. Just you."*

Shaky, Angie exhaled, staring at Zeke's fist.

Jamboree stepped up beside Lucas and said, "What's your favorite color?"

Confused, Angie said, "What?"

"Color," Jamboree said. "What's your favorite?"

"Um . . . all of them, I guess. Except for puce. Well, and heliotrope. And fuchsia, eggplant, neon carrot. I really don't like neon carrot. Oh, and green-yellow, salmon, beaver, desert sand, fuzzy-wuzzy. I really don't like those." Angie paused. "Blue. I like cerulean blue."

Before Angie's mind could fill up with panic, Jamboree continued. "What's your favorite thing to do when it snows?"

Angie grinned. "To try and catch snowflakes on my eyelashes."

Zeke smiled.

"How many times have you seen your favorite movie?" Jamboree asked.

"Forty-two."

"What's the square root of a hundred thirty nine?"

"Eleven point seven," Angie said.

"How many liters of water are needed to fill an Olympic-size swimming pool?" Jamboree asked.

Confused, Zeke looked back at Jamboree.

Confidently, Angie said, "Two million, five hundred thousand."

"What do you wish for more than anything else?" Jamboree said.

Angie paused, then looked at her brother.

"For Wang to get to hug our sister one more time."

Wang swallowed, clearing his throat of the emotion balling up in it.

"And for my mother to get it together," Angie said to Jamboree. "And for . . ." Angie closed her eyes, exhaled, then opened them. "And to be heard. I want to be heard."

Lucas stepped closer to the stage. "And how are you going to do that?"

Angie looked at him.

"By not running from my story," she said.

Lucas nodded. "Who are you, and what do you do in the world?"

Angie locked onto Zeke's fist, still in place. "I'm Fat Angie. I sing with the band Go Feral. And this is our revolution."

"Yes," Zeke mouthed to Angie.

Angie continued talking to the camera, threading her personal story with humor and heart and all things Angie.

When she was done, Zeke held out their fist for a knuckle bump.

"You did my abuela proud," Zeke said.

"I think I have to meet her," Angie said.

There was a loud banging on the warehouse door.

"I got it," Wang said, jogging off.

"Okay," Lucas said. "Chloe. You ready?"

"I guess," she said, passing Angie at the stage steps, playing her 3DS. Chloe plopped into the chair. "Not that any of us want to follow that."

Finster stabbed a plastic fork into an oozing pile of cheesy chili tots. "Put the game down, punk," Finster said to Chloe.

Frustrated, Chloe set it down.

Angie met Jamboree on the warehouse floor.

"Thanks," Angie said.

"You did it," Jamboree said.

"Yeah," Angie said. "Because you . . ."

And without warning, without provocation, Angie's past-ish and present were about to collide. Because stepping through the tarp with Wang—was KC.

Jamboree looked at Angie.

"I—I don't, um . . ." Angie said to Jamboree. "I'll, uh—be back."

Angie headed toward KC. Wang passed her, saying "What the hell?" as Angie continued toward KC and her belly-button-revealing custom crop top that read:

"Did I spill something?" KC said, noticing Angie staring at her shirt.

"No, uh-uh," Angie said nervously, looking anywhere besides the phrase scrawled across KC's chest.

"This is pretty massive," KC said.

"Yeah," Angie said, uncomfortably. "I guess. Um—"

"So, that's Lucas Waite, huh?" KC said, looking past Angie. "He's definitely easier on the eyes in person. Taller."

Angie looked over her shoulder at Lucas—at the band's curious and obvious watch as they gathered around the food.

"I actually had a trifold poster of him on my wall when I lived in Beverly," KC said. "Part of my dabble in the world of pretend straightness."

Angie cleared her throat. "So . . . you're here . . . um, why?"

"Oh," KC said. "I saw Wang's post online. About you rehearsing here. Said he's the manager?"

"Yeah, sort of. Manager-ish."

KC nodded. "Anyway. I hadn't seen you in a few. Thought I might catch you post-rehearsal. Maybe a little Betty's Muy Mexican and a movie at my place. Not that I need to sweeten the pot, but I do have *The Legend of Billie Jean* already cued in the VCR."

Angie did savor any opportunity to watch movies on

video cassette. There was something comfortable in the often-degraded picture quality. In the squeaking of play heads. And while it was an antiquated technology, it was one she loved all the same.

"So, what do you think?" KC said. "I could just linger along the back until you're done."

That seemed like a very bad idea.

A very, very bad idea.

Angie was about to say as much when KC dipped her head around Angie.

"I thought that was the salacious red I saw in the vids," KC said, eyes on Jamboree. "You hadn't mentioned."

"Yeah, it's just . . . um."

And what was Angie to say? My girlfriend-not-girlfriend plays drums in my new band? Seemed like a hard sell of a topic to Angie's now ex-girlfriend, KC.

"Hey," KC said. "No need for exposition. Friends support friends, right?"

"Yeah," Angie said, uncertain.

"Especially with something as momentous as starting a band," KC said. "I don't want you to feel like you have to hide your new romantic lead from me. I'm here strictly as a supporter of the Angie revolution."

"Well, it's all of ours," Angie said. "The band."

"Sure," KC said. "So . . . can I linger?"

"It's just," Angie said. "Rehearsal. It's kind of a private thing—for now. We're all just so . . . focused."

"No prob," KC said. "I have absolute respect for the creative process. Can I at least just meet everyone before I jet? Just hellos. You rock sort of thing."

Angie considered the pros, the cons, all while feeling the innate curiosity of every single pair of eyes on her.

"C'mon," KC said. "It'll be succinct."

"Um, okay."

KC sauntered behind Angie. A saunter that flaunted her long, runway-ready legs met by a skirt that lurked three and one-half inches above the knee. The closer they got to the band, the more Angie wanted rehearsal to end.

"Hey, so," Angie said to everyone. "This is, um . . . KC. She's—"

"Torch, look at the patina," KC said, admiring Finster's leather jacket. "This is vintage, isn't it? Fifties?"

"Yeah," Finster said, surprised. "It was my granddad's."

Chloe's eyes darted between Finster and KC while she played her video game.

"I'm more leveled toward vegan leather. You know, humane society, but there's nothing like an original leather," said KC. "It's always full of story, you know?"

Zeke rolled their eyes.

"For sure," said Finster, wiping her hand on a napkin before offering it to KC. "I'm Fin."

"KC," she said, shaking hands with Finster. "KC Romance."

"Really?" Finster said, surprised by her name.

"Oh, like your name isn't weird," Chloe said to her sister, before glaring at KC's shirt.

"The shirt is rock central, right?" KC asked Chloe.

"I guess, if that's what you want to wear," Chloe said.

KC shifted uncomfortably in her stance.

"And you're either vegan or you're not," Chloe said. "Old. Dead. Cow. Shaped into a jacket shouldn't change that."

Angie laughed as Chloe went back to playing her game as if she hadn't taken KC down twelve and one-half pegs.

"So, um," Angie said. "That's Chloe. And Wang you know. Lucas."

"Hey," Lucas said.

"Loved 'Rainbow on the Ridge,'" KC said to him.

"Zeke," Angie continued. "And—"

Jamboree stepped forward, shaking KC's hand. "Jamboree."

"That you are," said KC. "And then some."

Angie did not follow the trajectory of KC's comment. Was it meant to be a compliment? From Jamboree's face it seemed perhaps not.

"So, thanks for stopping by," Wang said, directing KC out.

"Right," she said. "Hey, congrats, everyone. I love that you're entering Rock Riot. When I told Angie about the competition, she was beyond skeptical . . ."

Jamboree looked at Angie.

Angie looked at Jamboree.

The dueling cinematic looks were layered with one significant fact:

Angie had lied to Jamboree . . .

and she had just been caught!

The competition hadn't been a random Internet find as Angie had suggested. Rather it had been a seed sown by KC, and it was in the knowing of this that Angie watched something shift in Jamboree.

"But I said she'd be lethal," KC continued. "Just from the clips I've seen, I know the music is going to be riot."

"Thanks," Finster said.

Chloe now rolled her eyes.

It was becoming a very eye-roll-y room.

"Anyway," KC said, backing up. "I don't want to crush the creative process. Just wanted to say hey."

"No, stay," Finster said, a flirty tone in her voice.

Zeke leaned into Finster. "You don't wanna do that."

Finster raised a confused eyebrow.

"Thanks," KC said to Finster. "But I gotta go. Ang, walk me to the door?"

Angie sighed, following KC through the tarp.

"So listen," KC said, walking. "What about Betty's and a movie? When you're done?"

"Maybe . . . tomorrow?" Angie said. "This could go . . . for a while."

"Okay," KC said, stopping at the door.

Why was there a huge dramatic pause? Angie looked back toward the tarp, seeing Wang peeking along the edge. That's when KC hugged Angie.

An unexpected gesture, as evidenced by Angie, arms down, shoulders raised.

"Text me later," KC said, letting go.

Angie did a polite smile, waiting three and one-half seconds after the warehouse door closed before she headed back to the rehearsal space.

"Yo," Wang said.

"Yeah?" Angie said.

"I don't want to tell you your business, but . . ." he said. "Remember John and Yoko?"

John Lennon and Yoko Ono (n): Husband and wife. It has been long theorized that John's relationship with Yoko was instrumental in the disbanding of the world-famous band the Beatles. A band with iconic songs such as "Twist and Shout," "Help!," "All You Need Is Love," "Hey Jude," and "Let It Be."

Angie was uncertain, as was often the case when listening to Wang's pop culture analogies.

"Where you going with this?" she said to him.

Wang looked at Jamboree, sitting by herself.

"I'm just saying. As band manager. Don't Yoko it."

Angie laughed. "You get there were other contributing factors to the Beatles' demise."

"I get that KC is like all those factors in one."

Angie headed over to Jamboree. Taking her time, collecting as many of her high-speed thoughts as possible.

"Hey," Angie said to Jamboree. "About the competition thing—"

"You mean the one you found on the Internet?" Jamboree said.

"Yeah, that was . . . sort of untrue."

"What is the current definition of 'sort of untrue'? I'm just . . ." Jamboree said, "asking because it seems like you lied to me."

"Well . . . I mostly just—omitted?"

Jamboree nodded. "Is this all for KC?"

"What?" Angie said.

"The band?" Jamboree said. "The competition? Is it to get KC back?"

"No," Angie said, sitting beside Jamboree. "Like absolutely no. No to the twelfth power no."

Jamboree didn't seem convinced.

"You just heard me—what I said on camera," Angie said. "That was real. The band—has nothing to do with KC. Other than she mentioned the competition. Which I don't really know why I didn't tell you, and I'm sorry."

It was one of those uneasy moments of silence that

Angie truly didn't like, but there she was feeling it all the same.

"What just happened?" Angie said. "Her coming here? She just—does things sometimes. But we're not. We're just friends."

"She's definitely friendly," Jamboree said.

"She's . . . from Los Angeles."

Which meant what, exactly?

"Look," Jamboree said. "You get to be friends with whoever you want. Even with your stunningly sexy, bad-girl-vibe ex with an actual purple heart tattoo on her neck."

Angie didn't know what to say, so she said nothing.

"Besides," Jamboree said. "We're just friends too. Right?"

Angie waited for Jamboree to let her off the hook because she felt very hooked. Hooked on Jamboree in all the ways that were definitely, unequivocally more than friends. All Angie had to do was say—

"Jamboree," Zeke said, standing by the camera with Chloe.

Jamboree got up. As she walked away, Angie's inside voice was screaming to be outside. To turn to Jamboree, to call out—do what people did in the movies. Where they stood up, said a few well-written lines that conveyed the Grand Canyon size of their devotion. Only to be followed by—

"Jamboree," Angie said.

Jamboree turned from Zeke and Chloe.

Deer in headlights.

Deer in headlights.

Why was Angie a damn deer in headlights?

"Um . . . yeah," Angie said. "I'll be . . . here. If you need me."

What?

That was not a well-scripted response.

That sucked!

"Okay," Jamboree said, turning back to Zeke and Chloe.

Angie sighed, thinking Pat Benatar was right. Love truly was a battlefield. She simply wasn't ready to step onto it yet.

Chapter 17

Wang whipped into Oaklawn Ends distracted by a call from Lori. As they neared the end of the cul-de-sac, Angie saw Jake playing basketball in his driveway. She couldn't just pretend she didn't see him, the way she mostly had for the last week.

Angie got out of the Jeep, Wang talking to Lori as he headed inside. Ryan galloped from Jake's yard, meeting Angie in the middle of the street. She scratched his head as he jumped up and down, following her.

"Hey," she said to Jake. "How was the game last night?"

"We won."

Jake shot the ball. It banged off the front of the rim and bounced toward Angie. He held his hands out, wanting the ball back.

"Want a rematch?" Angie said, dribbling.

"Give me the ball."

"Um . . . okay." She passed the ball back to him.

Jake dribbled to the chalk-drawn free-throw line. "So you're talking to me now?"

"I wasn't not talking to you."

"Uh-huh," he said, aiming but missing the shot.

"You need to flick your wrist more at the end," she said.

"I know how to shoot," he said, rebounding the ball.

Beat.

"You going to tell me why you're so mad?" Angie said.

"You know why," he said. "I called you out about KC, and you act like I'm, what? The jerk?"

Jake shot from the far side; the ball whipped through the net. Angie rebounded it.

"I think you don't give her a chance," Angie said. "I think you never have."

"That's not true," he said, hands waiting for the ball.

She bounced it to him.

"When you two became a couple, I let it go," he said, dribbling. "Because I thought maybe I was wrong. Maybe she did really care about you."

"She did—she does."

Jake shook his head, standing at the top of the basketball key. "No, she doesn't."

He shot the ball.

"KC cares about KC," Jake said. "She just can't see past her own stuff."

Angie shook her head.

"All she's ever wanted to do is change you," Jake said. "What you watch. What you listen to. How you should think. I know you know it. You just don't want to see it."

"You know," Angie said. "You're dating my former archnemesis, and I let that go."

"Because she's not your nemesis anymore," Jake said.

"KC's not my girlfriend," Angie said.

Jake nodded, stepping out to the three-point arch. "That's why I see you with her between classes—"

"Some classes."

"Burger Top the other night?" he asked.

Angie had no quick, witty reply to wiggle out of said spotting. She had been with KC after a rehearsal. KC, who had been having a hard night and just needed a friend. And that's what they were. Friends. Nothing more. Despite the occasional presence—surge—of physical attraction. They were . . . friends.

Jake shot the ball. It bounced off the backboard and toward Angie. Ryan barked.

"If I'm supposed to accept that my former archnemesis—" Angie said.

"Who isn't your nemesis—"

"Stacy Ann Sloan, of all people, can change," Angie continued.

"Which she did," Jake said.

"Then you should believe KC can too."

Jake sighed.

"She just wants to be friends, Jake," Angie said.

"She's going to hurt you," Jake said. "I don't want to be right, but I think I am. And like you said, it's not my life. But you said to be honest with you. This is me being honest. KC's your blind spot."

Angie bounced the ball to Jake, petting Ryan before crossing the street. Jake didn't understand KC because he never had. Yes, she had a troubled emotional past. Yes, there was her continued struggle with self-harm. But for someone like Jake, who was a good boy from a once-good home with a dog that liked his name, there were things he just couldn't understand. Like Angie and KC's bond.

Angie pondered all this as she shut the front door of her house, surprised to see the pile of mail and baskets of overflowing laundry gone. She set her keys in the entryway dish, hearing her mother in the kitchen. The gifted KitchenAid, unboxed after two years in the hall closet, a carton of eggs, and various other baking supplies cluttered the marble island. Surely, it was the end of times if Connie was baking.

Angie stood in the doorway, watching her mother review what seemed to be a recipe. "Mom?"

"What are you doing?" Connie said, startled. "Don't creep."

"I wasn't," Angie said.

"People don't like it when you come up on them," Connie said.

"Sorry," Angie said.

Connie reached for her wineglass. "I tried to talk to your brother when he came in, but he ran upstairs."

"We were just going to . . ." Angie peeked into the oven, where a chocolate cake was baking. Connie baking? Jesus jumping on a golden glitter-dipped pogo stick . . . was she pregnant? Was that even a physical possibility?

"Order a pizza," Angie finished.

"We're having family dinner tonight," Connie said.

"Why?"

"Because we're a family," Connie said, reading the recipe. "That's what families do."

Not Angie's family. At least not since her sister's deployment, her parents' divorce, her dad stealing their dog, Lester—who hated his name—and of course, Nat's capture. Connie had become an expert at finding any and all excuses to avoid "family" dinners. They simply required too many refills of her Ativan. At least, that's what she said to her good friend Joan.

"Do you . . . um"—Angie paused, uncertain if she should ask—"need . . . help?"

Connie considered the offer. Then she turned the recipe toward Angie.

It was an unusual thing for Angie to stand beside Connie. To not feel the burden of disappointment and disapproval, of anger and . . . Angie took a deep breath, reading the recipe.

"I never understood baking," Connie said.

"It's kind of a science," Angie said. "Baking. They always say on Wang's cooking shows how anyone can scramble an egg, but tempering chocolate? Now that's something."

"Your brother watches cooking shows?" Connie asked.

"Yeah," Angie said. "All the time. You should see his Baked Alaska. And his macarons. His feet are perfect."

"When did he bake anything?" Connie asked.

"When you weren't here."

Connie laughed to herself. "Baking. It's like a foreign language. My mother never let me in the kitchen. Your aunt Megan, yes, but me? No. I wasn't allowed. It was study or work."

Connie sipped her wine, staring off into a memory of something. This was exceptionally unfamiliar terrain for Angie. She wasn't sure how to maneuver in it—standing so close to her mother. She watched her mother rub the back of her neck. The twinge of pain in her face as she did. The shape of her profile. How it looked like—

"What?" Connie said, noticing Angie staring.

"Uh, nothing," Angie said, looking back at the recipe. "So, part of the challenge is that Italian buttercream is kind of tricky. But—"

Before Angie could get out another word, Connie wadded up the recipe.

"Forget it," Connie said impatiently.

"No, it's doable, it's just harder to—"

"It's fine." Connie tossed the recipe into the trash. "I'll just use the premade frosting from the store."

Angie stood there, awkward and uneasy. Unsure of what to do, she gradually started to back away.

"I saw you didn't take the video down," Connie said, peering into the oven.

That was when Angie realized she'd been holding her breath. She quietly exhaled. "No."

"Why?" Connie said, looking at Angie. "Because I asked you to?"

"Because I don't think it's bad," Angie said. "Me. Singing."

"I see."

Connie was uncharacteristically quiet—calm. Perhaps inroads were being made. Angie cautiously said, "I joined a band."

Connie nodded, but not approvingly.

"We're really kind of good," Angie said. "Lucas Waite—he's been helping us, so we can enter—"

"Will you set the table?" Connie said.

Quiet.

More of-course-Connie-shut-Angie-down quiet.

Angie lifted three white plates from the cabinet, pressing them against her chest. "You heard me, right?"

"Four," Connie said. "Plates. Rick is coming over."

"Uh . . . what?" Angie said. "I thought you were over-over."

"It's just dinner."

It was never just dinner. This wasn't even the first time Connie and John/Rick had broken up. It had just been the first breakup that included the violent throwing of Indian food against the wall. A hint of the stain was still visible to Angie as she started to set the table. Maybe Connie was really pregnant. Worse. Maybe they were planning to get—

The front door opened.

"Connie," John/Rick called out.

Connie set the cutlery and napkins on the table.

"You gave him a key again?" Angie said to her mom.

Connie left the dining room. Wang was gonna be so—

"Wang," Connie called upstairs. "Dinner."

"You might want to let him just skip dinner," Angie said, standing in the entryway.

"Angie," John/Rick said, as if they hadn't seen each other in years. "How are you?"

"I'm fine John—Rick, I mean."

Wang slouch-stepped down the stairs, headphones blaring bass from around his neck.

"Hi, Wang," John/Rick said warmly.

Wang lingered on the fifth stair, glaring down at John/Rick. Trusted confidant John/Rick was not. Because the minute Wang's court-appointed therapist had decided to date his mom on the sly, their chance at a trusting, therapeutic relationship had been over. Plus, and with all sincerity, John/Rick was kind of a tool. It was simply a fact that could not be disputed.

"What are you doing here?" Wang asked him.

"Well, your mother and I have been . . . reevaluating what happened. Talking about our feelings around it."

That was a lie. Angie's mother had few feelings about John/Rick outside of his alleged sexual stamina. His ability to make her couldn't-get-it-together mother—ugh. Sex was a topic, like so many, that Connie had spoken at great length to Joan about. A topic Angie wished she could expunge from her memory, but such was the burden of eavesdropping.

"Talking about," John/Rick continued, "what it must have been like for you. Both of you."

"Fuck that. I was just hungry."

"Wang," Connie said.

"What?" he said. "I was."

"Well, we're going to have a do-over," John/Rick said, holding up two Styrofoam-box-filled plastic bags. "I've got everyone's favorite right here."

"My favorite is called You Leaving Right Now," Wang said.

Angie grinned-not-grinned.

"Stop," Connie said to Wang.

"No, it's okay, Connie. He needs to work out his feelings." John/Rick looked at Wang. "Your mom told me about your dinner with your dad. How he'd like you to live with him."

"So?" Wang challenged.

"It must've been hard to say no," said John/Rick. "Given your desire to be emotionally closer to him."

Was John/Rick actually attempting entryway therapy in front of everyone? Was that even a thing . . . therapeutically speaking?

Hoping to defuse the atomic anger vibrating off Wang, Angie reached for the bags, leading everyone into the dining room.

"There are some things I'd like us to talk about tonight," Connie said. "About next week. About us as a family."

Wang's music continued to blare from his headphones as he flopped into his chair.

"Wang," Connie said. "Turn off the music."

Wang was about to when John/Rick intervened. "You can leave it on, Wang."

What?

"If it helps you express your feelings by playing your music loud, then we both want to let you do that," said John/Rick.

What-what?

Connie did not seem particularly thrilled with John/Rick's approach as evidenced by her pause before retreating into the kitchen for a bottle of wine

Angie finished setting out the food. Her stomach noticeably growled as Wang leaned forward, perusing his options.

"I've bought outfits for both of you to wear for the interview," Connie said, uncorking a bottle of Shiraz.

"Isn't that not until next Sunday?" Angie said.

"Yes," Connie said, pouring John/Rick a glass of wine. "But I need you to try them on. Make sure they fit."

Angie's wouldn't. The outfits her mother bought her never did. It was as if Connie bought a dress one to two sizes too small in the hopes that they would fit Angie. Perhaps believing if she could shame her enough, she'd eventually be that number—that size—that girl in material that made her skin itch.

"I've made arrangements for you both to get haircuts this week," Connie said. "Angie, I want to put highlights in yours."

"Highlights?" Angie said, reaching for the rice spoon.

Her mother's eyes followed Angie's hand. Wang watched the interplay as John/Rick ripped a piece of naan in half.

Angie let go of the spoon. Clearly carbs were bad for the upcoming interview.

"And I've made an appointment for . . ." Connie said.

And that was when it started.

Wang began dumping mounds of basmati rice onto his plate. Stacking large, deep-fried squares of cheese, Wang constructed his highest Leaning Tower of Paneer Pakora yet. Angie's eyes volleyed between him, pouring an excessive helping of chicken tikka masala onto his plate, and her mother, who was surprisingly silent. He scooped heaping spoonfuls of saag paneer, shrimp curry, and spicy chutney. All while Connie and John/Rick simply sat there, saying nothing. What in the radical therapeutic process was happening? Not that Connie would ever criticize what Wang ate, but bad table manners were, in Connie's words, "absolutely unacceptable."

Wang took two pieces of naan and folded them along the side of his plate. And when the mountain of food had reached its maximum peak, he slid it to Angie.

"What are you doing?" Angie said.

"Take as much as you want," Wang said before looking at his mom. "She can't tell you not to eat my food. Just yours."

"Enough," Connie said.

"Connie," John/Rick said.

"I know what you said, Rick, but this is—" Connie said.

"Wang," said John/Rick. "You need to stop acting out—"

But before he could spout another condescending sentence from his online-social-work/TV-therapy education, Wang scooped up the plate and smashed it against the wall behind John/Rick. Connie sprang out of her chair. Shards of china and pieces of shrimp shot toward John/Rick. Angie watched the delicious delight that was Indian food ooze down the wall.

"Go to your room!" Connie said to Wang.

"Tell him to go to his room," Wang said. "Tell his punk ass to get out. Shitty boundary, motherfucker."

It was true. John/Rick had slept with their mother, but that was likely not Wang's intention.

"Go. To. Your. Room," Connie demanded. "Now."

"Gladly," Wang said, leaving.

What in the what had just happened? John/Rick reached for Connie, but she was in no mood. She sat back down in her chair, her head in her hands.

John/Rick looked at Angie.

Angie sort of looked at John/Rick.

Connie stared at her empty plate.

And that's when the fire alarm went off. The piercing, screeching scream slit through the room. Connie sprinted into the kitchen, knocking over her glass of red wine. Panicked, she grabbed a wet dish towel and clamped onto the smoking cake pan.

"Damn it!" she said, dropping the pan onto the floor. "Damn! Damn! Shit!"

Connie squeezed her right wrist, kicking the pan. Seeming to want to ensure its culinary death.

"Rinse it," John/Rick said, pulling Connie's hand under the running faucet.

Angie looked away from them and at the performance art their family dinner had become. Paneer cubes scattered on the floor. Spilled wine dripped onto the carpet. All of which would leave a stain. There could be no stains. No imperfections. The carpet was sure to be replaced before next Sunday. The wall repainted. Before the cameras. Before the questions.

The smell of smoke and charred chocolate cake permeated the air as Angie sat back down. Reaching for a piece of naan, she poured what was left of the chicken tikka masala onto her plate and ate. Alone.

Chapter 18

Angie had just closed her locker when KC dropped against the one next to it.

"This day," KC said. "A literal hell. How is it not Friday?"

"Because it's Wednesday?" Angie said.

"Thank the goddess for an early release day. I'm driving into the city. Picking up Health's *Get Color*, a Tegan and Sara, and Girl In a Coma . . . all on vinyl."

"Sounds fun," Angie said, shouldering her backpack.

"You should come with," KC said excitedly.

"Uh . . . I've got rehearsal at seven thirty," Angie said, the two of them walking down the hall.

"That's like a year from now, time-wise," KC said.

"Not exactly."

"Hey, Angie," said a girl in passing.

"C'mon," KC said. "I need some Angie time. It'll be ultra. Two young women on the lam but not. Traipsing through the moderately waxed floors of the hugely capitalistic Arcade Mall. Sampling the forbidden fruits of feminist fury from the clothing racks of Electra Threads. Blasting zombies and becoming Skee-Ball Olympians once again at the Arcade Wizard. Finishing, of course, with a food-court extravaganza because no mall trip is complete without a food-court extravaganza. All of this, before sundown and your rehearsal."

Angie laughed. "How do you do that?"

"What?" KC said.

"Make something ordinary like going to the mall sound so . . . not ordinary."

"It's a gift," said KC, holding the door leading to the student parking lot open.

"I was going to go home," Angie said. "Work on some lyrics we've been tweaking."

"Tweak on the ride," KC said. "Besides—what are you going to wear on Saturday?"

Oddly, Angie hadn't given it much thought.

"I don't know," Angie said. "Jeans. Politically charged T-shirt. My boots."

KC remained quiet. The kind of quiet that made Angie adjust her stance.

"What?" Angie finally said.

"Okay," KC said. "Can I be . . . honest?"

Angie's cautious shrug indicated KC could.

"I dig your vibe, but you've got an audience now," KC said. "Let's shift your thrift. As in thrift store look to something more you-ish."

"This is me-ish. I mean, me," Angie said, questioning her ensemble.

"But you want to be the absolute you for the competition video," KC said. "Think of it like this. Stars have stylists. People who dress them for photo shoots, red-carpet events. That's me, but with my dad's Sapphire Preferred."

KC flashed a credit card from her messenger bag.

"You stole your dad's credit card?" Angie said.

"Stealing is a crime," KC said. "Unlike your brother, I don't dabble in the dark arts of thievery. My dad gave it to me for emergencies when I was in Dallas. I can't be held responsible for him forgetting to ask for it when he shoved me out the door. And technically . . . this is an emergency. I need vinyl. You need a look."

Angie laughed. "It would be cool . . . to go into the city," Angie said.

"Yeah . . . ?" KC said, leaning back on her boots.

"I'm not sure about the shopping thing, but the rest sounds pretty fun," Angie said.

KC grinned, shaking Esther's truck keys midair. "You're not going to regret this."

* * *

Angie and KC had torn through the clothing racks of several stores. It was surprisingly not as uncomfortable to shop for clothes with KC as Angie would've thought, given their vastly different waist sizes. It wasn't a shameful thing. It was actually . . . kind of fun.

Three shirts, two plaid skirts complete with steampunk embellishments, and a vegan-leather jacket were the makings of an updated Angie. She was a vision to witness as she strutted alongside KC. Her skirt flirted three inches above her knees. Her black button-down wanted only to please her curves, her cleavage. This was shape, this was form, and it wasn't asking for permission.

Well, mostly. Angie felt a little if not a lot—uncomfortable-comfortable.

"You'll get used to it," KC said. "The clothes."

Carrying a tray with AstroDogs and smoothies from the food court, they plopped their collective shopping bags onto the seats beside them. Sipping her smoothie, KC swiped from one picture to another on her phone, showcasing the two of them trying on clothes, mugging for the camera, and just being silly. Where was this version of KC when they were dating? The one who was unafraid to surrender to the surrender—to truly let go of the element of mystery and fully play? Their shared pain wasn't in the forefront for once. It was just Angie and KC without the heavy. Without the hard. Without the hurt of what had gone wrong between them.

"Oh, wait," KC said, putting her phone down.

She dumped the contents of her purse onto the table, sifting through a series of ticket stubs, foils of Black Jack Gum, tampons, wadded-up tissues, audiocassettes, and—

"Grape-flavored dental dams?" Angie said, holding one up.

KC blushed. "Yeah. You know. Esther and protection. She's like 'You can love, but cover the—'"

"Sure," Angie said, putting it back down.

"Keep it. We've got a jar of them at our house," KC said. "Besides, you never know."

"I never know what?" Angie asked.

"If you'll need it." KC grinned.

Angie laughed. "Yeah, that's . . . so, um. No."

"Why?" KC said. "Seems like you might be into someone."

Quiet.

Super-uncomfortable your-ex-talking-about-safe-sex-and-the-girl-you're-into quiet.

"I, um . . . so," Angie said, leaning over the pile on the table. "What are you looking for?"

"Nice deflect," KC said. "I'm looking for . . ." She felt around the bottom of her purse. "This and this . . . or maybe this."

KC proudly held up eye shadow and several tubes of lipstick.

"Uh . . . I don't know," Angie said. "I already feel kind of out of place in the skirt-and-top look."

"I swear you look . . . absolute." KC bit at her bottom lip. "Infinitely suspending."

Angie smiled, tugging at the bottom of the skirt as if to lengthen it.

"You have legs," KC said. "You have shape. You don't have to baggy-hide it. Besides, you're an influencer now. People are looking at you."

"People have always looked at me," Angie groaned.

"Yeah, but not in the way they should've," said KC.

"I'm just not real makeup-y," Angie said.

"Just try it," KC said. "If you hate, we'll wash off."

Angie considered it, tugging at the hem of the skirt again.

"Please . . ." said KC. "You're gonna look R-O-C-K star. Trust."

Angie sighed and nodded. "Let the clown face begin."

KC tapped her brush against the eye shadow. "This is a one hundred and ninety-nine percent clown-free makeover. Besides. You have a complexion to slay for."

"I don't know about that," Angie said.

"I do," KC said.

The two of them looked at each other. Whatever sentences both of them were writing separately in their own hearts, neither was saying them out loud.

"Okay," KC said. "Lean forward. Closer."

Angie became transfixed by the alluring smell of KC's cherry ChapStick, an aphrodisiac that blurred the clearly stated friends-only relationship.

"Do like this with your eyes," KC said.

Angie closed her eyes as the bristles of the brush broke against her skin, tripping every possible nerve ending. Angie gulped, shifting in her seat.

"Relax," KC said. "I'm actually pretty good at this. When I was a kid, I used to sit and watch Esther make up her face all the time. Especially when doc-in-the-box Dad bailed. She'd apprentice at a tattoo shop in West Hollywood by day, glam it up by night. Sometimes she'd go out. Mostly she'd stay in and just have us pick an era and go wild with makeup."

A different brush stroked Angie's eyelid. It was smoother than the first. Like cotton.

"It was like we were on the best kind of island for two," KC said. "Sitting in front of a garage-sale TV, eating shrimp fried rice and crab rangoon. Reading books from the public library before bed—at breakfast. It was for sure a crappy apartment in a meh neighborhood, but it was so much better than when we moved to Beverly. What a shitshow."

KC set the brush down, considering her lipstick options.

"You've never really talked about it much," Angie said. "Beverly Hills."

"What's to say?" KC said. "I tried to fit in. I kind of did. Until I didn't."

"Until you started cutting?" Angie asked.

KC shook her head and shrugged. "This is the one."

"Nice deflection," Angie said.

KC grinned. "It was until I started realizing that fitting in was about being someone else. I'm me. That's what I do. I can't change that."

KC popped the cap and rolled the lipstick up.

"That's awfully . . ." Angie started.

"Trust." KC smiled.

Angie conceded.

"Okay," KC said. "Kind of stretch your lips like this."

KC leaned forward, slowly, gently swiping her Limitless Linger across Angie's lips. The same lipstick KC had worn on the Fourth of July. She and Angie, making out in the back of Esther's truck. Waiting for fireworks. Yearning to be touched, Angie was sure her virginity would end. As Terence Trent D'Arby played on the radio, the mood was set. KC's warm breath—her hand, squeezing Angie's waist. All things hard, all things imperfect could be erased . . . then the news. KC was leaving.

"There." KC leaned back.

A grin galloped from one corner of her mouth to the other. "Now that's absolute. A little eyeliner, depending how far you want to take it."

KC held up a compact mirror. Angie was taken aback. This was not the thin person living inside Angie. It wasn't the fat one either. This person? The one staring back at her was smoky and . . . mysterious?

"Too much mood?" KC asked.

"No, it's just . . ."

"Hot?" KC said.

"Different," Angie said, distracted by a trio of girls watching them from a nearby table. KC followed Angie's gaze.

"I just want to go one place," Angie said. "Where people aren't staring at me because of her."

It happened in Dryfalls. It happened outside Dryfalls. It happened in public restrooms and in grocery-store lines. Angie's sister and her family had been morbid celebrities— national treasures. A story of stories. She just wanted it to—

"Yes," Angie said to the girls. "She was my sister, and it was tragic and gut-wrenching, and no, please don't say you're sorry for my loss."

One of the girls said, "Who's your sister?"

What?

Another girl said, "You're Fat Angie, right?"

KC laughed, grabbing Angie by the shoulder, leaning in. "They're fans. *Your* fans."

This was an impossible notion for Angie to fully grasp, but there she was, trying to grasp it.

"Hey," KC said to the girls. "You want to take a selfie

with Fat Angie? Lead singer of the most badass new band, Go Feral?"

Angie slapped KC's leg.

"What?" KC said.

"Are you for real?" said the first girl.

"Always," said KC.

The girls rushed over, crowding Angie.

"What's Lucas Waite like?" said a third girl. "I saw you on Instagram with him. OMG. I'm, like, two degrees from Lucas Waite right now."

"I really love your song," said the second girl, her phone shaking in her hands with excitement. "Like, really love it."

Angie smiled warmly. "Thanks."

"Okay," KC said, raising her phone in selfie mode. "Say revolution."

"Revolution!" they shouted in unison.

Angie was still marveling at her mini-fan-club food-court experience as they were heading out of the city.

"Still thinking about it?" KC said.

"I just . . . wow," Angie said.

"It's pretty powerful," KC said. "What a song can do. What you can do."

KC took an unexpected exit off the interstate.

"We're going to make one more stop," she said.

"Where?"

"It's a surprise," said KC.

Angie checked the time on her cell. "We're cutting it kind of close."

"It will be super fast," KC said. "I called while you were signing foreheads."

"One forehead," Angie said.

They pulled up to Tank & Tara Tattoo. KC cut the engine.

"I'm not getting a tattoo," Angie said.

"Of course you're not," said KC, getting out of the truck. "We're getting you pierced."

"What—no," Angie said, following KC. "I have a fear of needles. A deep, long-standing fear of needles."

KC reached for the door.

"You can close your eyes. Plus," KC said, "it's like flossing but faster. You'll never feel it."

Angie flossed relatively slow and felt that KC's estimation of a fast and pain-free piercing was at the very least questionable. She followed her in all the same. Soon the buzzing sound of tattoo guns swarmed her ears. People piled onto a sofa, laughing, flipping through tattoo books. And KC? She bobbed her head and sang "Sad But True," which was pumping from the speakers along the walls. Ink and needles and body modification. This was KC's kingdom, and she walked like it.

"What can I do for you ladies?" said the woman with the name *Roxanne* tattooed on her arm. Among others.

"Piercing," said KC.

"Are you over eighteen?" said Roxanne.

"By two hundred," KC said, slapping a stack of twenties on the counter.

Angie's eyes widened. Was KC serious? This was clearly illegal. And unlike Wang, Angie was very anti-illegal regardless of her recent role in all things rebel and girl revolution.

Roxanne eyed the money. Then KC and Angie.

"You know you have to have parental consent," Roxanne said.

"KC," Angie said. "Let's just go."

KC flashed her belly-button ring. "I've been consented. More than once. And we just want something small and screaming for her."

KC pointed to a flaming dice in the display case.

Roxanne's eyes cut from the case to Angie. This was all bad, and Angie knew it.

"Besides," KC said. "I called and spoke to Deacon. He knows my mom. Said it was cool."

"Deacon's not here, and he should've never told you that," said Roxanne.

"C'mon, it's a belly-button ring," KC said.

"Belly button?" Angie said.

Roxanne slid the money back to KC.

"Here's the thing," said Tattoo Roxanne. "That ink on your neck? That was stupid. You don't know where you're going to be in ten years, if some narrow-minded tool will deny you a job that you want and deserve because of it. Hands, neck, and face are a no."

KC shook her head, laughing to herself.

"I'm just telling you this because I wish someone had told me," Tattoo Roxanne said to KC. "And you can flash that cash to a half a dozen shops in town who will gladly take it and not care, but not here. Not in my shop."

"And that is really fair," Angie stammered, pulling KC out of the shop. "Thank you, Ms.—Mrs. Roxanne."

The door hadn't shut when KC started. "Can you believe that?"

"That she was following the law?" Angie said.

"She's a hypocrite with ink remorse," KC said. "She doesn't get to just tell me what to do with my body."

"Technically, it was my body, and she kind of does," Angie said. "In the realm of tattoos and piercings, anyway."

"I just wanted you to have the full rock-star experience," KC said. "Not some guidance-counselor piercing lecture."

"I did . . . have the experience," Angie said, walking closer to KC. "Makeup and AstroDogs. Fan selfies and listening to Paws with the windows down like we were in some . . . really perfect movie. That was the experience. I don't need to poke a hole in my body. You know?"

KC smiled. "Yeah."

The two of them might have been standing about one and one-half feet apart. Somehow it felt much closer. Butterflies-in-the-stomach closer. Like their relationship had never actually ended closer. All of the things that had not worked out between them seemed to push away. It was in that moment of nearly debilitating closeness that Angie realized . . . the time.

"We have to go," Angie said, looking at her phone.

"Yeah," KC said, walking toward the truck.

Just like that, Angie had dodged her confusion about KC, and KC had thankfully let her.

Chapter 19

The traffic gods had not been on Angie and KC's side, and they pulled up to the warehouse over two hours late. While KC had boasted that time was fluid and belonged to no one, a jackknifed eighteen-wheeler with a chemical spill had proven otherwise. Time belonged to that accident.

Angie piled out of the truck, grabbing her backpack and shopping bags. Tugging at the hem of her skirt.

"Just explain," KC said. "Accidents happen. It's the nature of things."

"I'll talk to you later." Angie shut the door and rushed inside.

Lucas was on the stage, plucking at his acoustic guitar. Pencil tucked behind his ear, sheet music on a milk crate in front of him.

"Where is everyone?" Angie said.

"You were late. They practiced. They left."

"I said I was coming. I texted that I was coming."

"They hadn't heard from you in over an hour." He set his guitar on a stand.

"My phone died," Angie said. "And I . . ."

Lucas jumped down from the stage.

"You get that on Saturday you're singing for Plymouth Montreal," Lucas said. "That aside from being my friend, he's one of the most innovative producers in the business. Playing for him at his personal party is a genuine opportunity. Not that the competition isn't, but—"

"I get what Saturday is," Angie said, frustrated. "I'm not stupid."

Lucas paused, realizing he had somehow stepped on a very live emotional land mine. "I didn't say you were."

"You're talking to me like I don't know what Saturday is," she said. "I know about Plymouth and this special favor you've asked for. I know that I'm supposed to warm up before I sing. That I'm supposed to emote—dance—feel the music when our songs aren't even fully done. I know that I'm supposed to work eleven hundred thousand times harder than everyone else because they actually know what they're doing. And I'm still making mistakes." Angie paused. "I know all of that, and still I'm here every day. Early. Late. Dealing with my mom about this stupid interview and the filming at school and school—I try to push it all out of my head every day because I want this. I need this. Okay?"

"I know you do," he said. "And I see all of that. But for the band? They don't know how to trust yet. This is that part where you are learning what you all are—if it's real. You can't be late. Not the way you were."

"What does that mean?" Angie asked.

"I think you should talk to them. C'mon." He grabbed his keys off a folding chair. "They were heading to The Slice. They're probably still there."

Angie and Lucas sat in a swath of silence. No music playing from the radio. No conversation. Just the occasional squeak of the truck and rattle of coins in the cup holder. When they pulled up, Angie saw Finster busing tables. Jamboree, Chloe, Zeke, and Wang at their usual horseshoe-shaped booth. Angie suddenly felt very outside of what had been a very inside feeling.

"Be honest with them," Lucas said.

"About what?"

"That this matters. That they matter. That this viral fame stuff isn't in your head."

Frustrated, Angie got out. "I don't know how being late to one rehearsal could make them think that it doesn't matter. That this isn't everything."

Angie walked away from the truck and into the boisterous pop music and cool neon lights of The Slice. The smell of garlic-butter pizza crust and melted cheese soaked the air. A group of kids cheered from the air-hockey table in the back.

Finster stepped away from wiping a booth down, lumbering a bus tub packed with plates and cups and cutlery covered in red sauce.

"Hey," Angie said to Finster.

"Your lipstick is smeared," Finster said, giving her little more than a glance as she walked by.

Angie reached for her mouth, checking her makeup in a mirrored sign on the wall, desperately trying to wipe it from her face. She could see everyone huddled around Zeke, laughing at something on their video camera. She tugged at her skirt, straightened her shirt, and headed toward them. The closer she got the more unmistakably quiet they were.

"Hey," Angie said.

Nothing.

More nothing.

Finally, when Wang was about to break the silence—

"You were late," Chloe said. "I'm in seventh grade, and I know not to be late."

"I texted," Angie said. "There was an accident on the interstate. Traffic. For miles. Sirens. Ambulances. The whole thing."

Angie surveyed the temperature that seemed to be dropping.

"Yeah, we checked," said Wang.

Finster slipped in the booth beside Chloe, sampling a piece of stuffed cheese pizza. "You were a no-show."

"I showed—" Angie said. "Late, but I . . . I was just explaining. Accident. Traffic—"

"No, Wang showed us that part."

"So . . . ?" Angie said. "It wasn't my fault."

They said nothing. Angie looked to Jamboree, who leaned away from the table, staring at her plate.

"What is going on?" Angie said. "Lucas is acting weird, and now . . . I mean, c'mon. Everyone's been late once to something."

"I'm never late," Chloe said, crossing her arms over her chest.

Finster took a sip from Chloe's soda.

"Ewww," Chloe said to Finster. "Now I can't drink it." She slid her cup toward her sister.

"Girl, just be for real with us," Zeke said.

"Real about what? I just told you."

Wang looked away.

"We all saw," Finster said.

"Saw what?" Angie said.

And before Chloe could blurt anything out, Jamboree scooted out of the booth, heading outside.

"You messed up bad," Chloe said to Angie.

Angie followed Jamboree, her backpack slapping against her butt, shopping bags twisting around her fingers.

"Jamboree," Angie said, rushing out the door.

Jamboree stopped short of her car.

"What is going on?" Angie said. "I'm sorry I was late, but—"

"What are we?" Jamboree said, turning toward Angie.

"What?"

"Us? You. Me," Jamboree said. "What are we?"

Angie stood suspended in an Angie silence.

"Just when I think we're . . . something maybe," Jamboree said, "KC spins back around."

"It's not like that."

Jamboree pulled out her phone. A few taps later, she faced her screen to Angie. And there it was. The mystery of everyone's quiet. In full and vibrant color, it was . . .

Angie and KC, cheek to cheek at the makeup counter.

Swipe. Angie and KC in the dressing rooms.

Swipe. Angie and KC and the groupies from the food court. Sparkly purple heart border around the photo.

"You're trending," Jamboree said. "Twitter. Instagram. #FatAngie. #GoFeral. My personal favorite comment: 'Fat Angie in the wild,' because that's . . ." Jamboree laughed to herself, tucking her phone into her jeans pocket.

"It's not . . ." Angie started. "I mean, it isn't . . . it's—we went shopping."

"And apparently signed foreheads."

"It was just . . . they were fans. Of *me*? Can you believe that?"

Jamboree didn't say anything.

"C'mon," Angie said. "You know me. You know me better than . . . it was just—"

"I don't want to do this," Jamboree said. "I don't want to be this person."

Quiet.

This-is-serious quiet.

"Jamboree," Angie said, walking toward her.

Jamboree stepped back. "I don't care what we are."

"You don't mean that," Angie said.

Jamboree nodded. "I mean everything I say. Do you?"

Angie lowered her head. She wanted to fix this. She needed to fix this. But when she looked at Jamboree, all she saw was . . . hurt. Hurt that Angie had caused because she couldn't say—

"I wanted to be fine with you and KC being friends," Jamboree said. "Because she was so important to you. Because you said it was over. But . . . I look at those pictures and . . . that doesn't look like just friends."

Angie couldn't dispute her. To do so would've been a lie. Angie was terrible at the art of lying. Incredibly much so. There was something there in those photos. Even if Angie didn't fully understand it.

"I gotta go." Jamboree headed to her car.

"Um . . ." Angie said. "Are you, um . . . quitting? The band?"

Jamboree paused; her car door open. "No. It means too much to all of them."

"Well, maybe not Chloe," Angie said.

"No, especially Chloe," Jamboree said. "This is the first time she's actually been respected—gotten respect for her talent and not been dismissed." Jamboree shook her head. "This may have started because you wanted to enter a competition and have Joan Jett see you. But this is bigger than that now. It's not just about you."

Just as quickly as Jamboree got into her car, she was gone. Angie's stomach literally hurt. Her head spun as she uncomfortably pulled at the hem of her skirt.

Wang strutted out of the restaurant. To-go box in tow, he stood beside his sister.

"Are you mad at me too?" Angie said.

He chuckled. "Yo, I screw up on the regular. This is kind of weak on the scale of a Wang misdemeanor. They're just a little run up about it."

"Jamboree is more than . . . run up. She's really mad at me."

Wang scratched his chin. "Should she be?"

Angie shrugged. "Maybe."

Angie looked through the windows of the restaurant. Zeke and Finster talking. Chloe in the arcade.

"I hate this feeling," she said to Wang. "Like I'm always disappointing someone. No matter how hard I try—what

I do. It's like Nat sopped up all the genetic perfection. She disappointed no one."

Wang considered it. "I don't know. Like, is it worth it?"

Angie looked at him.

"Perfection," he said. "Shit ain't real. It's just . . . maybe she didn't disappoint Mom or Dad or this town 'cause she got out of here before she could. Maybe she was full of fuck-up. Dying just pulls that out of the equation, you know?"

Angie did know. The equations were as follows:

Death + Natalie = Eternal Perfection

Attempted Suicide + Fatness + All Things Angie =
Eternal Disappointment

"I've been thinking," Wang said. "We're different. You and me."

Never had truer words been uttered. Of this much Angie was certain.

"We just put it out there, you know?" he said. "Sometimes it's jackpot. Sometimes it's not." He paused. "With them. Just let 'em know you weren't skipping out for this"—he looked at her outfit—"KC makeover."

Angie nodded.

"Is this actual leather?" he said, touching the jacket.

Resigned, she said, "Vegan."

"Huh."

Angie adjusted her backpack. "I'm going to go talk to them . . . be real," Angie said. "Wait for me."

"Only if we can stop and see Lori," he said very cutely.

She shook her head. "Why not?"

With her hand on the door, Angie took a deep breath, trying to sift through the thousand and two thoughts colliding in her head, focusing in on the most important one: *I'm in this band because of all of you.*

She pulled the door open and went inside.

Chapter 20

Being back in KC's bedroom was familiar in a way Angie hadn't expected. Among the feminist posters and KC's Wall of Thoughts So Twisted with its latest edition of all things bizarre, such as a photo of a stolen car on top of a house in California. Nicholas Cage's Egyptian tomb in a New Orleans cemetery. Magnetic Man, aka the holder of the Guinness World Record for most spoons on a human body. All of this had been added to her wall. All things eccentric and KC.

Angie looked at herself in KC's mirror. The highlights Angie's couldn't-get-it-together mother had forced into her hair. The outfit KC had bought her. The plaid skirt with steampunk embellishments. The black top with the word

SCREAM scrawled in white across it. Who was this Angie? In KC's lipstick and salon hair and fiery eye shadow with blends of ash and mauve. In a few hours, she'd be standing in front of Plymouth Montreal. The reality of it was oddly terrifying because she knew the music. She had studied stage presence and all the things Lucas had—

"Hey," KC said, carrying in a tray of food.

She kicked her bedroom door shut behind her.

"Don't slam the door," Esther said from the other room.

"What we have is something a little reminiscent of days past." KC sat on the floor at the foot of the bed. "C'mon."

Angie clumsily shifted to the floor, adjusting her skirt several times.

"We have Wisconsin baked cheese," KC said. "Fried with a splash of oil in our cast-iron skillet. Gives it a char and grit taste not found in the nonstick variety."

Angie grinned.

"And we also have an assortment of fruits, including my personal fave, Flame Seedless grapes. Here, try one."

KC held one of the enormous merlot-colored grapes out, waiting for Angie to open her mouth. She did, but awkwardly. It released a sweet, sugary juice into her mouth.

"Right?" KC said.

"Um, yeah," Angie said, feeling uncomfortable but not entirely sure why.

Friends feed each other grapes, right? There were two guys in her math class who threw food across the room and into their mouths all the time. Sometimes they even picked it up off the floor when it ricocheted and ate it. While eating a germ-infested food item off the floor was disgusting, it was still normal in the realm of food tossing. This grape had been washed. It was both clean and—it didn't mean anything.

Did it?

"And," KC continued, "we have a variety of crackers, hummus, and of course, chilled sparkling apple cider in official Toy Story tumblers."

KC grinned, handing Angie a cup of cider.

"This is really swell," Angie said. "But honestly, I don't know that I can really eat."

"Still nervous?" KC said. "About tonight?"

"Tonight is kind of everything," Angie said. "Plymouth Montreal. I mean, how is that real? Me, in a band. Singing . . ."

"Because you are stellar-amazing," KC said. "You seen the 'Rebel Girl' view count? It's over four million. And that BuzzFeed article."

"I know, right?" Angie said.

"They didn't mention your sister once," KC said. "It was all you."

"Well, and the band," Angie said.

"Mostly you," KC said. "As it should be."

Something about that didn't feel right to Angie. Why should—

"Hey," KC said. "What's going on? In the brain tank?"

"Everything. Nothing. Just . . . I can't . . ."

"What?" KC said, eating a grape.

Angie shrugged.

"You can tell me," KC said. "We're friends, right?"

"It's just . . . There are so many good things. Still. I can't seem to get the noise out of my head. This . . . I don't know how to describe it. And my mom. She's been on me all day about the interview tomorrow. Coaching me. Telling me what I'm supposed to say. How I'm supposed to say it. Smile, but not too much. Shoulders back. Head up."

KC slathered hummus on a cracker. "It's a documentary though, right?"

"Yeah," Angie said.

Not that it mattered to Connie. It was a commentary on Natalie. Any and all commentary about Natalie was scrutinized under the bloodshot eyes of Connie. There was one way to talk about Nat: Connie's way.

"I just . . . uh." Angie put her head in her hands.

"Hey," KC said, putting her hand on Angie's back. "You are gonna slay tonight. It will be beyond ultra—beyond ultra-even."

"I just want to shut it all off," Angie said. "The interview, my mom, the fear. Just get up onstage and do what I know. Without the noise."

Angie drew her knees toward her chest, resting her

elbows on them. KC sat quiet beside her. Then all at once she got up.

"I'll be right back," she said.

Angie sighed. Her eyes were following the pace of the chaos of KC's bedroom when she saw torn photos in the trash can. She reached for them, noticing—

"Okay," KC said, quietly shutting the door and locking it behind her. "I've got the answer to your problem. Well, at least one of them."

KC sat beside Angie with an ice-cube tray of Jell-O and a baggie of chocolate chip cookies.

Angie eyed them. "Jell-O and cookies? This is what I need?"

"I present to you Noise Be Gone," KC said.

Angie stared at the orange, red, and blue Jell-O shaped like diamonds.

"A couple of these," KC said, holding up the tray. "And a few bites of Mike's Relax Stash, and you'll be good to rock."

"What's in it?" Angie asked.

"It's all natural," KC said. "He's got like anxiety and glaucoma."

This all struck Angie as surprising. Esther's boyfriend didn't even wear glasses, and he never seemed nervous. Perhaps it was the medical effects of Jell-O and cookies.

"Trust," KC said, swallowing an orange diamond. "Noise Be Gone."

KC held the tray out to Angie. Reluctantly, she scooped out the sizable jiggling Jell-O.

"Raspberry," KC said. "Don't chew. Just—"

It slipped down Angie's throat. A trail of warmness followed.

KC chased down her second one, following with a bite of the cookie.

"It just takes the edge off," KC said, holding out the cookie. "You're gonna be so relaxed."

Angie hesitated.

"You want to get up there and let loose, right?" KC said.

"Yeah," Angie said.

"This is your loose."

Angie took a small bite of the cookie. It crumbled in her mouth, the taste surprisingly kind of like—

"Basil," Angie said.

KC grinned, taking another bite. "It's definitely not basil. Maybe a distant relative. I've never actually checked."

KC lifted an emerald-green Jell-O diamond out of the tray and offered it to Angie. "Diamonds are a girl's best friend."

One diamond became two. When two became a number Angie had lost count of, she realized it might be time to slow down. Between the Jell-O and the cookies, she definitely felt relaxed. Very, very relaxed. And a little . . . light-headed.

KC started laughing. Then Angie started laughing. Soon they were laughing and leaning into each other. KC nudged Angie's shoulder with hers. Angie nudged back. It was a nudge fest at the foot of KC's bed.

Angie's cell vibrated. A text from Zeke.

"I really gotta go," Angie said. "I'm already late as it is."

"Stay," KC said. "Just a little longer. I'll drop you."

"You can't drop me," Angie said.

"Why?" KC said. "Because of your girlfriend?"

Angie sighed.

"No," Angie said.

"I missed you." KC's fingers touched the side of Angie's hand. "Like, really missed you."

Angie's stomach twist-fluttered. Her face went flush. When KC had first left and in the weeks that followed, Angie had missed her to Saturn and back. Assuming that were astronomically possible in the realm of missing. And there KC was—no longer on Saturn but sitting beside her.

"What exactly are we doing?" Angie said.

"You tell me." KC grinned. "I'm not ulterior and motive. I mean, maybe a little-ish. I mean, yeah, we have history and there's a definite energy. I mean, for me there is."

KC looked at Angie in that way Angie had always wanted her to. The way she thought she had looked at her on the Fourth of July. Back of the pickup truck. "Sign Your Name" smooth sexy through the radio. That was the KC Angie had fallen head over heart over head twice for. That was the girl mixtapes were made for—the one who assured there would be get-back-together scenes in movies.

KC loved Angie.

And Angie—

KC leaned forward. Their heads tilted, Angie's beginning to spin. That's when Angie felt it. KC's lips brushed against hers. That revolving smoothness of Luscious Linger lipstick from both of their lips. Everything past was zooming into the present. Angie kissed KC back, not entirely sure what was happening—why it was happening. Feeling something wasn't right, she said, "We didn't work out."

"We could," KC said, still kissing Angie. "You get the invisible. The edge. That's why . . . you. Me . . . connect."

Angie pushed back. Feeling the weight of Jell-O and Mike's Relax Stash cookies. "What do you mean?" Angie said.

"You get the pain," KC said, sliding her hand behind Angie's neck. "You get the pull of it. The suicide ride . . . the noise of everything. My cutting. We get darkness. We—"

"Stop," Angie said, scooting back. At least, she thought it was back. She was feeling very disoriented.

"What?" KC said. "Tell me you're not feeling this—between us."

Angie had no idea what was happening. Her body was a confused yes, but something was wrong. Like sitting in her sister's room with Wang. The way everything had been . . . staged.

"This doesn't make any sense," Angie said.

"Why not?" KC crawled toward Angie.

Angie's eyes darted around the room. To the trash can. She reached for the ripped photos. Trying to puzzle them together and then—

"You slept with Avocado-Green-Hair-Girl-with-All-the Piercings, didn't you?" Angie said.

KC paused midcrawl.

"When you were in Dallas," Angie continued. "You slept with her."

KC sat back on her legs. Sighed. "It didn't mean anything. It was just a thing."

"You think that makes it better?" Angie asked. "It *should* mean something. Having sex means something to me."

"Angie, it was . . . she and I were . . . cliché to the nth power. We were drinking—just messing around and—people have sex, Angie. It's not always theme songs and soft-focus cameras. Sometimes it's just hard and fast, and hot and it feels good to just be—"

"Not with me," Angie said.

"C'mon," KC said. "This. What we were doing just now . . ."

"Uh, I'm so stupid," Angie said.

"Don't . . . complicate this."

And there was the word. The word of all words that Angie wished could be erased from the lexicon.

Complicate—complicated—in whatever freaking tense it could exist, she wanted it expunged.

"What is wrong with you?" Angie said. "The pain connection? I'm just the fat girl with the fat problems that made you feel, what?"

"That's not—" KC started, but Angie was not done.

"You slept with her after a few weeks, and barely . . . what with me?" Angie said. "You get that I thought it was me. Something wrong with me. My body. My size."

"You're beautiful."

"Quit lying, KC. Quit bullshitting me."

And all that was cool and mysterious about KC had drained from her face. She was simply a girl in an expensive rebel-wannabe outfit who had been called out.

Angie wobbled when she stood up. The room tilted horizontally.

"I want you, Angie," KC said, standing, slipping her palms onto Angie's face. "You can't tell me you don't want me. You don't want us."

Angie pushed her hands away. "Actually, I can. That's how consent works. I don't consent to any of this."

Angie headed for the door.

"Angie, stop," KC said. "Just talk to me."

"You never wanted to be friends," Angie said. "This . . . this was the goal right? This is what you wanted."

"Angie, I love you," KC said.

"You love . . . the *Dateline* special you saw. Before you came to Dryfalls. These clothes, this hair—hair that I hate, by the way. And the viral video."

"Angie, we get each other," KC pleaded. "You and me. We see each other."

"Trauma?" Angie said. "Trauma . . . bonding isn't love."

Angie walked out the door, KC following.

"I'm not going to let you end it like this," KC said. "Angie—"

"Hey, girls," Esther said, coming out of the kitchen.

Angie blurted out, "KC stole Mike's Relax Stash, which I ingested because of its medicinal purposes for anxiety. Not glaucoma."

"You gave Angie pot?" Esther said to KC.

"You gave me pot?" Angie said, horrified. "That's illegal."

Angie had sunk to the nefarious and uncouth standards of Wang. What was to become of her now?

"Was there pot in the Jell-O?" Angie asked.

"KC!" Esther said. "My room. My fridge. My things."

Esther rested her hands on Angie's shoulders. "Honey, are you okay? Do you want me to call your mom?"

Sweet Baby Jesus in a designer diaper, hell no! Angie did not want Esther to call Connie.

"No," Angie said. "Please. I just . . . I need a ride."

"Sure," Esther said. "Of course."

Esther grabbed her purse, turning to KC. "We are going

to have a long and hard talk about this when I get back. And don't listen to Jewel."

KC looked at Angie.

Angie looked at KC, tilted at a one hundred eighty degree angle, as she walked into her room and slammed her door, Jewel's "Foolish Games" sad-blasting from her stereo.

Chapter 21

Angie stumbled into the warehouse. Lights, cameras, and a lot of action were happening all around her. People milling about on sofas and chairs. The transformation from empty warehouse to posh party was unbelievable. The tarp that had separated the stage from the rest of the warehouse had been replaced with sheets of cascading amber lights. Lights that were likely not moving as much as they seemed to Angie.

Zeke, or what seemed to be three of them, peeled through the curtains, walking toward Angie. Angie tried to refocus her eyes. To distinguish which of the three was actually Zeke.

"Where have you been?" Zeke said.

"Sorry," Angie said.

"It's cool," Zeke said. "We were just worried you got locked up with your mom. So, listen. A couple of friends from AV Club are helping with cameras, and . . ."

Angie tried to listen to the three Zekes, but it was so—

"Dude, are you drunk?" Zeke asked.

Angie tried to adjust her eyes again. It was no use. There were three Zekes until there wouldn't be.

"I need something," Angie said, stumbling toward the buffet table.

"Angie," Zeke said.

"This . . . wasn't me," Angie said, ambling forward. "I was . . . and KC. And then she . . . tried to make a pass at me?"

"Wonder where she got that idea," Zeke said.

"Don't," Angie said. "It is not . . . we're not . . . I am. Not."

The Zekes shook their heads. "Girl, I can't be messing with all of your romance drama right now. There are hundreds of people here."

Angie finally managed to get to the buffet table. Her focus was distracted by a five-foot ice sculpture of—

"What are you on?" Zeke said, seeming very close by Angie's estimation.

"Um . . ." Angie swayed. "Jell-O. Some kind of cookie."

"Did you eat a pot cookie?" Zeke whisper-shouted.

"Seems likely," Angie whisper-shouted back. "KC said they were Esther's boyfriend's special Relax Stash. He's got glaucoma or glycemia or something with a *g*. What is this I'm holding?"

Angie was holding a carrot.

A baby carrot, to be precise.

It wasn't a mysterious food to anyone except Angie.

Zeke rubbed the back of their neck. "Okay. Look, you got to sober up. Two of the four bands have already performed. Angie?"

"What?" she said, annoyed. "I'm potentially drunk, not deaf."

"You're potentially drunk *and* high on the most important night for all of us," Zeke said. "Girl, what were you thinking?"

"I was so nervous and . . . it wasn't me," Angie said. "It wasn't . . ."

Zeke grabbed the carrot from Angie's hand and piled it on a small plate with some gourmet tortilla chips, salsa, and chunks of cheese.

"Sit here," Zeke said, pulling Angie to a chair. "Eat this. I'll be back."

"That was very . . . Terminator of you," Angie said before poorly impersonating Arnold Schwarzenegger's infamous line. "I'll be back."

The three possible Zekes shook their heads as they walked away, a trail of movement following behind each of them.

Angie ate slowly, methodically. Chewing exactly eleven

times between bites. Just as Sharon had at the Chinese buffet. Angie's jaw soon got tired. She set the plate on the floor, under the chair, almost falling forward as she did. She adjusted herself upright. This time determined to make her way to the stage.

She could do this.

She could make this happen.

She was Fat Angie, after all.

The warehouse—everything in it was spinning left to right. She tried to steady her staggering walk. Clutching to the backs of chairs as she tried to walk around people. She had never felt anything like this. It was a woozy, Tilt-A-Whirl carnival ride minus the carnival.

Angie teetered up the stage steps.

She fell forward into Finster.

"Whoa. You okay?" Finster asked, holding Angie up.

"Oh yeah," Angie said. "I'm good. Ready to rock the roll."

Finster steadied Angie as Jamboree stepped from around the drum set.

Jamboree gradually came into focus for Angie, who immediately said, "Wow . . ."

Angie's eyes traversed the trail of red stripes streaking along the legs of Jamboree's tuxedo pants. Continuing up, Angie advanced to Jamboree's feminine shirt and masculine tie. A kaleidoscope of sequins glistened along the collar and possibly in Jamboree's eyes.

"You look so . . ." Angie reached for Jamboree's hair. "Your hair is *so* soft. Is that . . . like, the conditioner? I always wanted to ask. There are so many things I want to ask . . . say—"

"Are you drunk?" Jamboree said, Chloe approaching.

"That is a common question tonight," Angie said, considering it with sincerity. "Um, maybe? I don't know. I've never been drunk. I've seen my mother drunk. Like *a lot* drunk. Queen Blotto. But I don't know, um, how it feels. Just . . . how it looks. And since I can't see myself yeah I don't know maybe."

Jamboree was not amused. Neither were Finster or Chloe. Especially, Chloe.

"Look, don't worry," Angie said to all of them. "I. Am. So . . . relaxed. All my nerves are just . . . poof."

Angie laughed.

"Shit," Finster said.

Wang stepped into the unhappy huddle. "Yo, what's going on?"

"Ask Drunkapalooza," said Chloe.

Wang leaned into Angie. "Are you blotto?"

"Do I look like Mom?" Angie said sincerely.

"Yeah," he said.

She overly shrugged. "I guess so."

Angie chuckled for four, as no one else seemed to think anything was funny.

"I . . . need something," Angie said.

"What?" Chloe said. "A Breathalyzer? An AA meeting?"

"Chloe," Finster said.

"What? Why are you all acting like this isn't a big deal? It is *totally* a big deal. She's going to ruin it."

"I was thinking water maybe," Angie said. "To flush it all out faster."

"It doesn't work that way, Ang," Wang said.

"I'm in seventh grade, and I know that," said Chloe. "You're so selfish. I should've joined the Chess Club. No one shows up drunk to Chess Club."

Chloe walked away.

"Chloe, I got this," Angie said. "It is body bagged."

Wang shook his head.

"What?" Angie said to him. "You say stupid stuff like that all the time."

"Yeah, because I'm stupid," he said. "You're not."

"Hey." Lucas leaned between Wang and Finster. "Ready?"

The frustration was clearly palpable, but Angie wasn't going to succumb to the band's worry.

"We're ready," Angie said.

"Just do what you know. It will be great," Lucas said, before walking to the DJ booth.

Jamboree pulled Angie to the side.

"Look, I'm fine," Angie said.

"You are not fine. You are not you."

"Yes, I am," Angie said defensively, tugging at her skirt. "This is me."

"This is you?" Jamboree said.

"At least I'm not ashamed of who I am," Angie said. "I didn't date a bunch of loser guys to play straight."

Ouch.

Unbelievable ouch as Jamboree stood wounded and without comment for the next five to eleven seconds. Time was feeling fairly fluid to Angie right then and difficult to track.

"Wow," Jamboree said. "I'm going to pretend that's Drunk Angie and not Angie Angie."

"It's Fat Angie," she said. "Four million views and climbing. I'm not the same joke-nobody anymore."

"Okay," Jamboree said, backing up. "Just so you know. You were never a joke-nobody. Not until now."

Jamboree left Angie standing there dazed, confused, and not entirely sure why she had lashed out. Angie tried to shake it off, noticing Finster staring at her. Well, a few Finsters.

"What?" Angie said to her/them . . . the Finsters.

Finster shrugged and plugged in her bass. "Nothing."

"This is *so* unprofessional," Chloe said, kicking on her effects pedals.

Lucas grabbed the microphone and turned to the crowd. The band cleared the stage. Finster stood between Angie and Jamboree.

"Once again, thank you all for celebrating Plymouth's birthday slash Bands on the Rise event," said Lucas. "As

I've said, it's an honor to host Plymouth and all of you here at the future yet-to-be named large-scale concert stage, rehearsal space, and recording studio."

Angie was distracted by a smudge on her shirt. Regardless of how much she rubbed it, it refused to fade.

"Angie," Finster said. "You okay?"

"I'm one hundred"—she adjusted her skirt—"and ninety-nine."

"Go Feral!" shouted Lucas.

Clapping rose as the band stepped onto the stage. The warehouse lights lowered. The stage lights breathed on. Angie clung to the microphone. She looked out into the audience. The crowd shifted—it swayed. It could have been a thousand people or a few hundred. It was impossible for Angie to know. She took a deep breath, nodded toward Chloe.

Chloe walked to the edge of the stage. The heels of her shoes drummed a tempo as she did. Then—she exploded with a grungy, gritty guitar solo. Finster and Jamboree followed. Angie banged her head out of time with the beat, missing her entrance. She whipped the microphone off the stand and rushed to catch up. That's when the Tilt-A-Whirl in her head transitioned into a jackhammer effect. She shut her eyes, focusing on the lyrics and not the room gyrating up and down. Her whole body felt lighter than it had ever been. Like she could almost float off the stage.

She opened her eyes, hoping to shake off the seismic

jittery ricochet of lights and people. It wasn't working. Her balance went loose. She dropped to her knees along the edge of the stage, singing to the crowd, sweat running down her armpits. Then she fell backward onto the stage. Somehow she still managed to sing, only she wasn't entirely sure what song she was singing. There were words and whirling and flashes of light and Finster standing over her—spinning out of Angie's orbit because that's when it happened. As things did when it often seemed it could get no worse. A heartbeat pulsed in Angie's stomach. Its driving beat thrust into her throat. Sweet goddess of the Ohio River, Angie was going to—she lurched forward and threw up onstage. Puréed baby carrots, salsa, tortillas chips, and whatever else had been inside her had projectiled its way out.

The band stopped playing, relenting to an echo of "Ewwwwww . . ."

When she could heave no more, Angie tottered to her feet; microphone still in hand. Lucas rushed toward her as she careened into the drum set. The banging of the bass drum—the crash of cymbals—was followed by an audible gasp from the crowd.

Angie looked up at Jamboree.

Jamboree looked down at Angie.

The DJ quickly resumed his electronica playlist. Jamboree walked away.

Lucas and Wang lifted Angie out of the drum set; her legs buckled.

"This wasn't me," Angie said to Lucas. "This wasn't . . . me."

"I know," Lucas said.

The world was a blur. It was a hazy, confusing, falling down, getting up, falling-down-again place of utter destruction that Angie just wanted to pretend wasn't real right then. But it was.

And there was absolutely nowhere to hide from it. It could get no worse.

Chapter 22

From behind a pair of sunglasses, Angie stared at a professional set of film lights cluttering her living room. Her head throbbed—pounded—her stomach sore from vomiting twice when she had gotten home from the party. All of that seemed to pale in comparison to what lay in front of her.

Behind a trio of chairs, perched on the fireplace mantel was the dented and mauled urn that had once held Angie's sister's ashes. The ashes that Angie had, without her mother's permission, poured into the Ohio River. The urn that had all but vanished since its return from Angie's road trip. Its unexpected resurrection truly felt like a bad omen.

Omen (n): An occurrence believed to foreshadow a future event. A good omen might be a twelve-game winning streak. A bad omen might be black butterflies and ravens descending on a wedding reception.

Angie had become acutely keen to the way of bad omens. Her life often felt like one long walk under a ladder. And after blowing the gig the night before and having a hangover the size of Texas, she wanted to be anywhere but in front of a set of cameras and lights with Lucy the Interviewer asking her fake questions about a real loss. Especially with said bad-omen urn lurking behind them, knowing it was empty but full of the many things Connie could not forgive about her.

Connie adjusted Wang's tie. "It is one hour, Wang. You can do one hour."

Wang stared at Angie. Angie, who had officially joined the ranks of Club Hungover. Sunglasses covered her exhausted eyes, her boot laces untied, her dress so ill-fitting. This was a girl regretting the night before and what lay ahead.

"Change your shoes," Connie said to Angie.

Angie reached for a bottle of water from the craft services table. "The camera can't see my feet."

Wang grabbed a bag of Fritos. "We need to talk," he said to Angie.

"Later."

"So that's it?" he said. "You're just gonna—"

"Later, okay?"

Annoyed, Wang walked into the living room, stepping through the tableau of light stands and cables and fake plants before slouching on the sofa, dress shoes on the coffee table.

Angie watched Connie check her makeup in the downstairs half bathroom, making every effort to perfect the face of grief, sorrow, and the American mother. Connie caught Angie's reflection in the mirror.

"What?" Connie asked.

"You look fine," Angie said.

It was a surprise compliment from Angie. Even to her, but it was exactly what she was thinking.

"I look tired," Connie said.

"You are tired," Angie said.

Connie flicked the light off. "Take off the sunglasses."

Angie sighed. She just needed this to be over . . . fast! She followed her mother into the living room.

"Feet off the furniture, please," Connie said to Wang.

Wang literally suspended his feet inches above the coffee table. Without question, he planned to defy her at every turn for making him do the interview.

Connie walked over to him. Angie eavesdropped on the whisper-threat of behave-or-lose-your-Jeep. Wang's feet hit the floor as he got up and followed his mom to the chairs the film crew had arranged for them.

Connie was asked to sit between Wang and Angie.

Immediately, she struggled to get comfortable. She asked both of them to scoot their chairs over.

"Um, they can't," said the camera guy. "We have the seats set for the shot."

"Oh," Connie said. "Sorry."

Angie and Wang scooted back. A noticeable discomfort emerged from Connie as she flashed a phony smile toward the lens.

Wang's tie, purposely crooked, was noticed by an intern, who promptly fixed it as someone else stepped in to mic each of them up.

"As we talked about, Connie," said Lucy the Interviewer, "this documentary is part of the extended look at your daughter's life. We'll release it online in conjunction with the feature film. Give our audience a look inside the real story of Natalie's family and hometown. The people who knew her best."

Connie nodded, smoothing out her blouse.

"Are you interviewing Mrs. Randall?" Angie asked.

"Who?" said Lucy the Interviewer.

"Mrs. Randall," Angie continued. "She was Nat's junior-high basketball coach, but she started working with—"

"Mrs. Randall isn't part of the story." Connie dismissed the interruption with a smile.

"What do you mean?" Angie said. "She started coaching Nat when she was six. She went to all of Nat's games."

Connie leaned in to Angie. "We'll talk about it later."

Angie's jaw clenched. It wasn't a we'll-talk-about-it-later lean in. It was a be-quiet one, and it pissed Angie off.

The camera began recording. The interviewer shifted in her seat, unfurling her fake smile. Angie looked at Connie, who was also performing for the cameras. It was a sickening scene of fakeness. From the lights to the camera to the fake plants all creating a fake scene of what felt like a fake family. The urn, watching all of them, from the mantel.

"Connie, Wang, Angie. Thank you for opening your home and hearts to us," said Lucy the Interviewer. "I think there are a lot of questions on people's minds as the anniversary of Natalie's funeral is approaching. Can each of you tell me what it has been like for you as a family this last year?"

Wang was starting to speak when Connie reached for his hand. "It's been the most difficult challenge we have faced," she said. "First with her missing and with the public way she had to sacrifice herself for our nation's freedoms. But with the support of our community, our family, and God, we're able to . . ."

God? Did Connie just say the G-O-D/Lord Savior/man/woman/they-them supreme? The same supreme being she cursed on the regular for taking her daughter—the good one—leaving her in the most dire of emotional straits? The same God who was the King supreme of the church she had said was an "institution only in it for the collection plate"? Was this the God Connie was referencing? Because if so, Angie and Wang seemed collectively confused.

Wang withdrew his hand from his mother's.

"Wang," said the interviewer. "What has it been like for you?"

He looked to his mother. One slipup, and he could forget his Jeep keys for the rest of the year.

"It's been hard," he said, looking away.

That was it? A mammoth level of grief and anger and heartache, and he'd cowered to Connie with a three-word reply. Not even a genuine one.

"Connie, can you tell me about getting the call from the president? The urn he had custom-made for your daughter's ashes."

"What?" Wang said.

Connie forced a smile, nodding. "We were all surprised."

That was an understatement, given that Wang and Angie had just found out.

"What was your reaction, Angie?" asked the interviewer.

"She's not in the urn," Angie said.

Connie glared.

"Well, she isn't."

"The urn is a symbol for us," Connie said. "A metaphor of how we honor her. Keep her service and her memory close."

"But it's empty," Angie said, under her breath.

"I couldn't hear her," said the sound guy. "Sorry, Lucy, I didn't mean to interrupt. Just wanted to let you know."

Connie leaned in to Angie. "Stop."

"Angie," said the interviewer. "You and your sister were close."

"Yes."

"Tell me about that."

Angie waited for her mother to interrupt. She didn't.

"She was kind of the best," Angie said. "Not just because of basketball or the school clubs. All the community service. I mean those things were important to her. But . . . the thing that made her the best kind of person was how she'd see you." Angie paused, remembering. "It didn't matter if you were her friend or someone she just met, she had this way of making you feel like you were the only one in the whole world that mattered right then."

Angie smiled.

"She was a prankster," Angie continued. "Huge prankster. She loved singing in the car even though she was pretty bad."

"She wasn't that bad," Connie softly corrected.

"She was scared sometimes," Angie said. "Scared of the world. Of who—how to be in it."

"Well," Connie said. "We're all scared of the world when we're eighteen and embarking on something new."

The interviewer waited for Angie to continue.

"You want to know what Natalie was?" Angie said. "She was a light in a sometimes really dimly lit world. And I miss her every day."

"You really loved her," the interviewer said. "What a loss. A war hero, a hometown hero. She's been hailed America's fallen angel by many. Angie, I was hoping you could take us back. To that fall afternoon in the gymnasium. When it was falsely reported that your sister's body had been found."

"I'm sorry, what?" Connie said. "Why is that relevant?"

"Our producers felt it was important to address Angie's attempted suicide," said the interviewer. "For other young people who may identify with Angie's experience."

"It was a difficult time for all of us," Connie said. "Having to never know if or when Natalie was coming home. Angie's experience—her reaction—came from a place of depression and—"

Connie was attempting to sterilize Angie's very personal experience into a digestible sound bite. There was nothing digestible or sound-bite-y about attempting suicide. It was extreme and desperate and filled with so many things said and unsaid. It was loud, up close, and distant. And most of all, it didn't belong to Connie.

"That's not true," Angie said to Connie. "That's not what happened."

Connie smiled for the sake of the cameras.

"We are still coming to terms with . . ." her mother said.

Angie was tired of people putting things in her mouth.

Her father at the buffet. Her mother, erasing her experience.

". . . And as we do—" Connie said.

"Don't take my suicide attempt and covertly couch it into something you think people want to hear."

Wang's jaw dropped.

"Excuse us," Connie said, pulling Angie up by the elbow and into the hallway.

"Mom," Angie said. "I'm sorry, it's just—"

"I want you to stop it."

"Mom—"

"Stop trying to ruin this."

"*This* is a documentary," Angie said. "It's supposed to be the truth. About her—about us."

"And you think you know what that is?" Connie said. "The truth outside of your myopic, attention-needing point of view?"

"I think I don't need you to spoon-feed me my answers," Angie said.

"Excuse me?"

"Why can't you just—Natalie was literally dismembered," Angie said.

"Okay, enough."

"Beheaded. Crushed into pieces—they didn't even find all of them."

"Go to your room. You don't deserve to be a part of this."

Connie started back toward the living room.

"Neither do you," Angie said.

Whether it was the deranged effects of Angie's first and decidedly last hangover or her own resolve, she had just challenged her mother in a way she never had before.

Connie turned on her heels and walked back to her daughter. Angie flinched.

"You are grounded," Connie said. "Now go to your room."

Angie stomped up the staircase and slammed her bedroom door.

This day? It just needed to end.

The day would not end. At least, not with Angie's bedroom door still on the hinges. John/Rick had popped the pins out and had the door off before dinner. Privacy was clearly a thing of the past. What did it matter? The gig had been ruined. The band was ignoring Angie's texts. And the only one who wanted to talk to her was KC. KC was the last person Angie wanted to talk to then, if ever again.

It was a moment worthy of big tears if Angie had had any to shed in her pillow. She simply could not manifest them. It was too hard.

Dinner consisted of a note on the counter from Connie.

Gone out. Check freezer.

Angie grabbed a pint of Ben and Jerry's hidden behind the frozen vegetables and low-calorie dinners. As she headed back to her room, she noticed the urn still on the mantel.

The urn, the symbol, the metaphor. The thing between her and her mom. It was a problem Angie didn't know how to fix. A solution she couldn't solve. Mathematically, there seemed no formula to change the outcome. Too many variables. Too many—

The front door slammed shut.

Angie looked at Wang, tossing his keys into the entryway dish.

"Figured you'd still be sleeping off your foray into stupid," he said.

Angie shook her head, heading upstairs.

"You GOT DRUNK!" he said. "You blew the gig. That's not your MO."

"I'm sorry I encroached on your position as family bad seed," she said.

"Uh-uh. You don't get to do that. You don't get to make this shit like it's my fault. The band—everyone came together because you wanted this."

"Are you really calling me out? If you're not baked, you're throwing back beers with Criminal Cody or your former trio of wannabe bad asses. You screw up every night and get a Get Out of Jail Free card. I do it one time, and I need to be like, what? On the cross? At least I wanted something—tried to do something besides riding my sister's coattails."

And it was then that Angie wounded Wang in way she could not have foreseen, his seemingly directionless life spotlighted in a way that felt tender and raw and deliberate. He seemed to shrink, grow smaller in front of her. Only to then—

"Yeah, okay." He swiped his keys from the dish and left.

Angie squeezed the slightly softer pint of ice cream. She sat on the stairs, popped off the lid, and began to eat. One spoonful after another after another after another, and when there were no more spoonfuls to eat, she stared at the empty bottom of the container. Feeling sick and sad, she wanted to disappear inside it. Only there was nowhere to hide.

Chapter 23

Sunglasses on, Angie dragged through the minefield of the Monday-morning/first-day-of-spirit-week halls of William Anders High. Her Saturday night onstage lushcapade played in a continuous loop in her mind and possibly on her classmates' phones.

She traipsed through the throngs of students decked out in their favorite pajamas, all of them celebrating the over-the-top explosion that was homecoming week in Dryfalls. Hallways were decorated in television-show themes, lunchtime activities scheduled in the quad, and of course, music playing through the intercom between classes. It was a convection oven of cheer and joy, and Angie . . . felt none of it.

Her life, she had decided, could get no worse.

"Hey, Fat Angie," said Courtney, her gaggle of gossip girls a half step behind.

It could get worse.

"I was thinking you could sing at my uncle's funeral this weekend. Seeing how *dead* your performance was Saturday."

Wisdom would dictate that Angie ignore Courtney and simply walk away because Courtney was clearly baiting her. Angie wasn't feeling particularly wise as she stepped into Courtney's face and shouted, "Fuck you!"

The flock fell silent. Their newly self-appointed queen bee had been called out! And with the f-bomb no less, which was not a word actively in rotation for Angie.

"Screw you, psycho," Courtney said, stepping back uncomfortably.

Angie pushed through the jagged slit along clear, plastic draping, stepping into the sophomore hallway of *The Walking Dead* fandom. Red handprints in water-based paint, per the homecoming decoration regulations, stretched from the floor to locker doors. Life-size character cutouts lurked beneath split black garbage bags along the walls. Caution tape tethered to chicken wire fenced in an army of the undead.

Angie was almost to her locker when she saw KC through the maze of morbidity. With a couple dressed as a shark and a panda standing between them and all the strangeness of what had been said, it was all just too much to deal with, so Angie headed to first period.

All morning, Angie sank into one desk after another, praying for the day to somehow end before lunch.

The day did not end before lunch, which now included the documentary crew filming, so Angie skirted the homecoming celebrations in the quad and retreated into the gym. She hunched over her phone, sending her fifth likely-to-be-unanswered text to Jamboree. The other seven to Finster and Zeke had also gone with no response.

Angie's world felt very much over, prompting her to eat like the asteroid was coming, as evidenced by her three double-cheeseburger wrappers, two paper boats of fries, a Twix bar, and one Diet Sprite.

She hadn't been particularly hungry.

Angie looked down at the blank page of her therapeutic journal, glaring its stark whiteness back at her. She had been looking at it for approximately two and one-half minutes. It felt much longer. Everything did.

"Write the first thing that comes to mind," her therapist had told her.

"Things don't always come . . . to mind. What am I supposed to do? Just make stuff up?"

"Write whatever you're feeling or not feeling."

"I don't know how to do that," Angie had said.

"Then write that. Write what you don't know how to do."

Angie reluctantly pressed her ballpoint pen tip to the page.

The age of my mind
Confined in the moment you said good-bye

I realize that's not the end
But this is where I go . . . begin
When the noise of the world gets so loud
The crowd crowding around
The chanting of jersey numbers and high-score lovers
I want to be a version of me that isn't you
A light without a shadow
This moment can't be random
I clamor—get loud and demanding
Everything I've been told
"You don't know what's best
Wait until you're old—er"
I'm old enough to know what death is
To fall off the edge
To wish for forgiveness
How old do I have to be
To finally be a star in a sky full of dreams

"Angie?" Coach Laden said, emerging from the locker room.

"Hey, Coach," Angie said, closing her journal.

Coach Laden climbed the bleachers. "Hiding from your life?"

"You have no idea." Angie's strained smile quickly disappeared.

"The film crew was in here this morning," Coach said. "Your mom too."

Angie didn't say anything.

"She showed me a video of the actress who's going to play your sister. She . . ."

"Doesn't look like my sister at all?"

"Yeah. Excellent ball player." Coach Laden laughed to herself. "She's just not . . . the embodiment of her."

Angie nodded.

"Maybe after some rehearsal," Coach Laden said.

"The weird part," Angie said, "is when everyone sees that movie, they're going to think that's her. The way she talked, walked . . . laughed. Maybe she will be like her, but she'll never be her."

"No," said Coach Laden.

"And that love story in the script," Angie said. "It's so stupid. It's like *Twilight* for war heroes. I wish her fiancé was in it instead."

"Fiancé?"

Angie sighed. "Yeah. She was engaged."

"Wow . . ."

"Weird, huh?" Angie said. "If she hadn't been taken, she'd be married right now. He's really nice. He came to the dedication ceremony."

"What did your mom think of him?" Coach asked.

"She doesn't know. My mom doesn't know a lot of things when it comes to Nat or . . . me . . . Wang. And if she does, she just . . . revises them to fit in some kind of story that isn't about us at all."

Angie stared at her boots, feeling the weight of everything really sink in.

"As much as I hate the movie and the book deal," Angie said, "I thought the documentary thing might be . . . some kind of real? We were sitting there yesterday. All these lights and cameras and microphones—pointing at us. It just wasn't . . . real."

"Is that why you're lunching alone in here?" Coach asked. "Avoiding the film crew?"

Angie shook her head. "I screwed up. I screwed up really bad this weekend. And I don't know how to fix it . . . if I can fix it."

"Most things are fixable," Coach Laden said.

"I don't know," Angie said. "I'm in this band. Go Feral."

Coach Laden smiled.

"And we're good. Practicing *all* the time. Writing songs and laughing and listening and—even Lucas Waite was helping us. And Saturday we had this performance, so we could film ourselves for a competition." Angie shook her head. "And I blew it. Like, really blew it. Now we don't have any footage. And none of them are talking to me. Which I get. It's just . . . when I was in here and you asked me what I wanted, for the first time I knew. Like really knew. I wanted to be heard. My whole life someone has always been speaking over me or telling me what to say. But music? Singing? That's not about being in anyone's shadow. It's about just being me. Anyway. It doesn't matter. I'm grounded until

I'm eighteen, and no one is talking to me."

Coach Laden sighed. The two of them sat quietly, and then out of nowhere, Coach said, "My older sister plays the oboe."

"What?" Angie said.

"Oboe. It's a musical instrument."

"Yeah, but . . ."

"She's really good. She plays professionally. When we were kids, I wanted to play the oboe because my mother loved the oboe. It was her favorite instrument. See, everyone in my family is a musician. Singers, songwriters, percussionists, violinists, guitar players, accordion. If it's musical, they can do it. Except for me. I can't sing a note—or play an instrument. My mom used to joke that I was 'musically dyslexic.' It used to make me feel very alone. Unseen. Then one day I'm at my grandmother's, and I pick up a basketball. And that was my music. That was where I belonged."

"Are you telling me to play basketball?"

"I'm telling you not to give up," Coach said. "If music is what makes you be heard, then do that. You're not someone who quits. You're someone who endures."

Angie considered the sage advice from Coach Laden.

"Talk to your bandmates," Coach Laden said. "Admit whatever got in your way, and promise them and yourself that you won't do it again. And don't break that promise."

"I'm never doing what I did again," Angie said, the memory of hurling closer than she would prefer.

"Do you still have time? To get together and record your video for this competition?"

"I mean, yeah, assuming they'll talk to me," Angie said. "And even then, we have to record it at a legitimate gig. Something people attend and pay for."

"How many songs do you have to perform?" Coach Laden asked.

"Two," Angie said, sighing.

"Play homecoming."

Angie laughed. "Right."

Coach Laden seemed to be serious.

"I'm serious," she said.

She was, in fact, serious.

"I'm the senior advisor and faculty chair for the homecoming dance."

"You're serious-serious," Angie said.

"I can give you two songs," said Coach Laden, standing up. "Can give you three if you need it."

Coach Laden had literally thrown Angie and Go Feral a bone, a second chance—whatever the phrasing was, it was an opportunity to still submit their music.

"Let me know by tomorrow morning," Coach Laden said. "That way I have time to coordinate a few things."

"Yeah," Angie said. "Definitely."

Coach Laden started down the bleacher stairs.

"Coach," Angie said.

Coach Laden turned.

"Thanks," Angie said.

Coach Laden smiled and continued down the bleachers, across the court, and into her office.

Angie reached for her phone, dropping a group text. Asking the band to meet her at Lucas's at seven thirty p.m. Begging them for one last chance to explain. And offering free pizza because who didn't want to eat pizza as Angie groveled?

Angie shouldered her backpack and mimed opening her nonexistent bedroom door before she went downstairs. Connie's dinner-and-drinks evening with the filmmakers and John/Rick was the opportunity Angie needed to sneak out and meet the band.

She quickly locked the front door and was at the end of her driveway when Jake's car pulled up across the street. He got out, slinging his backpack over his shoulder. The two of them stood in silence. Then . . .

"Hey," she said.

He nodded.

"I'm on my way to meet the band," Angie said, walking toward him. "At least, I hope they're meeting me."

Jake looked away.

"I'm sorry," Angie said. "About fighting you . . . about KC. I still think you're not entirely fair about her. What she meant to me, but you were kind of right. I do get lost."

"You know, I never feel like I can trust what's going on

with us," he said. "Like what's going to set you off. First you're mad at me for dating Stacy Ann, which I can understand. But then I call out KC for what she is, what she's done, and you're mad at me for that."

"I got mad at you for not trusting me to make my own decisions—my own mistakes, Jake."

"You mean like getting plastered—pissing off the people who really care about you?"

Quiet.

"You're my best friend, Angie, and I miss you when you go silent. When you . . . push me away. But I'm kind of over it. Because it . . . it hurts."

Angie sighed.

"Sometimes," Angie said, "it's like I've got a hundred emotions about three things at the exact same time. And I always feel like I'm fighting against what happened in the gym that day. The way that one moment limits me . . . to you. Jamboree. My dad . . . my mom. I'm more than a moment."

"I know that," Jake said. "But truth? Do I ever get scared—it could happen again? Yeah because I watched you after KC left. How dark you got. How hurt and hopeless."

"But I didn't try to hurt myself," Angie said. "And at some point, you have to trust I'm not going to. That I can say when I'm in trouble."

Quiet.

"But you're right," she said. "About me not really being,

um, a good friend. About . . . pushing you away. And I'm sorry."

Jake rubbed the back of his head. "Me too."

"Friends?" Angie said.

He grinned, putting his arms around her.

"Always," he said.

"You really need to shower after practice," she said.

He let her go.

"I gotta go," she said. "Picking up a pizza bribe on the way there."

"Want a ride? I downloaded that new group you like. Imagine Dragons."

"The whole album is out?"

"Yeah," he said. "I knew you'd nerd out on it."

As Angie got into Jake's car, she decided good things were coming. There was just too much upward momentum.

Chapter 24

Angie stood with two extra-large pizzas, one with meat, one without, realizing that Lucas was the only one at the warehouse.

"Maybe they just need some time," he said, taking the pizza from her.

"They're never late," Angie said. "It's Chloe's mission to torment me about being on time."

"You can't blame 'em," he said.

Angie sat on the sofa. "I know. I just . . . I've never done anything like that before. Drink. And . . . I'm definitely never doing it again."

"Maybe wait until you're of age," he said. "Focus on moderation."

He handed her a cup of water.

She forced a smile.

"I keep thinking that my sister would never have done that," Angie said. "She'd never blow anything."

"You can't know that," he said. "It's easy for the dead to be perfect. My mom talks about all the ways my dad did everything right. But the thing I remember most about the two of them was their fights. Over money, dreams . . . shit that you just don't think about when you're a kid."

Angie looked up at Lucas's dad's office. Lucas craned his neck to see it.

"Everyone had a theory," Lucas said. "Of why it happened. Of what he did. Was it the failing business? My mom having an affair? She didn't, by the way. Everyone made up some story about the demise of Samuel Waite. The press, the town. Nobody wanted the real story. The story that wasn't about the business or my mom or me. He was just a guy who couldn't get out of his own head. Who couldn't ask for help."

Quiet.

"Do you miss him? Your dad?"

"Yeah," he said. "Of course. All the days. But . . . I tried to use the band as a way to run—erase all the noise. That's not how it works. You gotta deal because it goes wherever you go. You know?"

"About what happened—Saturday," Angie started. "I—"

The warehouse door opened. Angie stood up as Zeke,

Finster, and Chloe trailed in. No Jamboree.

"Hey," Angie said to them. "Thanks for coming and—"

"Finster said there was pizza," Chloe said.

"Yeah," Angie said. "Half-cheese, half-supreme."

"At least you got that right," Chloe said, taking a paper plate from Lucas.

Finster and Zeke collapsed onto the couch.

"Something to drink?" Lucas asked them.

They looked at Angie.

"Um, no." Angie's cheeks flushed with embarrassment at having to confront the stupidity of her brief but consequence-filled foray into underage drinking.

"What happened, Angie?" Finster said.

"Oh, I know what happened," said Chloe. "Drunkapalooza and her ex were—"

"Just let her speak," Finster said.

Chloe sat on a stool, chewing, stewing, and clearly already done with Angie.

"I got . . . scared," Angie said. "Scared I'd mess up. I mean, it's Plymouth, right? And I kept thinking what if I go off pitch or space out? I didn't want to let you down."

"So, getting drunk was . . . ?" Finster asked.

"It wasn't what was supposed to happen," Angie said. "KC—it was a couple of . . . Jell-O shot things."

"You did Jell-O shots?" Chloe said. "I'm in seventh grade, and I know that's stupid."

"Yeah, um, it was," Angie said. "I just wanted . . . to relax. To calm down. And I didn't realize . . . until I did realize that things were . . . out of control."

They all listened. Zeke, of course, filming.

"So, you weren't trying to get drunk?" Finster said. "Party?"

Angie shook her head.

"Why didn't you just talk to us?" Finster said. "Tell us what you were feeling. That's what we're about. All of us. Being real. Not doing that thing we've all done in other bands."

Zeke nodded.

Chloe continued to chew.

"Look," said Finster. "What's done is done. We can't qualify for the competition now, but that doesn't mean we can't be a band."

Chloe put her plate on the coffee table. "Until she freaks out again."

"Chloe," Finster said.

"For real, Fin," Chloe said, looking at Angie. "This competition meant something to all of us, Angie. Yeah, I get you're sorry, but you messed it up for all of us. Not just you."

"There are other competitions," Lucas said.

"Yeah, but this was ours," Chloe said, turning to Angie. "It was mine."

Angie sighed. "You're right. And it still is."

Everyone waited.

"We can play homecoming," Angie said.

"What?" Zeke said.

"Homecoming?" Finster said.

"Sweet!" Chloe said, turning to Finster. "I get to take a date."

"Coach Laden is the faculty chair of the dance," Angie said. "She said we could play. Homecoming fits the rules of the competition for a paid gig, and if Zeke edits fast enough, we can still hit the deadline."

"Yeah, but . . ." Finster said. "It's homecoming. It's kind of a classic heteronormative pop-hits experience in Dryfalls. Not exactly our demographic."

"Music is our demographic," Angie said. "What we can do with it. Look, I'm not going to be afraid . . . to be who I am anymore. I want to play our music. Our way. This is our chance."

Finster looked at Zeke. Zeke looked at Chloe. Chloe, well, she continued to stare at Angie.

"You choked trying to sing in front of those people at The Slice," Chloe said. "How do we know Dr. Jekyll and AA Angie won't show up?"

Angie considered the question.

"Because this is where I belong," Angie said. "And I'd want to play homecoming even if we weren't entering the competition. Because making it isn't about the votes." Angie looked at Lucas. "You start a band because you have something to say. Because you want to do or be something better than who you are without it. Otherwise, why are you doing it?"

Lucas grinned, nodding.

"Angie, that speech," Zeke said. "Epic on camera."

"What?" she said.

"Can you do it again?" Zeke said. "Just take a longer pause when you look at Lucas."

Angie was trying to process how to proceed with Zeke's direction when the door shut behind her. She turned.

Wang strutted in. "What up, Fin? Z, Chloe."

"Hey," Angie said. "I didn't think you'd be here."

He nodded toward Lucas. "Wannabe musical Mr. Miyagi dropped a text. Said you were gonna eat crow. Didn't wanna miss it."

Angie softly smiled. "How much crow do I have to eat?"

"Whole fucking bird."

They laughed.

"I'm sorry," Angie said. "About what I said."

Wang pulled her into a hug. "Yeah. You should be."

"Shut up," she said, holding on to him.

"What are all y'all looking at?" Wang said to everyone else. "Get over here and hug this out. Y'all are lucky I'm managing this band."

One by one, they all huddled together, intertwined in a group hug. Holding on, holding one another up. Only one part missing, and she was the most important part to Angie's heart.

Wang pulled up outside Jamboree's house. Blinking slime-green lights christened the imperfectly trimmed bushes lining the front. An oversized spider climbed along a glowing orange web.

Wang craned his neck past Angie, admiring the scene of tombstones, inflatables, and glowing paper bags with stenciled pumpkin faces.

"Damn, Halloween goals for sure, huh?" he said as Angie got out of the Jeep. "Hey. Want me to wait?"

"No, it's okay," she said.

"Just you know, like . . . be real with your shit."

"What does that even mean?"

He dropped the gear into drive. "It means, maybe tell her how you feel."

Angie considered the possibility of finally say-saying it. She'd considered all day.

"See you at home," he said.

Angie watched as the taillights of Wang's Jeep disappeared into darkness. She had started toward Jamboree's front door when she heard the echo of music. Angie followed the sound, which led her to the side of the house. To the RV.

Angie stood there, watching Jamboree sitting on the bench-to-bed combo, spinning a drumstick in one hand, flipping a textbook page with the other. There she was. There she had always been. And Angie just had to—

"Hey," Angie said, startling Jamboree. "I'm . . . sorry. I didn't mean . . ."

Jamboree put the stick down, committing only to walking as far as the edge of the bed.

Angie jammed her hands into her jeans pocket, clearing her throat. "I, uh, texted you. Eleven times—which in certain circumstances might be considered excessive, but I figured in the current circumstances might qualify as, um, reasonable."

Jamboree didn't seem amused.

"I was worried that maybe," Angie said, "your phone might've fallen through a black hole or down a well. A well without a bucket. Not that I've seen a lot of wells in Dryfalls lately, but, um . . . I guess—"

"I didn't want to talk to you," Jamboree said.

"Yeah," Angie said. "I guess that could have been a possibility too."

Angie was in free fall, scrambling to come up with something—anything that wasn't a combination of ramble-stammer.

"What do you want, Angie?"

She wanted so many things. The list was extending by the second. She wanted Jamboree to play homecoming with Go Feral. She wanted to ask Jamboree to homecoming. She wanted to fix all the ways she'd messed things up between them. Most of all, without question, Angie wanted to profess her heart-aching, gay-girl-gay, utmost love for Jamboree. Because it was, as Angie had surmised, what she truly felt. If only she had a set of index cards memorized for this particular situation. She just needed to—

"So, I . . . um," Angie said. "I owe you an apology. I owe you, um. A lot more than that."

"You hurt me," Jamboree said. "And I know I've hurt you . . . when I disappeared—ghosted you. When I couldn't deal with what I felt . . . for you. But I thought that was over. I thought we were . . . I don't know what I thought."

"No, you—it wasn't you—it was me mostly, and—I just . . . that sounds like every single bad breakup cliché."

Jamboree shrugged. "It doesn't. Because we were never together."

Angie looked helplessly at Jamboree.

"And that's probably for the best," Jamboree said.

There was no way that could ever be for the best. Not for Angie. Not for Jamboree. And . . . definitely not for Go Feral. They'd come together for Angie. She needed to come together for them.

"I get that . . . um," Angie said, "you don't want to talk to me. And I . . . I can respect that. But I got the band a second chance. We can play homecoming."

"Zeke called," Jamboree said. "They told me."

"Oh," Angie said. "What did you . . . um, say?"

Jamboree nodded. "I said I'd play homecoming, so

Finster and Chloe and Zeke could have their shot. Because we're good enough to have that shot, but then I'm done."

"Oh," Angie said.

Quiet.

More awkward truly heart-aching silence.

"I need to get back to my chem homework," Jamboree said.

"Sure," Angie said. "Yeah, that's important. Chemistry and all. I guess. Um, so I'll see you at rehearsal."

"Yeah," Jamboree said.

Jamboree closed the RV door.

Angie headed home, her head dropping. Her chin doubling. Her heart absolutely shattering. But she had made a promise to the band to show up, and she intended to keep it.

Chapter 25

The rehearsals started early. The rehearsals went late. It wasn't just the same two songs over and over. It was talking and listening. It was listening and laughing. It was Zeke, roaming with their Steadicam and asking questions. It was cheeseburgers and salads and tacos and smoothies. It was Lucas and Angie, debating the theory of music or the failure of it. It was Chloe actually having fun, excited about playing homecoming. It was Wang and Lucas, discussing the business of managers, and what it might take to succeed at it.

And it was also all of them together, sometimes standing on the rooftop with one of Lucas's old telescopes. All of them, looking up. Angie stealing glances at Jamboree. Jamboree stealing pieces of Angie's heart when she looked away.

By Thursday night, the band had decided what songs to play for the homecoming dance. Their final run-through ended with Lucas and Wang clapping and whistling. With Zeke, fists in the air, shouting, "Now, that's a revolution!"

It was really happening. They were actually good. Maybe even better than good.

Angie turned to Jamboree, sitting behind the drum set. The distance between them seemed to almost narrow. Angie had started to walk toward her when—

"Hey," Zeke said. "Y'all come check this out."

Everyone huddled around Zeke's laptop, Angie's and Jamboree's arms lightly touching before Jamboree switched places with Finster.

"So, I've been working on the intro video," Zeke said. "This is what it looks like so far."

Zeke hit the space bar and they all watched.

Angie stands on the replica *Heather Runs* stage, with a lone light on her. "I've been bullied."

A series of fast cuts timed with explosive drumbeats shows Angie being knocked down on the basketball court by Stacy Ann. Angie shoved by Gary Klein.

"I've been belittled."

Angie walks through the halls being mocked.

Angie sits alone in the quad.

Angie looks into the camera. "I've been told I have nothing important to say. And then I grabbed a mic."

Clips from the Cincinnati performance pop on the screen. The crowd cheering. The live video pulls back to the online post as the view counter speeds to over two million.

Angie looks into the camera. "I'm Fat Angie, and I sing for the band Go Feral."

The title GO FERAL scrawls across a black screen before being scratched out as a steady set of drumbeats leads into a montage of the band being interviewed and various B-roll.

"Go Feral," Angie says.

"Is a band of outsiders," says Finster.

The band walks in slow motion through downtown Dryfalls. A cool, queer nod to *The Wild Bunch*. An American flag flaps outside a barber shop. Women with yoga mats turn in near unison as the band struts past them.

Jamboree, sitting on the stage, says, "Our music challenges words like—"

Chloe: "Freak."

Finster: "Fat."

Angie: "Flirt."

Jamboree: "Behaved."

Chloe gnashes her teeth at the camera.

Angie marches around the stage while singing.

Finster flashes her flannel button-down open, a homemade FAT & FERAL REVOLUTION T-shirt underneath.

Angie: "Our music isn't just political—"

Chloe: "We're definitely political."

Angie: "Our music is political and unapologetically woman."

Jamboree: "The kind of woman who doesn't have to fit into a boxed version of being polite because—"

Finster: "I'm tired of guy bands where my sound and my ideas were irrelevant. Just play what we tell you. Be . . ."

Chloe: "Tame. Forget that. I'm in seventh grade, and I know that."

Clips from songwriting sessions. The band writing together. Flipping through journals. Plucking strings. Each of them, being heard by the others.

Angie says to the camera: "To know who we are . . . is to know our music."

Finster: "Our voice."

Jamboree: "It's like the history of rock 'n' roll and punk—alternative."

Chloe: "Without rules. Expectations."

Angie: "Feral."

Zeke hit the PLAY bar, stopping the video.

"Well?" Zeke said.

"That is badass, Z," Finster threw Zeke a high five.

"I got a few thoughts," Lucas said, sitting beside Zeke.

Chloe pulled Jamboree to the side, showing her possible outfits for homecoming on her phone.

Finster shook her head. "She's boy-sick."

"I can't relate," Angie said, grinning.

Finster laughed. "Me neither."

"Fin," Wang said, phone pressed to his ear.

"I'll be back," Finster said.

After several deep breaths, Angie awkwardly approached Jamboree.

"Hey, um," she said to Jamboree. "Do you think . . . we could talk for a second?"

Jamboree looked at Chloe. "Text me what you pick."

"That was, um, really great," Angie said, walking with Jamboree. "What, uh, you suggested. About the song. Earlier."

"Thanks." Jamboree slung her purse across her chest.

Chloe's eyes ping-ponged between the two of them while playing her 3DS.

"Yeah, um . . ." Angie said, her confidence waning. "So, uh, I wanted to talk you about . . ."

So many things. About all the mistakes Angie had made. About her immense regret for not simply telling Jamboree the day KC came back what she felt—how scared she felt, and—

"I kind of need to get going," Jamboree said, walking around Angie. "My parents. Dinner."

"Sure . . ." Angie said.

Angie stood there, watching the door close behind Jamboree. She sighed, sitting beside Zeke.

"You could not have possibly done any worse," Zeke said, scrubbing through footage on their computer.

They stopped at the first songwriting rehearsal. It was

Angie and Jamboree, sitting side by side. The two of them, laughing and leaning into each other. Falling hopelessly, madly, and quite completely in—

"Love, right?" Zeke said. "Like that's just . . . pure. Lucas wants me to add it."

Angie lowered her head.

"You know," Zeke said. "Jam and me . . . we push. We pull. That's just us since she got back. That's ours to figure out. I hope. But this." Zeke pointed to the screen. "That's how things are supposed to be."

"She won't talk to me," Angie said.

"You kinda crushed her," Zeke said. "You made her think she was special—"

"She is."

"Special to *you*." Zeke paused. "Girl, you gotta dig deep and finally bury this KC thing. Be like sana, sana, you know? Cleanse that shit out for good."

While not familiar with the sana, sana reference, Angie got the gist of it.

"I gotta take off," Zeke said, closing their laptop. "I'm going over to Raquel's."

"Wait. What?" Angie said.

"I know, right?" Zeke said. "I actually got her to give me/us another chance. Darius is always telling me humility goes a long way, so I gave it a try. And I don't think it hurt that I wrote her something a little melty too. Power of the pen."

Angie shook her head, smiling. "So you're taking the chance."

"I'm taking all of them," Zeke said. "I'm done being mad about this bag. My family. I just need to keep straight in my head that whatever happens next, it's on me. Pues, it's like mi abuela says—"

"In her infinite Mexican wisdom," Angie and Zeke said together.

They smiled.

"A woman is always more than the story people try to write for her," Zeke said. "¿Que no?"

Angie smiled.

"Plus, my abuela is never wrong," Zeke said.

"She's kind of the smartest person ever."

"She kinda is." Zeke headed for the door, throwing Angie a final wave before leaving.

"Hey," Finster said to Angie. "See you tomorrow."

"See you," Angie said, watching Chloe trail behind Finster, playing her 3DS.

Angie stood there, eyes closed, thinking. And it was in this moment that Angie began to hear a sound. It wasn't the sound of Lucas and Wang, talking on the stage. It wasn't the makeshift kitchen faucet dripping into the sink. It was something inside of her. A note that had become a chord. A chord that had become—Angie dug through her backpack, pulling out her therapeutic journal. She flipped through the pages. Then stopped.

“You ready to take off?” Wang said, jumping off the stage.

“Um, you go,” Angie said.

“You sure?” he asked. “Mom’s probably gonna be hella pissed.”

“Yeah. I just need to stay for a little while longer.”

He nodded, walking backward. “Okay, but text when you get to the front door. I’ll come downstairs, so you don’t got to deal with Mom solo.”

When Wang was gone, Angie looked back at her journal. There was something there that she needed—

“Lucas?” Angie said, walking toward the stage.

“Yeah.”

“I need a favor . . .”

It was nearly one a.m. when Angie unlocked the front door, gently clicking it closed. Her phone had died, so she couldn’t drop an SOS to Wang. She managed to make it to the third stair before the living room light turned on. The classic but unexpected cliché of being busted for coming in late on a school night while grounded had just happened. There was no escape. Only surrender. Angie took a deep breath and walked toward the living room.

Connie sat on the sofa, a glass of wine on the coffee table in front of her. The urn standing guard from the mantel. The room was full of bad omens as Angie cautiously sat across from her couldn’t-get-it-together mother.

Silence.

More distinctly uncomfortable silence.

So much unsettling silence that Angie finally said, "Mom, I—"

"Your brother said you were studying for an exam," Connie said, reaching for her glass. "I'm not familiar with midnight study groups when you're grounded."

Connie took a drink of her wine. A substantially large drink. From the slight sway of her body, it was likely not her first glass or possibly bottle of the night.

Connie shook her head. "I try . . . to understand you. As different as you are from me, I try. The way you . . . make a mockery of your sister's memory."

"That's not true—"

"The interview," Connie said, in inebriated lawyer mode. "That performance in front of the cameras?"

"Performance?" Angie said. "I was—I was trying to tell the truth. Mom. Why can't you see that? Why can't you see what she—was? Not that bedroom you've staged. The clothes you've dry-cleaned."

"You are never to be in that room," Connie said, getting up off the couch.

"Mom, please."

Connie walked into the kitchen, and surprisingly, Angie followed.

"Why can't you see?" Angie said. "She was messy and kind of a klepto. Can't she be a hero *and* that? Because she was—"

"I think I know my own daughter," Connie said, throwing two empty wine bottles into the recycling bin.

"Which one?" Angie said.

It was an unexpected comeback that seemed to have caught Connie off guard. A rarity in the art of argumentation for Angie. Then—

Connie laughed to herself. "I'm not going to be baited. You want a reaction. You always want a reaction."

Angie shook her head. Frustrated and angry and—

"Not everything is about your grief, Mom."

"I hope you never know what it's like," Connie said. "To watch a coffin go into the ground—"

"God, it was empty."

"It was a metaphor," Connie said.

"The urn is a metaphor. The casket is a metaphor. Wang and me. We're all metaphors."

There was nowhere for Connie to hide. Not at the bottom of a wineglass. Not in the kitchen with a marble island between her and Angie.

"I'm going to bed," Connie said, turning off the kitchen light.

That simply wasn't good enough.

"When can it just be what it is?" Angie asked, following her mom.

Groggy, Wang stumbled downstairs.

"When is it that she's just gone," Angie said. "And we're here and that's enough to—start over."

"Start over?" Connie said.

Quiet.

"Start over what?" Connie seemed bewildered. "What is there to start over, Angie? You have no respect for me. For this family. For yourself. Look at you. I mean, really look at you."

Wang shook his head. "C'mon," he said, ushering Angie upstairs.

"You are grounded, Angie," Connie said from the bottom of the stairs. "You either come home and stay home, or I will find a solution."

Angie paused at the top of the staircase, looking down at her couldn't-get-it-together mother.

"Just forget it," Wang said.

Connie seemed smaller from that distance to Angie. Not the invincible, high-priced, corporate attorney who eviscerated adversaries and decimated Angie on the regular. The Connie at the bottom of the stairs wasn't invincible. She was frail and fragmented. The way she had been at the half-birthday party.

"C'mon," Wang said. "You can crash in my room."

And so Angie did.

Chapter 26

Wang blazed down the road, exceeding the state-mandated speed limit per Angie's glance at the speedometer.

"Relax," he said, adjusting his tie. "The one thing I'm good at is driving."

Beyoncé's "Single Ladies" burst-clapped through the speakers, bass bouncing, vibrating around them. At the chorus, Angie and Wang synchronized their sways, bumping left, then right, singing at the absolute top of their lungs as they pulled into the parking lot outside the gym. A homecoming banner and tethered blue-and-gold balloons welcomed them.

"This is really happening," Angie said, watching a group of couples stroll into the gym.

He laughed quietly. "Crazy, right?"

"Really, with that word?"

"Look at you," he said. "A year ago . . . everything was like . . . now you're playing homecoming. You get that, right?"

"Mostly," Angie said.

Wang stayed quiet.

"I just keep thinking maybe . . ." Wang said.

He ran his hand along the bottom of the steering wheel.

"What?" Angie asked.

"You think I could be a good person?" he asked.

"Yeah," Angie said. "I think you already are."

He chuckled. "I don't know about that, but it would be pretty cool, huh? Me on the right side of things. Using my 147 IQ for good, not evil. I mean, not Jake good."

"Well, no one is Jake good," Angie said.

"You are," Wang said.

The two of them looked at each other. The moment was genuine in a way few had ever been.

"Thanks," Angie said. "For . . . getting me the clothes. For getting me."

Wang pulled his door handle. "Let's go show 'em what badass looks like."

The two of them walked side by side, dressed in tuxedos, climbed the gymnasium steps, and swept through a shimmering curtain of gold-and-navy streamers. Bass pumping. Throwback dance music stomping the floors, climbing the ceiling. Angie and Wang stepped onto the crowded basketball court, lights spinning. Homecoming was—

"Wow," Angie said softly.

Massive!

Twinkle lights pulsed against sheer fabric draped from the rafters. Metallic stars dangled from near-invisible string. Disco balls hung from each of the basketball rims. There was a glow-in-the-dark moon near the stage. It was an extravaganza in glitter and light and excitement. It had lived up to its Night Under the Stars theme.

Wang was tugging at Angie to follow him toward the stage when something stopped her. Through the hordes of kids dancing, milling near the retracted bleachers, there she was: KC Romance. The girl who had sworn off any and all traditional teen events had broken her own golden rule by showing up to the homecoming dance. And she was a sight to part any and all seas as she wove her way across the dance floor. Her leather jacket sashayed against her perfectly fitted red dress. She was lust in motion—she was ache in transition—and as she narrowed the gap between herself and Angie, it seemed an inevitable reunion was in the making.

"I'll meet you by the stage," Angie said.

"I don't think that's a good idea," Wang said. "And I know this because I'm the master of bad ideas."

"I'm okay," Angie said to Wang, who wasn't convinced. "I promise."

Though she wasn't entirely sure she was.

Reluctantly, Wang stepped along the edge of the crowd as KC made her way toward Angie.

"Hey," KC said. "A burgundy tux looks good on you."

"It was Wang's idea," Angie said. "He seems to be full of good ones lately."

KC nodded.

"I didn't think you'd be here," Angie said.

"Who knew going stag would make three chaperones, including Coach Laden, stop and talk to me about being stag. Besides, I didn't wanna miss this. It's all I've been hearing about all week—Go Feral playing at homecoming. Kind of felt like an in-person soiree."

"It's just a couple of songs," Angie said.

"It's more than that."

Angie considered it. "Yeah. It is."

"Look, um," KC said. "I'm sorry."

"For?" Angie asked.

"Pretty much everything . . . since I got back." KC looked down at her boots. "The way I acted. Not being a hundred percent honest with the whole . . . just being friends thing."

"Hey, Angie," said a girl in passing. "Can't wait."

Angie smiled at the girl, leaving her in the uncomfortable moment of standing with her troubled, beautiful, complicated ex-girlfriend.

"I don't know," KC said, "how so much changed so fast."

"Maybe it wasn't all that fast," Angie said.

"Maybe," KC said. "Someday, who knows, right? Maybe we'll, like, really be friends. I don't know when, because just saying that . . . hurts so much."

And there was KC. The real KC. The one who, when she did put her emotions on the table, reached into Angie. Made her remember why they had fallen in love.

Zeke waved Angie to the stage.

"Look," KC said. "I know you gotta go. I just wanted to say that."

Angie started to walk away but stopped. This wasn't a walk-away moment. This wasn't a take-the-easy-way-out.

"You know," Angie said to KC. "You'll always be the first person I loved."

"That's something, right?" KC said.

"Yeah," Angie said. "It'll always be something. It just can't be everything."

"Yeah . . ." KC said. "I know."

"Bye, KC," Angie said.

"Bye, Angie . . ."

And after an exchange of soft-hurt, mildly sweet smiles, Angie walked away from KC Romance. With each step, her stride became fuller. Her stance became taller. Her heart . . . lighter.

Zeke met her at the stage steps.

"You okay?" Zeke said. "I saw you with . . ."

"I'm good," Angie said.

Zeke nodded. "You look dope and dapper. Once again affirming that clothing has no gender. But . . ." Zeke slid a cerulean-blue rose out of their pocket. Pinned it to Angie's jacket lapel. "Now perfection."

Angie smiled. "Definitely."

That's when Angie noticed them. The film crew setting up along the edge of the gym floor. Zeke's eyes tracked Angie's direction.

"Damn, they got nice gear," Zeke said, turning back to Angie. "Did you know they'd be here?"

Angie nodded.

"But your mom . . ."

Angie shrugged. "Not everything's about her. Tonight's about us. All of us."

Zeke half grinned, putting their hand on Angie's shoulder. "I got your back, girl. You know that, right?"

"Yeah. I know."

They cut behind the closed stage curtain. Angie saw Jamboree talking with Finster.

"So, Raquel and I have two cameras ready, and I'll roam with a third on Steadicam," Zeke said, noticing Angie was less listening to them and more watching Jamboree. "You talk to her?"

Angie shook her head.

"Girl, whose story is this?" Zeke said. "Pues, it's yours. Don't let fear write it for you."

Angie nodded.

"Zeke," Wang called from the side of the stage.

"I'll be right back," Zeke said.

Angie straightened her tuxedo shirt and walked toward Jamboree, en route to her drum set.

"You look . . ." Angie said to Jamboree. "Speechless. I mean, you make people speechless. Um. Cool pants."

Cool pants?

"Thanks," Jamboree said. "It's kind of uncomfortable for me to drum in a skirt."

"Sure," Angie said. "I mean . . . that makes sense."

Quiet.

Loud awkward quiet.

"So," Angie said. "I really wanted to say . . ."

The hurt on Jamboree was tangible.

"There's nothing to say," Jamboree said, picking an envelope up off a drum. "Just . . . be you. Tonight."

"Yeah," Angie said, nodding. "You too—I mean, good luck or don't break a drumstick or drumhead or . . . um, yeah. You know."

Angie turned away from Jamboree, her mind spinning with all the things she needed—wanted—to say.

Lucas walked across the stage. "You ready?"

A thought occurred to Angie. "Almost."

She reached into her jacket pocket and pulled out the birthday hat she'd worn onstage in Cincinnati. She fixed it onto her head, the string bulging against her chin.

Zeke approached Lucas and Angie.

"Not the hat," Zeke said. "Please not the hat."

"You know," Angie said. "It contains me."

Lucas grinned.

"Ay," Zeke said, leaving the stage. "It's not good on camera, you know."

"Just do what you know," Lucas said to Angie. "No matter what."

"No matter what."

The curtains were drawn open. The band gathered off-stage. Chloe scooted next to Angie, wearing a skinny black tuxedo that made her more badass than usual.

"Hey," Chloe said. "Don't mess up."

"Thanks," Angie said.

"I'm not going to mess up," Chloe said.

"I know."

Jamboree stood beside Chloe. Finster leaned in, fist-bumping Angie. "Revolution ready."

Angie took a deep breath.

"It's my revolution," she said quietly to herself as Coach Laden signaled the DJ to stop playing.

"Good evening, William Anders High," said Coach Laden. "I want to thank our amazingly supportive principal, Mr. Warner."

People kind of clapped.

"And the creative homecoming dance committee for making tonight's celebration truly a Night Under the Stars . . ."

Angie looked at Jamboree. Jamboree looked at Angie. Chloe looked up between them.

"Performing original music is Dryfalls' own," Coach Laden announced, "Go Feral!"

There was a mix of clapping and confusion as Angie and the band stepped onto the stage.

A guy shouted, "Whale!" from the back of the gym.

Angie would not cower. She would not cave. She would not be reduced to the ignorance of an insecure boy.

She grabbed the microphone and shouted back, "Where?" pretending to peer through the lights and the crowd. "I'm guessing you weren't referring to what's between your legs."

A noticeable "Oooooo . . ." echoed.

"All right," Coach Laden said. "Enjoy the music without name-calling or you'll be escorted out."

Coach Laden officially handed Angie the microphone and left the stage.

Angie adjusted the microphone, looking out at the hush of hundreds of students. She saw Jake and Stacy Ann near the front. Wang and Lori. KC at the edge of the crowd near the film crew. Angie could do this. She just needed to breathe. She just needed to . . . see Courtney in the middle of the gym floor, mouthing, "Eat shit, fatty."

It was then that Angie grinned and began to sing.

"I . . . Oh, I . . . I . . .

Am more than ready
to be this provocation . . ."

Explosive bass solo, followed by Chloe's electric guitar slide-grind. Jamboree came in and the tempo pumped. It was . . . on fire!

Angie marched around the stage, pacing her crescendo, singing with depth and grit and small vocal runs. The party hat bobbed as she owned the stage with all that was big girl revolution!

She stepped away from the mic during the instrument solo. Finster moved to the edge of the stage, changing up the solo with a little extra Fin jazz-grunge, before returning to the original bass line as Chloe slid in beside her. Jamboree circled the toms several times. Then—

"Wait!
Just wait.
Not gonna concede to a woman's place."

Angie was all go and no stop, climbing on top of a theater platform behind the drum set. The crowd roared.

"Hey!
Who's coming with me?
Revolution or envy?
Don't wait!"

The band stopped playing and . . . there was a sound of—exhilaration.

"Yes!" Zeke shouted from below the stage.

Angie looked at Jamboree, smiling at her. She'd done it. She'd actually, really, done it. She climbed down the platform, throwing a look to Lucas offstage. Then she approached the front of the stage.

"It's homecoming, WAH!" said Angie.

Cheering! Clapping! It was all happening.

Chloe grinned.

"What do we like more than winning and going to state?" Angie asked. "A sexy, loud, teen revolution!"

Everyone cheered!

Chloe marched to the edge of the stage, kicking her cable, launching into a solo for the ages.

Angie gripped the mic. "This is for all the girls out there who are *done* being someone else's special."

Jamboree broke into a pounding percussive rollout with Finster a beat behind. Angie danced around the stage, completely in tempo. Reinventing herself with her own stripped-down fabulous fat-girl momentum. Head banging, body swaying, birthday hat snapping off and flying into the crowd. This was Angie's moment, and she was going to own all of it!

Angie whipped the microphone off the stand, letting loose her big, impressive voice full of ethereal punk rock rage.

"I see you at the edge of the party.
Eyes down.
Chocolate on your lip.
You're a rebel in a wrinkled T-shirt.
Don't give up . . .
Never quit!"

Angie danced around the stage; fist pumping with the beat.

"Daddy brings balloons to your party.
Mommy drinks wine to escape.
You won't be the martyr of this story.
You've got too much life to live
Yeah!

You're a . . .
Special Girl.
Special Girl.
Don't hide that face.
Special Girl.
Special Girl.

Wear your lipstick crooked and your hair out of place."

Finster grinned at Angie. Angie grinned back before turning to the crowd.

"They always like to push you.
The girls in your gym class.
They don't know you're a warrior.
They don't know you're a fucking badass!
Yeah!

Special Girl.
Special Girl.
Don't hide that face.
Special Girl.
Special Girl.
Wear your mascara thick and your hair out of place."

Angie pranced to the edge of the stage.

"Let's show them what special really means.
I wanna hear you scream."

The band screamed!

"I wanna hear you scream!"

She pointed the mic toward the audience. They returned with a raw collective pep rally battle cry.

Angie held her hand to her ear, waiting. They screamed again.

She slipped the mic onto the stand, lowering it as Chloe

approached. But Chloe wasn't there to sing. She was there to drop some Chloe original spoken word:

"Acceptance is an act of resistance.
We will not be commodified.
With magazine makeup tips and tricks
to amplify
Privilege over power
Power over inclusion.
A woman's place is in the revolution
Of equality, justice, and the pursuit of being chingona!"

Finster let out a grito that roared through the gym. Cheering followed as Chloe stepped away, slaying guitar chords as she did. Angie marched back to the mic.

"You are a vision of chaos,
Strength, and ease.
You scare the flock because
You're the real Homecoming Queen yeah!

Special Girl.
Special Girl.
Don't hide your face.
Special Girl.
Special Girl.
Now you know your real place!"

The band sang:

"Special Girl.
Special Girl."

Angie ran her finger down her cheek singing:

"Let your mascara streak."

All together:

"Special Girl.
Special Girl."

Angie jumped in the air.

"You're a beautiful mess.
Ohhhh yeah!"

The band together:

"Special Girl.
Special Girl."

Angie grinned wildly.

"The world is ready for your wrinkled T-shirt."

The band:

"Special Girl."

Angie:

"You're perfect ooo yeah . . . !"

The band:

"Special Girl.
Oh so so special . . ."

Angie sang:

"Wear your hair dyed . . ."

Angie marched to the edge of the stage, stopped, and said:

"I'm nobody's special girl . . .
And neither are you."

The band hit their final majestic chord. The crowd roared! Phones in camera mode pushed forward. This was it. This was that moment. Angie exhaled, laughing to herself, feeling suspended in all of what had just happened.

"You did it!" Finster said, arm over Angie's shoulders.

There was a sound. It wasn't the crowd, chanting a jersey number or a fallen hero's name. It was . . .

"Angie! Angie! Angie!" that the audience chanted.

Well, most of them. And in that most, Angie couldn't believe it. No shadow. Just her and Finster and Chloe and Jamboree, who was already leaving the stage.

"Come on," Finster said. "Let's pack out and go celebrate."

Angie looked at Lucas, standing offstage, then Finster. "I have one more song."

Lucas stepped onto the stage with an acoustic guitar. The crowd went wild!

Confused, Zeke looked at Wang, who was shouting, "Go, Angie!"

Lucas pulled two stools to the center of the stage.

Zeke mouthed "Girl, what?" to Angie.

"Hey everyone," Lucas said, adjusting his microphone.

Girls screamed.

"So," he said, tuning his guitar. "I've been lucky enough to work with this band, with this young woman the last few weeks."

"Go, Angie!" someone shouted.

"And," Lucas continued, "it reminded me what's really great about music. When it comes from a place that really matters. And tonight . . ."

He looked to Angie, who said, "We're going to sing something we wrote. Together."

A wave of clapping trailed off as phones popped up vertical. The anticipation of a Lucas Waite/Fat Angie song was palpable.

Angie looked offstage. Jamboree's back was to her, and she seemed to be showing something to Finster.

Lucas began to play. Not like the front man of Rancid Reign. He played like the musician Angie had grown to know. This was the real Lucas Waite.

Angie took a deep breath and began to sing with an unsettled ache:

"Constellations entertain us
Late night on top of the RV.
The world above dictates
The world inside of you . . . and me."

Jamboree stepped up beside Chloe, actually listening.

Lucas leaned into his mic.

"Everything I've seen seems easy
When it's the hardest thing I've done."

Angie continued:

"How do we make sense of this
When all we know how to do . . ."

They sang together:

"Is run."

A few loose cheers echoed through the gym as Lucas continued to play. He and Angie leaned into their mics and harmonized.

"I've been running . . .
Looking for what's real
In all the things that mean nothing.
Without you here,
Scared and afraid
To find a way home.
To find a way . . . home."

The film crew closed in along the bottom of the stage beside Zeke. Angie raised her mic.

"I regret the things I couldn't say
Every single day."

Lucas:

"Haunted by a memory
That I still can't explain."

Angie echoed:

"Can't . . . explain . . ."

Lucas:

"We tell our story
in good-byes."

Angie:

"No more good-byes . . ."

Lucas:

"We tell our story . . .
We tell our story . . . tonight."

The crowd was captivated by Lucas and Angie singing.

"I've been running . . .
Looking for what's real.
In all the things that mean nothing."

Angie:

"All the things . . ."

Together:

"Without you here.
Scared and afraid,
To find a way home."

Angie:

"Find my way home . . ."

Together:

"But maybe there's a different way
To finally . . .
Belong."

Wang beamed from below the stage, cell phone recording. Jake slipped his arm over Stacy Ann's shoulders. The world as Angie knew it seemed to expand, not contract as she raised her mic.

"I'm sorry that I hurt you . . . ohhhh.
I'm sorry I didn't . . . understand."

Lucas:

"I'm sorry I couldn't listen."

Together:

"Everything inside me
Wants to change."

Angie:

"Everything inside you . . ."

Together:

"Wants to change . . ."

It was then that Angie noticed that KC had all but vanished from the crowd. She took a deep breath. An ease washing over her as she gripped the mic and sang.

"I thought I saw you
Just the other day."

Lucas:

"A ghost from a different time
That I know can't stay."

Angie:

"But if there is a chance
To make things right,
I'd start by saying . . ."

Together:

"I've been running . . .
Looking for what's real
In all the things that mean nothing.
Without you here . . .
Scared and afraid.
To find a way home
To find a way . . . home

But maybe there's a different way
To finally . . ."

Angie:

"Belong . . ."

The guitar faded out as claps rose. Angie smiled at Lucas. Wang sprang up on the stage, hugging his sister.

"That's some doing-the-crane singing shit!" he said to her.

She laughed.

Coach Laden approached the edge of the stage, beaming.

Angie knelt. "Thanks for this."

"You. Are. Exceptional," Coach Laden said. "Never stop."

The DJ rolled out a pop-music hit as the band started to pack out their gear. Angie walked toward Jamboree, waiting at the side of the stage.

"Hey," Jamboree said.

"Hey."

"How long had you planned that?" Jamboree asked.

"Um, it wasn't a plan?" Angie said. "It was . . . a feeling. I have a lot of feelings. My feelings have feelings about my feelings. Which is a really strange thing to say . . . now that I've said it. Um, out loud."

"You really hurt me. Confused me," Jamboree said. "One minute I think maybe you like me. And then I try to be close and you . . ."

"I do—like you. So much like. Um, you."

Jamboree reached into her purse and pulled out a black envelope.

"This was on the drum set tonight," Jamboree said.

She slid out a set of index cards with a blue Post-it stuck to the front.

This is what Angie wanted to say
the morning KC came back.
It's still true. —Jake

"Is it?" Jamboree asked. "True?"

Angie was nervous.

Angie struggled immensely with such on-the-spot situations.

Angie didn't want to be the person who struggled with such on-the-spot situations anymore.

"Yes," Angie said. "It is."

Jamboree looked at the cards. Then at Angie. "Why didn't you just ask me? How could you think I wouldn't have said yes? I told you . . . what I feel—how I've felt for so long."

"I . . ." Angie took a deep breath. "I never asked . . . anyone . . . out." Angie paused, then. "I get that it's normal for you, but for me—"

"Nothing about us is normal for me," Jamboree said. "And yet it is. Wanting to be with you is the most normal thing I've ever felt. I thought you knew that."

"It just got so built up in my head," Angie said. "You know, after we weren't friends for so long, and then we were, and then it was . . . so good. Like, *so* good. I didn't want to mess it up or to lose it. I didn't want to lose you again."

Angie looked down at her boots, trying to be the kind of brave she knew she could be. Feeling the wave of feelings that wanted her to run. But no more running.

"So, it wasn't because of KC?" Jamboree said. "Coming back?"

"Her coming back . . . didn't change what I felt for you," Angie said. "It confused things. I confused things. Because when she left, I was crushed. I guess I was afraid to be crushed. But I'm not afraid of that anymore."

"How do I know you won't change your mind?" Jamboree asked. "Get scared? Confused? Pull away?"

Angie reached for the index cards, staring at the blue Post-it before peeling it off. She began to read.

"I've been thinking a lot." Angie cleared her throat. "And I wanted to talk to you about some of it. If that's okay. Cool. You know, the last few weeks, spending time with you. It's been really—the best kind of happy. I thought about that because I saw this funny commercial the other night about mouth guards. I didn't know they made those kinds of commercials. Anyway, you were the first person I wanted to tell."

Jamboree listened.

"It happens a lot," Angie said. "Things come up, and you're the first person I want to tell. I mean, yes, as a friend, because we're friends. Good friends—great friends. But you know, because, um. Anyway, I know things have been kind of whirl and wind, so maybe it's too soon to ask, but I was wondering if you'd be maybe interested in being my girlfriend? In fairness, I should give you a few legitimate reasons to consider not being my girlfriend. For one, I don't get puns, and I'm super socially awkward sometimes. Which you've probably noticed . . . like right now. And my podiatrist says one leg is actually longer than the other, so that might make for weird slow dancing at some point. Though I'm getting inserts."

Jamboree smiled briefly.

"And, um," Angie continued, still reading. "I'm sad sometimes, and I don't always know what to do with that, but I'm trying. Reasons you should, um, absolutely date me—despite the previous cautionary ones: I'm . . . funny. I didn't always know that, but I am. And I can dazzle you with my infinite knowledge of random factoids. I have stockpiled a few today just in case you need proof."

Jamboree grinned, then pulled it back.

"And I, uh, love so many things about you. Your clumsiness and the scar on your left elbow . . . the way you snort laugh when you're really happy . . . how you pronounce 'iridescence' and make it sound like the best word ever. With the exception of when you say 'love.'" Angie paused, then. "When we're . . ."

Jamboree pressed her fingers against Angie's lips.

"You had me at mouth guard," Jamboree said.

They laughed.

"So now what?" Jamboree asked.

Angie flipped over the last card.

"My plan was . . ." Angie said.

IF NO = Run (not literally)
IF YES = Don't geek out (literally)

"I didn't plan that far in the cards." Angie smiled bashfully.

"What do they do in the movies you like?" Jamboree asked.

A flash of film scenes carousel-spun through Angie's mind. But it was the song the DJ slid into that removed just the right one from the vault . . .

"In *Pretty in Pink,*" Angie said. "Which is hugely flawed, but . . . um, I'd follow you into a parking lot and . . . kiss you."

Jamboree wrapped her arms around Angie's neck. "You can do that right here."

Angie leaned forward and kissed Jamboree Memphis Jordan, her official gay-girl-gay girlfriend.

And it was hot!

Chapter 27

Greasy pizza trays and pitchers of mostly melted ice cluttered the three tables Angie and the band had shoved together at The Slice. Even after midnight, the place was packed with a post-homecoming dance crowd.

For Angie, it was the commercial-perfect scene she had always imagined. Jake and Wang, hedging bets on who the future air-hockey champion would be the second the table was free. Stacy Ann telling an elaborate joke to Jamboree. Finster and Chloe getting along. Zeke filming the whole thing while Raquel filmed Zeke.

It was a queer, straight, gender-nonconforming, racially diverse chosen family dinner. And even if it felt kind of like the Last Supper before Angie faced the inevitable social crucifixion that awaited her at home, she planned to make the most of the night because she had earned it. It was hers. Finally.

Jamboree squeezed Angie's hand under the table. Angie squeezed back.

"Hi," Jamboree whispered, leaning into Angie.

Angie blushed. The body does what the body will.

The waitress started clearing off the table. "We're closing in five minutes."

Angie looked at Jamboree. "I don't want this night to be over."

"It doesn't have to be."

Moment.

"Everyone's coming back with me to Darius's," Zeke said to Angie and Jamboree. "You in? We could watch the footage in his home-theater room. I'm just saying. Eighty-four inches in sixteen-by-nine."

Angie got up. "That could be fun. It's just . . ."

Angie looked at Jamboree.

"Look, I know y'all are official now," Zeke said, as they headed out the door. "But don't go all cocoon-couple for the next few months. We've got things to do. Tonight is just the beginning."

"Ay, give them a break," Raquel said.

Surprising Angie, Zeke conceded.

Wang draped himself across his sister's shoulders. "You riding with Jam or me to Darius's?"

"I think I'm going to skip the after-after-homecoming soiree."

Wang pushed back, hand over his mouth. "Snap, crackle,

and all the way pop! It's time. Don't worry. I got you."

Wang slid his iPod out from his back pocket.

"This is what you want. My personal, mood altering, *Hit This* top-ten playlist."

"Oh my goddess, stop," she said. "It's a random movie and a cuddle. Which is a pretty big night for me."

"It's always a cuddle and a movie," he said. "Until it isn't. Seriously, check this."

Hit This Playlist

Let's Go Party, Addy Tran, featuring 365daband

Welcome To the Jungle, Guns N' Roses

Mac + Devin Go to High School, Snoop Dogg & Wiz Khalifa

Brick House, The Commodores

Photograph, Nickleback

Whip It, Devo

The Sound of Silence, Simon & Garfunkel

Climax, Usher

Angel, Sarah McLachlan

Angie's brow furrowed. Make-out mood setter this was not.

"'Angel' by Sarah McLachlan?" she asked. "That is like the saddest song ever? This playlist is why girls throw full cans of unopened soda at your head. You get that, right?"

"Dude, I'm right about this," he said.

"Not a dude and—"

"Think about it," he continued. "Who's made out with more girls?"

She sighed. "It's likely you."

He grabbed Angie's hands. "Don't panic. Just act like you're riding a bike."

"You know I don't know how to ride a bike."

"It's a metaphor," he said. "Don't be weird."

It was a mathematical impossibility. Angie was weird. And that was okay.

"We're just going to watch a random movie," she said. "Really."

"Uh-huh," he said. "I know what movie you're gonna be watching."

Wang began to obnoxiously thrust his hips. It was so immaturely cliché. Angie planted his iPod against his chest. "Thank you, but not necessary."

"You're gonna be cryin' for this later," Wang said as his phone chimed. A striking seriousness crossed his face as he read his text.

"Is it Mom?" Angie asked him.

"Nah," he said, but it wasn't a *nah* kind of face. "Yo, have fun. You killed it tonight. Killed it."

"Sure you're okay?" she asked.

"Go," he said. "I'll see you tomorrow."

"I'll be home tonight. To face the wrath of Mom."

"I keep telling you she's not going be back from John/Rick's until tomorrow. They're too busy touching their feelings."

"That's so gross," she said.

Wang threw a nod to Jake before jumping in his Jeep and peeling out of the parking lot. Because of course he needed to make a notable exit.

Angie turned back to Jamboree, waiting by her car.

"You sure you don't want to go to Darius's?" Jamboree said.

"Yeah," Angie said. "I mean, unless you—wanted to."

"I'm good," Jamboree said, getting inside.

Drops of rain tapped the top of Angie's head as she slid into Jamboree's car. Jamboree turned over the ignition and Boston's "More Than a Feeling" blasted through the radio. They pulled out of the parking lot and toward Jamboree's, singing the chorus in unison.

"I love this song," Angie said.

"I know."

Inflatable pumpkin patches, witches, and black cats swayed in the wind en route to Jamboree's. Orange and green lights outlined the eaves and window trims of houses. Leaves swirled from yards and swept across the road.

It was pouring rain when they pulled up to Jamboree's house.

"Wanna wait it out?" Jamboree asked.

After a shared grin, they both jumped out of the car, running for the side of the RV. Jamboree dropped her keys.

"I'm sorry," she said, picking them up.

When Jamboree stood up, Angie slid her hand behind Jamboree's head, pulling her into a kiss. The sparks—the thirst—the surrender. Both of them rendered helplessly not helpless. Kissing as if nothing else in the world mattered. Not the pelting of rain or the lashing, bitter-cold wind. Their clothes were drenched, sticky-pressed against them. Jamboree clung to Angie's hips, leaning into her. Angie ached . . . all over!

They finally exhaled. Their breath formed puffs of clouds from the cold.

"I, um . . . was that . . . okay?" Angie said.

"Yeah." Jamboree rested her head against Angie's. "But I'm freezing."

"Same."

They laughed as Jamboree unlocked the RV door and climbed inside.

"Here," Jamboree said, handing Angie a beach towel. "Take off your jacket."

Angie draped it across the passenger seat while Jamboree pulled a pile of clothes from the loft. "I think I have a T-shirt and shorts you can put on."

"They won't fit," Angie said, towel wrapped around her, shivering.

Jamboree looked over her shoulder. "Yeah. They will."

After sorting through the clothes, Jamboree held up the red T-shirt, made humiliatingly famous on their road trip:

I Wish You Were Pizza

"Really?" Angie said.

"And here are my band-camp warm-ups."

"Thanks," Angie said.

Jamboree looked at Angie.

Angie looked at Jamboree.

It was in this shared moment Angie felt herself not entirely sure what to do next, so . . . she retreated.

"I'll go change," Angie said, heading toward the bathroom.

Angie suddenly realized what now was—she and Jamboree in the RV after homecoming. Maybe Wang had been right. Maybe Angie bypassed the cuddle and a movie and went straight for—

She closed the bathroom door and began to change, her mind racing. Angie had gone from proclaiming her love for Jamboree to wearing her warm-ups. Was this the natural progression of a teen lesbian relationship? Was this the clothing version of the much-joked-about U-Haul effect?

"Do the warm-ups fit okay?" Jamboree asked through the door.

"Uh, yeah," Angie said.

They were snug, but they would do. What wouldn't do was the reality that Angie didn't look like Jamboree. Angie's mind began to spin out into the troublesome trifecta of doubt, fear, and insecurity as she stared at the stretch marks along her hips. Angie had stretch marks and scars on her wrists and—she had to stop. To stop freaking herself out.

Angie took three slow, deep breaths per her therapeutic process. Reminding herself, all tonight had to be was a cuddle and a movie.

Angie stepped out of the bathroom. Jamboree got up from the bench-converted-to-bed. The glint of the Christmas lights sparkled in her eyes.

"See?" Jamboree said. "They fit."

"Yeah," Angie said awkwardly.

"You okay?"

"Yeah," Angie said.

"I was thinking." Jamboree slipped a cassette tape into the antiquated boom box. "Since we didn't dance at homecoming."

Jamboree pushed play. After a few seconds of scratchy tape silence, a romantic guy-with-guitar song came on.

Super-awkward Angie stepped toward Jamboree. Where to put the arms, the hands. They laughed.

"How about this." Jamboree put her arms on Angie's shoulders.

Angie lightly held onto Jamboree's waist. Her much smaller waist.

The two of them began to slow dance, under twinkle lights and rain still rapping against the RV.

"I used to pretend this was happening," Jamboree said.

"Really?"

"Yeah," Jamboree said. "Really. Less rain. More ocean outside the door."

"I like that."

Quiet.

More nervous quiet.

"What are you thinking about?" Jamboree said.

"Everything. Nothing."

"Ah. Return to the existential."

Angie smiled, considering. "A little. What are you thinking about?"

"You. Me. Here."

"I like all those words," Angie said.

"I was thinking about the way you kissed me. Outside."

Jamboree's hands slid along Angie's shoulders and to her waist.

"How . . . I wanted to kiss you like that for so long," Jamboree said. "I wanted to—"

Jamboree's lips slipped ever so slightly apart before she pressed them softly against Angie's. The sensation pulsed—ached. Angie's heart and thoughts were wide awake as she leaned into Jamboree. Her fingers fell along the bottom of Angie's T-shirt, brushing along her hips. Touching her—Angie stepped back.

"I, uh." Angie didn't know where to start. "I, um . . . don't look like you."

"No, you look like you," Jamboree said. "I like you. I more than like you."

"But I, uh," Angie said.

"Hey," Jamboree said. "We didn't stop being friends. Tell me."

Angie lifted her T-shirt, looking away. Jamboree reached out, touching Angie's stomach, sliding to her hip.

"I didn't want to freak you out," Angie said.

"By stretch marks?" Jamboree held the bottom of her shirt up. "Left and right side. Not that it would've mattered if I didn't. Don't you get it? I'm into you. My heart. My . . . everything is into you."

This feeling—inside Angie. It wasn't simply a rush of hormonal ecstasy as had been described in her health class. It was deeper. It was longer. It had a shape and a taste, yet it was nothing she had ever felt in this specific way before.

"What?" Jamboree asked.

"I love you," Angie said quietly.

Jamboree smiled, her palm on Angie's cheek. "It's about time."

Jamboree eased closer to Angie, her breath escaping in an almost whisper against Angie's lips. "I love you, Angie."

Their lips brushed against each other before crashing into a kiss so intense—so full of closeness. Different from anything Angie had ever felt.

Somewhere in the midst of heads turning, breath escaping, Angie and Jamboree stumbled onto the bed. The two of them, side by side. The whole moment felt like a race and a wreck. Misplaced hands—elbows. Both of them agonizing to find a rhythm in the clanking of teeth. In Angie jamming her elbow into Jamboree's ribs. Only to then get her hand tangled in Jamboree's hair before they bumped heads. This was not Angie's fantasy of sex. It was her worst nightmare.

"I'm sorry," Angie said.

"No, I'm sorry. This is kind of . . ."

"Different," Angie finished.

"Very," Jamboree said. "Maybe we should . . . slow down?"

"Oh, yeah," Angie said. "Sure. I mean, we could cuddle-movie—I mean, cuddle and watch a—"

Jamboree kissed Angie's rambling into silence.

"I just meant . . ." Jamboree said. "Slower. Not necessarily stop. Unless you want to. Stop."

"No, I just," Angie said. "I've never had an ending where I got the girl. Like this."

"Me neither."

They laughed.

Angie looked at Jamboree. At her frizzy damp hair. Her soft smile. The freckles she used to draw constellations on. Jamboree had always been her person. Not just that night, but all of them. Even when Angie couldn't see it.

"Are you going existential?" Jamboree said.

"No," Angie said.

"Confession?" Jamboree said.

Angie nodded.

"I don't really know what I'm doing," Jamboree said. "As evidenced by me not knowing how to—where to touch."

"Me neither," Angie said. "I've never . . . with someone. I mean, you know? Assuming we were thinking about the same, you know?"

"I just assumed that you and—that the two of you would've . . ."

"Nope," Angie said.

The two of them looked at each other. Best friends. Girlfriends. What would that formula equate to?

"So, what do we do now?" Jamboree asked. "Now that our awkward is all out in the open."

"I think . . . we just keep doing what we're doing." Angie leaned in. "Kissing."

"I like the kissing. A lot."

Angie kissed Jamboree. "Being incredibly awkward."

"I'm officially good at that," Jamboree said.

"And whatever happens, happens," Angie said.

Angie didn't rush—she didn't fixate on the shape or size of her body, her perceived imperfections. She simply stayed there. Close to Jamboree. Both of them exponentially happy.

Chapter 28

Angie woke up with Jamboree draped across her chest, the two of them mostly covered in an unzipped sleeping bag. In the randomness of Angie's thoughts, it occurred to her that Mr. John Hughes, the famed Hollywood director she had once admired, would not have written such a scene in the movie of her life. Because Mr. John Hughes lacked the imagination for a world where two girls could wake up next to each other the night after homecoming. Especially a girl like Angie. It was then that she realized that she wanted a world where this kind of morning was normal.

Angie was midreach for the therapeutic journal nestled in her backpack when Jamboree's phone pinged, waking her up.

"Hey," she said, propping herself on her palm. "You're awake."

"Mostly."

Jamboree stared at Angie.

"What?" Angie said.

"There's something different about you," Jamboree said.

"There is?" Angie self-consciously wiped the corners of her mouth; worried about the possibility of a drool trail.

"Yeah." Jamboree leaned into Angie. "Did you have sex?"

Angie chuckled. "Funny."

"Seriously," Jamboree said. "You okay?"

"Yeah. You?"

Jamboree considered the question. "Yeah."

Angie slid the tip of her finger over Jamboree's arm, drawing—

"Constellations."

"Just one. A new one."

"What are you going to name it?" Jamboree said.

"Love."

Jamboree leaned in, kissing Angie, officially waking up all the parts of Angie. Their foreheads touched briefly before Jamboree kissed Angie's neck. The kiss was soft and tingly, and Angie squirmed. They were in the midst of a pretty passionate make-out when "Alien She" played on Jamboree's cell. A sign that Zeke was calling.

"You need to . . . ?" Angie asked between kissing.

"I'm good. Just let me." Jamboree fumbled for the phone, trying not to break from kissing, and rolled the call to voice mail.

"Is this really?" Angie said. "Us. This."

"Yeah."

As Angie leaned into Jamboree, her phone pinged.

"Zeke," Angie said, feeling along the bed for her cell. "I'm so going to punk their chi."

Angie refocused her eyes. Finster had texted a Twitter link. Lucas had posted the video of him and Angie singing at homecoming. It had been picked up by *Rolling Stone* and a host of news outlets. One headline:

THE WAITE ISN'T OVER

Jamboree leaned over Angie, reading. "Global sensation Lucas Waite performed at a high-school homecoming in his native Dryfalls, Ohio, surprising everyone with a new song and a duet with recently viral teen personality Fat Angie."

"What in the upside down?" Angie said.

"The original post has over four million views," Jamboree said.

"That's not possible," Angie said.

Jamboree wrapped her arms around Angie.

"Is it . . . possible?" Angie asked.

"He's Lucas Waite. You're Fat Angie. So, yeah, it's possible."

Angie looked at Jamboree.

"What?" Jamboree asked.

"You have drool on the side of your mouth."

"Oh my god! How long were you not going to tell me?"

Angie laughed. "I don't know. It kind of would have broken the mood."

Jamboree wiped her chin. "Is it gone?"

"Mostly."

Jamboree pinned Angie to the bed, her hair cascading down. The two of them—

"Alien She" played again on Jamboree's phone.

"Now I'm going to punk their chi," Jamboree said.

They laughed.

Jamboree reached for her phone as Angie's pinged. Angie looked. It wasn't Finster or Zeke or even Wang. It was Angie's mom. Somehow she had gotten Angie's number, and the message read:

Your brother has been arrested.

Come Home Now.

"Shit," Angie said. "I have to go."

Angie scooted to the edge of the bed, swaddling herself in the sleeping bag.

"You have to see this. It's—"

"I can't," Angie said. "Wang has been arrested. Of course he'd get arrested."

"That's why you have to see this."

There it was. Wang. In the vertical world of Snapchat video. Holding his mom's—

"No," Angie said.

"Yo, bitches," Wang said to the camera. "This is a three-K bottle of Pappy Van's best."

He took a swig and passed it to Criminal Cody, who was filming. When Cody handed it back, Wang held the bottle up high and poured it onto the street. Cody laughed, shaking the shot. Wang turned to the camera. "Now it ain't worth shit."

Cody followed Wang, getting into—

"Whose car is that?" Jamboree asked.

"Shit," Angie said. "John/Rick's."

The next shot showed Wang, Fast and Furiously Stupid style, street-racing Winter. Criminal Cody filmed the entire event passenger side, cheering Wang on. Right until—

Impact!

Angie gasped.

Airbags deployed. The phone stopped filming.

"I need to get to the police station—the hospital," Angie said. "Wherever he is."

"I'll drive you. Hey. He's okay."

"What if he's not?" Angie said. "I can't—not again."

"Your mom said he was arrested. He's arrested. We'll figure out where. I have a feeling people know."

Angie nodded, taking a deep breath.

"Okay," she said.

From fantasy morning make-out to rushing to get dressed, everything was spinning sideways. Angie simply needed to see Wang.

* * *

Zeke and Darius were waiting when Finster and Chloe pulled into the police station parking lot. Angie's damp tuxedo pants stuck uncomfortably to her.

"Hey," Darius said, hugging Angie.

"I feel like I haven't seen you in forever."

"I know," he said. "I'm sorry I wasn't there last night. The whole football/homecoming thing. It's hard to be around that. Not getting to play anymore, you know? But I saw the video. It was great. It was good, Ang."

"Thanks," Angie said before turning to everyone.

"What happened?" Finster asked Angie.

"I don't know," Angie said, noticing Chloe being unusually quiet.

"What?" Chloe said.

"Nothing," Angie said.

"Let's just find out if your dumb brother is okay." Chloe led them into the police station.

Finster leaned into Angie. "She's scared."

Everyone fanned behind Angie as she approached the counter. Her uncle Gabe stepped out from an office.

"Where's your mom?" he asked Angie.

"I need to talk to him," Angie said. "I need to see Wang."

"He's in a lot of trouble this time. He struck two other vehicles, unoccupied, thankfully, and the hardware store is now a drive-through. Not to mention driving a stolen vehicle while drunk."

"It was John/Rick's," Angie said.

"Yeah, he's not really happy right now," Uncle Gabe said. "I'm hoping your mom can talk him out of pressing charges."

"Charges?"

"Grand theft auto."

Of all the dumb things Wang had manifested, why would he do this? Now? When they were finally—

"I'll take you back," her uncle said.

Angie turned to everyone before following her uncle. He led her to an interrogation room, not a jail cell.

Wang raised his head from the table when Angie came in. A gash with dried blood tore across his nose. An oversize Band-Aid above his right eyebrow. His chin bruised. His hand wrapped in a splint.

"Hey," Angie said.

Wang lowered his head, picking dried blood off his thumbnail. "Don't look at me like that."

"How am I looking at you?" she asked.

"You're looking like, you know, when you're like 'What were you thinking, Wang? How could you be so stupid?'"

"What were you thinking, Wang? I mean, really?"

Wang slouched against the back of the wooden chair, shaking his head.

"Wang, this is for real," she said, sitting across from him. "What if Mom can't bail you out this time? Then what?"

He shrugged in that annoying I'm-acting-like-I-don't-care angry-teen-brother way that Angie knew was a facade. This made her mad.

Incredibly mad.

"Wang!"

He smacked his fist against the table. "I don't know, okay!"

"'I don't know' doesn't work. This isn't like all the other poser criminal stuff you've done. You stole John/Rick's car. You drag raced Winter? Why, because of Lori?"

Wang shook his head.

"You wrecked—drunk," she said. "That's DUI. That's license gone. What if somebody had gotten hurt besides you?"

"Nobody did."

"But they could've," Angie said.

Wang pushed away from the table. "But they didn't. Cody's fine. I'm fine."

"You are not fine."

Wang leaned against the wall, rubbing the toe of his Vans against the floor. "Look, it's gonna be cool. Okay? Mom will pay for the car. Sweet-talk John/Rick's stupid ass. It'll be fine."

"I don't know if you hit your head so hard that you forgot that Mom isn't even Mom anymore. She might—in your words—legit leave you here. And John/Rick—he wants to press charges."

Wang kicked at the floor.

"This is not looking good," Angie said.

"Whatever."

"Stop doing that," she said.

"What?"

"Acting like you don't care. Like none of this matters. Like it's no big deal."

He shook his head.

"It's a big deal, Wang."

"It's whatever!" he said.

"You said something to me last night. You said you wanted something more. Then be it. Be something besides this bullshit. Because it's bullshit. This isn't who you have to be."

"Just go."

"This isn't you," she said.

"Leave. Get out."

"I'm not going to leave."

"Leave, Angie!"

The moment seemed pivotal in that way that moments of true crisis were. After everything that had happened to Angie, to Wang. This was the time that she had to—

"Not leaving," she said.

He picked up a chair and pummeled it against the table; Angie stood up. He threw it against a wall. It collapsed to the floor.

"Still not leaving," she said.

They stood there in the loudest silence that had ever

been between them. Louder than when Nat said good-bye at the airport. Louder than staring at her empty casket at the cemetery. There was no lowering the volume of it, of what was happening.

"You wanna know the sum total of what I know?" Wang said. "I was a mistake. I showed up to the party seventeen years ago, and nobody wanted me. And then, here comes Dad and his adopt-a-son mission. He wanted me, so I end up here. And for a while, I thought, yeah, this could be what I am. I'm part of this family. I belong. Nat made everyone belong somewhere. But she enlisted." Wang rocked against the wall. "Dad split, you went crazy, and Mom . . ."

Angie walked toward him. He backed away.

"Wang . . ."

"You don't get it," he said. "I'm not you. I don't have anything special. Boosting that car—that's something I'm good at."

"Bullshit," Angie said. "It's like a costume you put on. Wang the Car Booster. Wang the Mistake. Wang the Hip-Hop Wannabe who can't admit he loves ABBA, Coldplay, Kelly Clarkson, and VPop."

Wang shoved past her. Angie stood beside him.

"You're actually a pretty great brother when you're not trying to be all those things that aren't about you. When you're the guy who teaches me about Vietnamese food and films and music. The guy who doesn't feel like he has to mute that part of himself for jerks like Winter or Cody."

Wang shook his head. "Whatever."

But it wasn't a whatever, and Angie would not be silenced.

"I thought we were in this together," she said. "You and me. *Mystery Science Theater* marathons. Obnoxiously oversize chocolate chip pancakes at two a.m.—us mocking John/Rick for his poorly appropriated Dr. Phil approach to social work. You managing the band. Us getting away from Mom, and Dryfalls. This . . . this isn't you."

Wang paced, trying to find some way to shut her out. Angie stepped in front of him.

"You're my brother," she said. "I can't lose you too."

His jaw clenched, tears streaking his cheek. She stepped closer, wrapping her arms around him. He tried to break away, but she held on.

Then he began to sob. Big heavy guttural sobs.

"It's all messed up," he said.

"I know."

"I can't make it better," he said. "I miss her so much, Ang. I can't breathe sometimes from missing her. I can't . . ."

Angie held on to him.

"It wasn't supposed to be like this," he said, his voice shaking. "She was supposed to come back. She was supposed to come back for us. Nobody ever comes back for us."

"We come back," Angie said. "We come back for us."

Angie held Wang, and in that unmarked time, they

stood there not devising a plan for his escape or talking about the fact that she had crossed the threshold of womanhood in Jamboree's RV. They were simply holding each other, knowing that whatever came next, they would face it together.

Chapter 29

Everyone fanned around Angie, leaning against the hood of Finster's car outside the police station.

"That's it. That's all I know," Angie said. "The DUI would be bad enough, but grand theft auto? If John/Rick doesn't budge, I don't know."

"But your mom will get him off?" Jamboree said. "Right?"

"My uncle Gabe said she was supposed to be here over an hour ago," Angie said. "I mean, it was a three-thousand-dollar bottle of whiskey and her boyfriend-not-boyfriend's sports car. So . . . yeah."

"Outlook is not good," Zeke said. "Damn."

Angie looked at Chloe, who hadn't said anything all morning.

"He's going to be okay," Angie said to her. "He's got, like, forty-two and one-half lives."

"What's he on, forty-one?" Chloe said.

"More like twenty-nine," Angie said. "I know he'll be okay. He'll be here making offensive jokes in no time."

Which was likely a lie, but Angie's need to comfort Chloe was greater than her need for full transparency.

"So, what are you gonna do now?" Finster asked Angie.

Angie shook her head, sighed. "Go home. Face my mom. I'm already grounded until I'm eighteen so . . . yeah."

Jamboree laced her fingers between Angie's. "I don't think you should go alone."

"We'll go with you," Zeke said. "We'll talk to her—explain about the competition. Why you left—"

"She doesn't care about—" Angie said.

Angie's phone pinged. Two missed calls from her dad. She definitely didn't need to hear a litany of reasons why he couldn't help Wang.

"All I'm saying is you can't go it alone, Ang," said Zeke.

"Maybe my dad could help," Darius said. "He's really good with mediation."

"The last thing my mom wants is a therapist coming into our house," said Angie. "I just need to—face her and—"

Just then, Angie's mother's SUV pulled into the station. A glint of sunlight popped off its perfectly detailed chrome, causing Angie to squint.

"Let me get your uncle," Jamboree said.

"I got it," Angie said, not entirely sold that she did.

Angie started to walk toward her mom. Angie's heart raced, adrenaline pumping. All as she tried to breathe. Slow, deep, therapy-take-the-wheel breathing.

Connie's pumps pierced the asphalt. She was dressed in a salute to the power pantsuit with no Zen of hope in her eyes.

"Mom, just let me—"

"Get in the car, Angie."

"Mom, I need you to—"

"Get. In. The car. Now," Connie ordered.

The smell of bourbon permeated the spaces between her sentences. Between the anger and rage in her eyes. Between everything a mother was supposed to feel for her child but—

Connie clamped onto Angie's upper arm.

"Mom—"

"You left the house—grounded." Connie pulled Angie, feet clomping.

Angie's face wrenched in pain. "Mom, you're—"

"Played at the homecoming dance, knowing the film crew would be there."

"Mom, stop it. Let go."

Connie's grip deepened. "You will not be crazy—not here—not now, not anymore. I don't care what your woo-woo therapist and your father say. I'm done. I'm sending you to Whispering Oak."

"You're not sending me—" Angie flailed, fought her mother. "Mom, stop it!"

Connie slapped Angie across the face. She struck her so hard—so unexpectedly—that Angie lost her footing.

"Angie!" Jamboree shouted.

Sound seemingly suspended—muffled. A quiet elongated between Angie and Connie—between Angie and everything around her. Her cheek searing, stinging. Angie looked at Zeke, shouting. At Finster, holding them back. At Jamboree and Darius rushing toward the police station entrance.

Angie turned to her mother.

Connie held up her red, pulsating hand for verification. This was an event she needed proved, because the action was too large even for her to believe. The surprise of having struck her daughter, so violently, so publicly, was setting in.

Angie caught her reflection in her mom's car door. The distorted, wider version of herself—the fat girl staring at the even fatter girl—the girl Angie's couldn't-get-it-together mother, the woman who couldn't understand, who couldn't be bothered saw as—

"It's over," Angie said, not entirely sure what she meant.

Connie began to emerge from her own shock as Angie stood up.

"Get in the . . . get in the car, Angie," Connie said, opening the driver's door.

What was the "it" that was over? Angie thought. What was—

"Angie," her mother said.

"No," Angie said, her epiphany manifesting rapidly. "No more loud whispers, no more leaning in and telling me to pretend for cameras, for people you want to please, impress, lie to. This, right now, this isn't about Nat or the movie or the book or whatever part of her life you need to emotionally freeload your bankrupt misery on. This isn't about anyone else but you and me." Angie paused, taking a breath. "This is about how much you hate me. That's what it is, isn't it?"

For the first time, Angie did not feel smaller. She did not feel ugly or stupid. She felt bigger. She felt huge, and it was in the girth of Angie's size that she continued, "You can say it. You can finally say all of it. You don't have to couch it in bullshit birthing stories. Say how much you wish I wasn't here, because at least that's real."

Angie's uncle Gabe started to approach, but Angie held up her hand.

"You have no idea what *real* is," said her couldn't-get-it-together mother. "Your whole life is a fantasy, Angie. I don't have that luxury. I have had to work. Hard. For everything—"

"I'm not bad at math."

"What?" asked her mother.

"You say, with immense consistency, that I am 'terrible at the art of numbers.' I am not bad at math. You are."

Connie's jaw tightened. Her shoulders straightened. All a physical tell that normally would have sent Angie into submission, but she simply wasn't finished.

"I just accepted it," Angie continued. "I accepted it because you told me it was true. That I was bad at math. Bad at how I dressed or ate or looked. You know what? My body isn't an apology I owe you anymore."

"I'm not going to be egged on. I'm not going to get into your manipulative cycle whereby you—"

"All you know how to do is have the same fight with me, Mom," Angie said. "The same fight about the same things, and you get mad, and I feel like shit, and then you tell me to change my shirt or my pants or my shoes, but I'm still me. I'm still me. And all I know how to do is have this fight and . . . be disappointed with you—with me."

"You done?" Connie said. "Acting out? Getting everyone's attention?"

Angie shook her head.

"I've spent the last year and half trying to fix myself—to be something you could love. You know, because mothers are supposed to love their daughters. But I think I finally get it. It's not that you can't love your daughter. You just can't love this daughter."

Connie gulped.

"And I can't fix that," Angie said.

They stood swaddled in a reality some people would likely refuse to believe: a mother unable to love her daughter.

Nevertheless, it was true. It was true, and Angie finally, completely, and painfully understood it. There was no size, no shape, no doing of anything that could allow Connie to love anyone other than Natalie.

"I'm sorry for your loss, Mom." Angie turned and walked away.

With each step closer to her uncle Gabe and Jamboree and Darius, Angie tried to imagine the world not collapsing around her—on her. There was a distinct pang—a heartache in knowing what she now knew. But there would be no more fighting between her and her couldn't-love-Angie mother because this was the end of their relationship.

Chapter 30

Angie stood beneath the basketball goal outside her aunt Megan's house. She stood there, head back, with her uncle's sun-bleached basketball, thinking about the hours she and her sister had spent focusing on getting a rubber ball into an eighteen-inch solid-steel hoop with nylon netting.

She dribbled the basketball three times and aimed for the right corner of the board. Elbow bent. Ball ready to release . . . she paused.

A dog barked in the distance.

Wooden wind chimes clanked a few houses away.

Leaves swept along the grass, crackling.

The world had not ended. It was all still happening around her. It was all still—

She released the ball. Nothing but the snap of the net.

Jake's car eased up along the curb. She walked to the end of the driveway.

"How you doing?" he asked, coming around the front of his car.

"Okay. But not. I don't know."

He nodded.

"How's Wang?" he asked.

Angie sighed. "In deep. Can you believe John/Rick wants to throw the whole book at him? And my mom. I don't know. I think she'll just leave him there this time. She's kind of over it."

Angie bounced the ball to him. Jake spun it between his palms before charging the goal for a lay-up. His stretch was long, fingertips almost touching the rim before he dropped back down.

"Think you'll stay here?" he said, rebounding the ball. "With your aunt and uncle."

"They say I can."

He passed the ball to her.

"What about your mom?" he asked.

Angie dribbled, then shot. "I'm not going back there."

She rebounded the ball and passed it to him.

"It's different, you know," he said. "Looking out my window . . . knowing you're not going to be there."

"I'm, like, eight miles away."

"I know, it's just . . . everything keeps changing."

He pressed the ball to his chest. "Sometimes . . . I don't know how to keep up. Your sister. My parents. You. Here. Everything used to be so . . . Play a sport. People cheer. Do good in school. Things just aren't simple anymore."

She nodded. "I think this is better. I mean, not Wang being in juvie, or your parents getting divorced, or my sister dying. Which kind of sounds pretty awful. I just mean, things kind of in the open. No lies. No hiding or pretending."

Jake sprang up for a jump shot. The ball bounced off the rim. "I guess."

"I had sex," Angie said, matter-of-fact.

He held the ball at his side. "Wow, what?"

"I know, right? It was definitely wow and what and nothing like on TV. Not that you don't know, but . . ."

He laughed.

"What?" she said.

"I don't. Know," he said. "I've never had sex."

He shot the ball.

"Yes, you have," she said. "Jake."

He dribbled the ball. "No. Official member of the Virgin Army. Live long. Going strong. Until it's right."

Jake Fetch was a catch of the highest magnitude. His humor, his heart, his kindness . . . his body. I mean, he was that thing young women were into. It seemed an implausible thing to Angie.

"But Stacy Ann?" Angie asked.

"Nope."

"Kendra Johnson? Frances Walker?"

He shook his head, a sly grin filling out his face.

"Wow," Angie said. "I had sex before you."

"You had lesbian sex before me."

"Lesbian sex is sex," Angie said. "I think."

"So, does this mean you're, like, official? Girlfriends?"

"I hope so. I mean, I think so. We're meeting for Mexican food later."

"It's official then," he said, shooting for three. "So, how was it? The . . . you know. Sex?"

"It was super awkward and super sweet and . . . sexy and scary. Really scary, and it felt . . . like I couldn't have done it with just anyone."

"So, KC . . . ?" he asked.

"We said our good-byes," Angie said. "I said good-bye. For real this time. She'll always be the first girl I ever loved. But just because someone loves you, it doesn't mean it's the love you need."

"That sounds weirdly mature."

"I don't know about that," she said. "I don't really know what to do now. I got the girl. This is the part in the movie where they ride off into the sunset. On a horse or a lawn mower. They don't show the part where things get instantly hard. Where your brother gets arrested. Your mom hits maximum psycho. They don't put that part in the movies.

Because it's real. People don't like real. They like to think it's going to be okay."

"Maybe it is going to be okay," Jake said. "Maybe real okay is different from movie-sunset okay, but I think . . . you just try to be happy in between the hard stuff."

"Now that was weirdly mature," she said.

"I keep thinking about you playing homecoming last night," he said. "Like seriously, could you imagine that a year ago?"

Angie shook her head. A year ago she was coming out of the haze of attempting to end her life. And here she was, even in the hard, living it.

"Last night was good," he said. "Better than good. Don't let all the hard stuff make you forget that."

Angie half grinned. "Wanna come inside? See my nautical beach-themed bedroom? Complete with distressed turquoise shutters, jars of seashells, and rope. Everything centered by a cool lagoon-blue bedspread."

"That does not seem you."

"It will be eventually."

In a surprising twist of early evening events, Angie's father's Prius pulled up behind Jake's car. Angie and Jake watched as he characteristically finished a phone conversation before getting out.

"Jake, how are you?" her couldn't-be-accountable father said.

"Uh, good. I guess."

Her dad opened the back door and out jumped—

"Lester!" Angie dropped the basketball as he galloped toward her.

Lester the family dog that had hated his name and wouldn't respond to it was overjoyed to see Angie. He flopped and plopped. Jumped and licked her in the face. It was a disgustingly Hallmark TV moment, but Angie didn't care.

"I had planned to bring him up in a few weeks," her dad said. "We call him Ollie. He seems to like it."

Angie held Lester's face between her hands, looking into his thoughtful eyes. "What about it? Lester or Ollie?"

The dog tilted his head.

"Lester/Ollie?" she said.

He pawed at her chin. Lester/Ollie it would be then.

"I'm gonna take off," Jake said.

Angie nodded.

"Text me later," he said. "Okay?"

"It's good to see you, Jake." Angie's couldn't-be-accountable dad held out his hand.

Jake hesitated before shaking. "Yeah. You too."

Jake headed for his car, looking over his shoulder before sliding into the seat and driving away.

"Jake's a good kid, huh?" her dad offered.

Angie continued to pet Lester/Ollie.

"I'm sorry it took me so long to get over here," he said.

"I didn't know there was a here to get to," Angie said.

"Your uncle called," he said. "To tell me what happened with Wang. With you. So I went to the police station. Talked to your brother. Tried to see what I could do."

"So . . . you came because of Wang." Angie stood up. "What are you doing here?"

"Well, I couldn't leave Ollie—Lester with your mom. Your aunt seems to be okay with him being here. With you."

"So you saw Mom?"

"Yeah. I went by the house."

Angie shifted her stance. "I'm not going back."

"I'm not going to ask you to," he said.

This surprised Angie.

"Well, thanks for Lester," Angie said. "Ollie."

Angie scooped up the basketball. Lester/Ollie followed her as she headed toward the house.

"Maybe you should come live with me and Sharon," her father said.

Angie paused. "Why?"

Her dad was confused. "I don't understand. You don't want to live with your mom. Which makes sense."

Angie nodded. "You don't want me, Dad. You're just trying to look like the good guy."

"Maybe I am a good guy."

"Maybe you are a good guy to a lot of people," Angie said. "Just not me. Or Wang."

"We used to be so close," he said, walking toward her. "You and I."

"It's because Nat always put me in the middle of the two of you. It's because Nat put me in the middle of everything. There is no middle anymore."

"It's not that simple," he said.

"It's not that complicated."

"You're fifteen."

"I'm sixteen," she corrected. "I'll be seventeen in a month. I don't eat at buffets anymore. And I'm gay—I have a girlfriend. I played varsity basketball last year. And I was good. I sing in a band now, and I'm really good at that. Someday maybe I'll be great. And yeah, I count things obsessively. And sometimes I can't get the thoughts of my dead sister out of my head, and I get depressed. And I use food to cope. But I'm actively working with Dr. Moreno to do better."

"Dr. Moreno?" he asked.

Angie sighed. "The woo-woo therapist as mom calls her."

"Right. I thought her name was—Sharon arranged it. She knows more about how to deal with . . . this sort of thing . . . than I do."

"Good for her, bad for you," Angie said.

"I'm trying," he said. "Angie, you're my special—"

"Don't," Angie warned. "Look, I'm different, okay, but I'm not special in the way you think."

"I didn't mean it that way—"

"Yeah you did, because you don't get me," she said. "You don't see me. You see fat, but you don't see Angie. I'm both, and it's actually okay. It's okay to be both, and I don't expect you to get that either."

He dropped his head.

"You want to do the right thing because you're a right-thing kind of person trapped in a wrong-thing kind of dad." She shook her head. "Asking me to move to Lexington, Kentucky, because you feel trapped in a . . . have-to and not an actual want-to is just stupid. I'm not doing stupid anymore."

"You're my daughter, Angie."

"I've always been your daughter. Where were you? After Nat went missing—after she didn't come back. Birthdays, holidays—everything was an excuse because you didn't know what to do with me without her putting me in the middle."

Lester/Ollie planted his paws on the knee of her jeans. She rubbed his head.

Her dad shook his head, seemingly dumbfounded. "I don't know what to say."

"At least that's real."

The echo of a plane flying overhead propelled them to look up.

"You and Wang used to wish on the planes that flew over the house," he said, eyes following the plane trail. "Every time I see a plane, I look up and wish."

Angie watched her dad: shoulders slouched forward, his wrinkled reprint concert tee. His dark-stained jeans frayed along the cuffs. His attire only mattered in that it didn't quite fit the idea of him. The idea of the man who didn't always try so hard to be someone else. Or maybe he did.

"I don't know what the right thing is," he said, fighting tears. "I thought I knew, and then . . . she went missing. And you, you fell to pieces, and Wang . . . got into so much trouble. And then, she came back. In so many pieces. I couldn't do anything for her. Or you. Or Wang."

He wiped tears from his eyes.

Quiet then . . .

The sound of Lester/Ollie panting. The wind chimes from a few houses over. The leaves scraping along the driveway. The world still there, again.

"You, um," he said, clearing his throat. "You going out for the team this year?"

"No."

"I bet you had a great jump shot," he said.

"It wasn't bad."

He nodded. "You always had good form. Follow-through. Even better than hers."

A ball of emotion swelled in Angie's throat.

"Maybe we could shoot a few hoops sometime or play some music," her dad said. "I bought a new bass."

"Yeah, maybe."

Quiet.

More quiet.

"I'm, um," he said. "I'm going to be in town for a few

days. Maybe longer. See if I can help your mother sort out this thing with Wang."

"Okay," Angie said.

"So if you need something," he said. "I'll be there. I'll . . . be here."

They waited. The moment traveled into the seconds. Seconds that narrowed the distance between them.

"Well," he said. "I'm going to check in at the hotel."

"Dad," she said.

Angie reached into her wallet, slipping out Staff Sergeant Hernandez's information. "Give this to Mom."

He held the paper, befuddled.

"It's Nat's fiancé," she said.

"What?"

"He came to the dedication ceremony," Angie said. "Mom doesn't know who he is." Angie paused. "I get that she hates me. For a lot of things but especially for pouring Nat's ashes out. I can't fix that because I know it was the right thing. But maybe . . . meeting him? Hearing the stories he has about Nat. Maybe it will help."

"Okay," he said, slipping the paper into his pocket.

Her dad walked to his car. Lester/Ollie sat dutifully at Angie's feet.

"Thanks for the dog," she said.

He halfheartedly smiled before getting in and driving away. Somehow they felt closer, even if only by a millimeter.

A millimeter was still something.

Chapter 31

Angie pressed her back against the outside wall of Lucas's warehouse, waiting for Jamboree. Her uncapped pen hovered over a blank page in her therapeutic journal. She'd promised her therapist she would continue to try to write her thoughts, even though the last few weeks since Wang's arrest had been hard.

She pressed the pen to the paper, took a deep breath, and began:

I used to want my life to be like an early-1980s/mid-1990s family drama because things always seemed to work out in them. Now I know something working out doesn't always happen in the way you expect. Sometimes it's surviving things. Things you couldn't imagine surviving, but there you are. Faced with red palms, shaking.

The sound of helicopters—tanks—IEDs. Basketballs dribbling and crowds. Stadiums shouting your name.

I've been thinking about what you asked me. In our last session. What the movie of my family's life would look like? Without my mom and a screenwriter fictionalizing it. To be honest, I think it would be kind of like me. Curvy, scarred, sweaty, awkward, um . . . hungry, tired, funny. Definitely musical and full of revolution. It would be about the places we went as a family and the places we didn't. It would be full of hope and probably a lot of despair. People don't like despair as much. I get it. But sometimes it's just that way. Until it isn't.

In that movie of us, my dad would definitely be flawed. My mom would be broken because it's all she knows. My brother would trade in his acting out for a way out. I'm not really sure what that would look like. And my sister . . . that one's hard. I guess she would be less invincible. More human. She'd be lonely and full of life. She'd be scared. Unsure. And she still wouldn't come home in the way we expected, but we'd find a place for her inside us all the same. Even when it was hard. Even when it hurt. Because it does . . . hurt.

One thing for sure, without question, the movie of our life wouldn't just be ours. It would belong to the town, to the basketball team, to Coach Laden, to Jake, to Jamboree. To everyone and everything that was touched by her and us. Because it wasn't just our story. It was never just our story.

Angie paused, looking at the crinkled WHY NOT? postcard from her sister.

It's like I said. Life is heart and ache. You can't have one without the other, but you can have both. At least, that's what I'm hoping for.

Angie jammed the postcard into her journal and closed it. Lucas popped out the warehouse door.

"Hey," he said, shivering from the cold. "Whatcha doing out here?"

"Waiting," Angie said. "For Jamboree."

"You doing okay?" He sat beside her. "Zeke told me you and your dad went to see Wang."

"Yeah, we did. He said to say thanks. For coming to see him."

"Of course," Lucas said.

"And for the books."

"Nothing like *Rick Rubin: In the Studio* and *Artist Management for the Music Business* to keep him busy."

Angie grinned.

"Any word about . . ." he said. "What's gonna happen next?"

"Yeah, um," Angie said. "Sounds like if he's willing to do rehab and therapy for real this time, followed by what will likely be a lot of community service and no license until he's twenty-one, he might be able to get out soon."

Lucas nodded. "That's good news."

"It's great news," Angie said.

Quiet.

"He'll be okay," Lucas said. "I think he's got his head in the right place. Seemed that way when we talked."

"I think so too."

Jamboree pulled up. Lucas stood up, dusted off his jeans. "Meet you inside."

Angie walked toward her girlfriend. Girlfriend! Swoon to infinity times pi!

"Hey," said Jamboree.

"Hey," Angie said.

A sense of bashfulness lingered between them as they leaned in and kissed.

"You look—" Jamboree said.

"You too. I mean, I'm—you do."

"Did we just use any sentences?"

"Not complete ones," Angie said.

"You nervous?" Jamboree asked.

"A little."

"Whatever happens—"

"Happens."

They kissed.

"Wow . . ." Angie said. "That never gets—"

"Nope." Jamboree smiled, hooking her arm into Angie's.

Everyone crowded onto Lucas's sofa. Finster on one end, grinning while passing a bowl of popcorn to Zeke. Zeke turned up the volume on the laptop speakers, grabbing a handful of M&M's from a dish on top of a stack of vinyl. Chloe closed her 3DS, scooping up a handful of popcorn. Lucas handed Jamboree a cup of water. And Angie . . . she waited.

Joan Jett appeared on the screen . . . greeting viewers. Ready to announce—

"And the winner is . . ."

There was a girl. Her name was Angie. And this . . .

was *her* story.

ACKNOWLEDGMENTS

For the young readers out there, books can be conversations and inspiration. They can get people excited or frustrate them to no end. Whatever the emotion, I celebrate you in conversation and hope something in you blooms from reading this book. That something ignites and sparks the ganas in you to tell your story.

The story of Fat Angie came to me while I was listening to a Lenny Kravitz song in a diner in snowy Madison, Wisconsin. Music has always been a big part of my storytelling and my life, and it takes center stage here. I want to thank the musicians who FaceTimed or emailed me and played music with me or for me while I worked on *Fat Angie: Homecoming*. Immense gratitude to Trust Bucket's Zola Neri, Grace Bloom, and Mel Ruiz. Your insight, politics, and music inspired me to dig deep. Dave Markey and Dave Bartlett, your band stories helped simplify what I tried to make musically complicated and encouraged me to trust what I knew. And Carrie G.—the midnight songwriting chats and shared love of music was everything.

Thanks to my editor, Joan Powers, who excitedly traversed Angie's journey all these years. Matt Roeser, your covers are art, and I'm ecstatic to have another one. I am so grateful for the nuanced work of copy editors Maggie Deslaurier and Maya Myers along with proofreaders Martha Dwyer and Lori Lewis. You make this book read good.

And thanks to my agent, Erin Murphy, who continues to create paths for me to tell stories that matter.

Much love to my brother, Kurt, and my Belgian family: Anouck, Ayden, and Esperanza.

From my surrogate family, Sally Derby and Frances Gordon, to my birth mom, Virginia Trujillo (whom I met for the first time while finishing this book), each of you has taught me that home can look like a lot of things. Zeke, Mags, and Greg, thank you for keeping me grounded through all of this. And Larry P. and Jann C., I continue to do the work on and off the page because of your insight.

Last but not least, thank you to a girl named Ruby, who came to my signing booth at the North Texas Teen Book Festival in 2017. This book is a nod to your strength and your story. And your story is a revolution!